ALPHA'S DARKLING BRIDE

ALPHA'S DARKLING BRIDE

LINDA BARLOW

ISBN 10: 91941982913
ISBN 13: 9781941982914
Linda Barlow Books
www.lindabarlow.com

Cover design by CrocoDesigns

For the latest updates and giveaways, subscribe to Linda's newsletter:
http://eepurl.com/yB2x5

Jess:

Cade Derringer wants me naked and vulnerable.

Screw that.

The last thing I need is a dirty-talking, bad

boy shifter crashing into my life.

Especially the wolf pack alpha, who never lets me forget that

the first time he saw me, I was stark-freaking-bare-assed.

Trouble is, I can't seem to stop losing my clothes around him.

But that doesn't mean I like him.

Nor does it mean I'll obey his sexy, arrogant orders…

Even if I am forced to marry the jerk.

Cade:

I've got no damn use for a wife.

Especially one with dark, mysterious secrets.

I'm a hunter. Chicks like her are my natural prey.

But Jess lights me up with mystic fire every time I nail her.

If she thinks that means we're fated mates, forget it.

I take what's mine, but I don't believe in fairy tales.

Alpha's Darkling Bride is a full-length, standalone novel
with hot sex, strong language, and an HEA.

AUTHOR'S NOTE

This romance is related to, but not technically part of, my *Shifters of Scotland* series, which contains, so far, two novels: *The Zrakon's Bride* and *The Zrakon's Curse*. A character from *Shifters of Scotland* series plays a minor role in *Alpha's Darkling Bride*. But all the books are standalone novels.

Alpha's Darkling Bride is also related to an out-of-print romance I wrote many years ago, *Hunter's Bride*. I had originally planned to update that romance for a contemporary audience, but I ended up writing a paranormal novel with new characters and a different plot. There are still some similarities—mainly that they are both set in Montana and involve a marriage of convenience.

DEDICATION

To Curt, my lover, partner, editor, and wise advisor. If there were such a thing as the sevmelle, I'm sure I would see it with you.

CHAPTER ONE

Jess

My mother was trying to fix me up with a vampire.

No, I exaggerate. If Cameron Malloch is a vampire, so am I.

Actually, we're both shifters, but unlike most shifters, we have more than one form. I'd always believed my only alternate self to be a wolf.

I didn't find out until I was older that I could also shift to a darkling. A ferocious winged humanoid with no moral code and a hunger for blood.

My mum, who had a practical side when she bothered to use it, figured that since she was part of the family who'd bequeathed me the multiform shifter gene, she ought to be the one to solve my demon problem.

"It would be the perfect match," she told me. "Cameron is a multiform shifter and so are you. He has a darkling side, too. Plus he's a very important man. He runs the Council of Protectors for all of Scotland."

"He's my cousin, Mum."

"He's only your second cousin. It would be quite legal."

Right. But I wasn't interested in Cam Malloch that way. Fortunately, he wasn't into me, either, except as someone to mentor and harass.

Mum wouldn't give up on the idea of an arranged Scottish marriage, complete with kilts, bagpipes and haggis. So I fled.

Which is how I found myself thousands of miles away from the Highlands in Whittier, Montana. Not such a dramatic change as it might seem. I was born here.

"Much though I hate to consider it," my grandfather was telling me as we drove the rugged road from Whittier to his ranch a few miles outside of town, "I might have to sell off a few acres of land."

"What? Why, Grandpa?" The beautiful expanses of meadow and forest with the Rocky Mountains looming majestically in the western distance had been in the family for generations.

"Well, darlin', I don't want to bother you with the details, but I've got a few debts to settle. Never fear, though. I do have an interested buyer in mind, a friend of mine. He's a fair man who wants to keep the land as natural and pristine as we do."

"Debts? How much? I have a little money set by. Maybe I can help. I'd hate to see you sell any of your ranch."

"Thanks, honey, but I can't take money from you. You're a young woman with a bright future." He started coughing as he gripped the wheel of our SUV. Ever since I'd arrived, he'd had

2

a bad cold. "You'll need your savings for yourself. Besides, it wouldn't be enough."

"How big are your debts?"

"A man's debts are his own private business. Don't worry. I got it covered."

But I did worry, and I hated to think about Grandpa suffering from money problems at this stage of his life. He was the only one left from my father's side of the family, and I loved him very much. If there was any way I could help out, I wanted to.

Meanwhile, I didn't like the sound of that cough. "Are you sure you're feeling okay, Grandpa? Your cold should be getting better by now."

"Tip-top! It's so good to have you home, pumpkin."

He'd insisted on driving, but I could see that he was weary. We'd been into town to do a little shopping together. He'd wanted to pick up some of the foods I liked, and I'd needed a few art supplies. I'd moved back to Whittier a little more than two weeks ago, and Grandpa and I were still trying to learn each other's ways.

My offer to do the driving had been brushed aside with his customary impatience.

For as long as I could remember, Grandpa had insisted on doing things himself. He liked to be in control, to run his own life, to be independent.

We were well into the countryside now, and I was enjoying the fresh air with the SUV's sunroof and windows fully open.

The evening was magical. The full September moon floated on a sea of wispy clouds. The breeze was warm and moist, scented with wildflowers and lodge pole pine. Crickets chirped, fireflies danced and the ground alongside the vehicle on the rough mountain road was bursting with the rich aromas of summer's end.

But as Grandpa weaved out of our lane, my sense of safety vanished. He corrected, but he seemed off somehow. Not quite as fit and sharp as he had always been. This was no great surprise, since he'd been stricken with cancer last year. He was in remission, but the treatment had taken a lot out of him. I'd been shocked at his gauntness when he'd picked me up at the airport.

As we headed up into hillier ground, we rounded a curve going a little too fast. I'd never thought of Grandpa as a man who thrilled to speed; so maybe his judgment was impaired. I was positive he hadn't been drinking; I'd have smelled it on him. I didn't make much use of my shifter abilities, but my sense of smell was hyper-acute, no matter what form I was in.

"Slow down a bit, Grandpa. If you're revving up for the Indy 500, could you do it when I'm not in the car?"

He glanced over at me, grinning. Just then two headlights spun out of another curve up ahead and came roaring toward us down the straight-away. They were oddly spaced—too far apart. A truck? Ground fog on this part of the road wasn't helping with the visibility.

As the lights approached, the distance between them shifted, and I realized they must be bikers. They whipped by on the other side of the road, their engines thunderous.

Grandpa must have been distracted, because he took the next curve too wide. I felt him fighting for control as the wheels started to skid. Shit! Just as I thought he'd managed it, we swung around the curve and were confronted with a bright light coming right at us. Another speeding biker?

The other vehicle was in the correct lane, but Grandpa had over-compensated. He reacted a split second too late. We veered into the biker's lane.

I lunged for the steering wheel, but I was belted in. Grandpa swerved to get back on our own side of the road, but the SUV was bucking wildly now. We skidded sideways, brakes screeching. Then we flipped and started to roll.

I wasn't sure what happened after that. My body responded as it did when confronted with a threat—I started to shift. Not consciously. I rarely shift on purpose anymore.

And of course, it wasn't my wolf that emerged. She never did in these situations. It was the Other, my wild, ungovernable self, the darkling. "She might appear at times of stress," my cousin Cam had warned me. "You must learn to control her if she does."

Much as I hate my darkling self, those wings are useful at times. As we came upright after the second roll, I exploded out through the open sunroof. I was soaring over the road before the

SUV had even stopped tumbling. I'd escaped, but I was muddle-headed, and it was difficult to think clearly.

My shifted brain took over and controlled my flight. As I soared over the road on my midnight wings, I used my improved vision to scan the tops of trees. The hillside. The road and the ditch beside it. There was thick ground fog all around, and I knew I carried my own dark aura when I was in this form. I was grateful for that, since it helped to disguise me, but the fog was hiding my grandfather.

Where was he? Had he shifted, too? He couldn't shift to a winged creature; he was a simpler being than I. He was an ordinary wolf shifter. He wasn't twisted like I was. It wasn't Grandpa's side of the family where the taint lay.

I tried to focus the seething thing that was my mind and the terrifying thing that was my body. I didn't want this ferocious flying self. What I needed was my wolf.

Control the shift. You're in charge. Take the form you prefer. Don't allow the creature within to dominate you.

Bones I hadn't felt cracking cracked anew. Pain washed through me as my body realigned itself. My skin prickled as hair sprouted. My skull groaned as my nose and jaws lengthened. The wolf shift was more dramatic than the darkling shift since darklings resembled the human form in all but our wings, our claws, and our eerie elongated bones.

I dived, and flight turned to a giant leap as the ground approached. There. *There.* I landed on all fours, my paws scrabbling for balance. I growled and shook my head. I lifted my tail like a jaunty flag. I felt good as my wolf. I loved her. But lately she hadn't come when I'd summoned her. The Thing insisted on coming instead.

The air was full of the smells of countless small creatures—rabbits and mice, squirrels and foxes, cats, dogs, skunks, and chipmunks, birds of all varieties, groundhogs and deer. And the droppings, urine, and musk of all living creatures as well.

But I also smelled the human world. Burning rubber and vehicle exhaust. The dust and grime from a million particles that had just dislodged in the crash. Fire? No. Blood? Yes.

I bounded toward the wreck. All my bones and muscles ached, but I didn't think I was hurt. I'd escaped before the SUV had shuddered to a halt. But Grandpa? I was freaking out, not seeing him anywhere. He was here, though. It was his blood I was smelling.

It should have been his instinct to shift when danger threatened, but he was getting old and losing his edge. Had he escaped the SUV? Had the window been open on his side? I couldn't be sure.

As my eyes adjusted from human to darkling to wolf, I darted around in crazy circles, searching for Grandpa. I could hear soft, anxious whines coming from my furry throat.

The SUV had rolled over several times and landed off the road in a ditch. It was lying on its side.

Where was he, dammit? Was he trapped in the wreck? Injured? Dead?

And what about the other guy? The one on the motorcycle whom we had nearly rammed?

As soon as I thought it, I felt something. I can't really explain what it was—you know that sensation you sometimes have when you're being watched? I had that. But even stronger. It felt as if someone had lassoed me with an invisible rope and was hauling me in.

My gaze was drawn up toward the road, and the fog seemed to clear for me. I saw the motorcycle first, its headlamp still illuminated. It stood across the road at an angle, but it had not overturned.

The biker was standing beside it. Straight and tall, legs braced and hips cocked in an arrogant fashion. He was staring down at me.

Good. He wasn't dead.

Something about him was familiar, but it was too dark to see his features. He didn't rush to help. He was probably pissed off, given that we'd almost collided with him. Although, come to think of it, he'd been going a lot faster than we had. Too fast for this curvy road. He'd materialized out of the fog, right in front of us.

I knew he was also a shifter. A wolf, and an alpha. I could always sense other shifters. All of us could.

If he had been in his animal form, his body would have been rigid and his tail high in the air, signaling his dominant status. Expecting me to submit.

A primal stab of terror reverberated through me. Shit. I pushed it down, taking a deep breath. My adrenaline was pumping, but that must be from the crash.

As for the dude up there, he didn't look injured.

Screw him. I tore my gaze away. Where the hell was Grandpa?

There. One of the car's doors was open. And then I saw him. He was lying on his back in the ditch, tossed free of the SUV, still in his human form. He looked broken.

No! My heart screamed as I sprang toward his limp body. I was shifting again even before I landed in the dirt at his side. I ignored the pain as my body reshaped itself to my naked human form.

Grandpa was naked too. That meant he must have started to shift right before the impact. He was unconscious. There was blood.

The darkling in me thrilled to the blood in a way that made my human self sick to my stomach. I heard the sound of something crashing down the hillside, but the roaring of fear for my grandfather was so loud in my ears that I paid it no mind. My head was pressed to Grandpa's chest, my fingers to his lips. Could I hear a heartbeat? Was there breath?

I couldn't be sure. I could see from the weird angle of one of his legs that there were injuries, broken bones.

I felt rough hands on my body, pulling me away. I resisted, but the hands were strong.

"Let go of me, dammit!"

"Get out of the way," a deep, authoritative voice said. "Haven't you caused enough trouble? Was that you driving? Are you drunk?"

It must be the shifter. What a jerk. "No one's drunk, but my grandfather is elderly. He needs help."

"Step aside, lady." The word he used was "lady," but he said it in the same tone as he might have said "bitch." "I know what I'm doing, I've got some EMT training. Give me room."

I couldn't bring myself to step away, but I did make space. It would have been hard not to. He had that alpha voice—confident, commanding. People did what he told them to do.

I knew that voice. I hadn't heard the rough, impatient tone before, but I recognized the husky timbre, the Western drawl. I couldn't place him in the dark, though. I hadn't been around these parts long enough to know the members of the local wolf pack. At least, not since my early teenage years.

It didn't matter. Whoever he was, introductions could wait.

The dude dropped down in the dirt and started examining him, his large hands moving over my grandfather with a certain expertise.

"I can help," I said. Grandpa wasn't responding. "Tell me what to do."

"Call for an ambulance. There's a phone in my back pocket. Pull it out and use it."

I did it without even thinking. I guess I must have noticed with part of my brain that the ass covered by the leather pants was firm and trim, but I was wrapped up in Grandpa, not focused on this biker dude.

I dialed 911 and gave our location as best I could. I'd just finished explaining what had happened when the guy kneeling over Grandpa ordered me to hold the phone close to his mouth.

He snarled something into the mouthpiece, adding, "broken leg, possible internal injuries, pulse weak but steady, breathing okay, possible concussion, lacerations but no arterial bleeding noted. What's your ETA?"

Ten minutes, they reported.

"Okay," the man said, shoving the phone back in his pants and continuing whatever he was doing to help Grandpa. "They're on their way."

"How is he?"

"I think he's stable, but I'm no expert."

"You said you were an EMT."

"I said I had some EMT experience. Volunteer fire department stuff. But I'm not a fucking physician. What the hell were you doing, racing around that curve? Don't you know how dangerous this road can be at night?"

What a tool! "You were the one speeding."

"Are you hurt? You got out fast. Couldn't you take him with you? That was some fucking high leap."

My heart kicked against my ribs. What had he seen? He had to know I was a wolf. No alpha would fail to pick up on that. Besides, I was standing here bare-assed. The biker was still fully clothed, so he obviously hadn't needed to shift to avoid the crash. He was jerking off his leather jacket to lay it over my battered grandfather.

This gave me a glimpse of broad, muscled shoulders and a tall powerful body. He was young and strong. My human eyesight wasn't as keen as my wolf vision, but it was good enough to see that this was one fine specimen of a man.

I remembered with some effort that he'd asked a couple of questions. "I think I'm okay. Not injured. What about you?" He didn't look hurt, but it seemed only polite to ask.

"I wasn't the one who lost control and crashed my vehicle."

As he said these words, he turned his head so we were face to face. His expression changed. Mine must have done the same. I knew the bastard, all right.

"Cade Derringer?" Goddamn. He was the alpha wolf, leader of Grandpa's pack. They were friends, too. Grandpa talked about him constantly.

He grinned. Derringer's smile was charming—oh, he was a charmer all right. Melting women's panties off wherever he went. I'd met him on two occasions since I'd been back in Montana. Both brief, and both hot.

He had actually put his hand on my ass, almost the first moment we'd met. He'd made it clear that he couldn't wait to get me alone so he could work his sexual mojo. According to the local gossip, any woman the alpha wanted, the alpha got.

Worse, I'd sensed that Grandpa wanted the same thing Cade did—me in the alpha's arms. That was all I needed—my grandfather trying to fix me up with his friend. What was going on with all these people trying to hook me up? I suppose it was because I was twenty-four and had never had a serious boyfriend. Why couldn't they just leave me to sort such matters out myself?

Anyway, who cared about that? Here I was, standing before this man naked, with Grandpa injured, maybe dying. And all because the alpha leader of the Whittier wolf pack was still the wild motorcycle-riding hothead that he'd been as a teenager. Yeah, I remembered him from then, too, even though Mum and I had left town when I was thirteen.

Back then, Cade Derringer's dad had been the alpha leader, and his youngest son had been infamous. Everyone in Whittier had known Cade as the biggest bad boy fuckup in town. His high school class had voted him Most Likely To End Up Dead Or In Prison.

He'd had a motorcycle then, too. He'd even joined one of the local motorcycle gangs, something that was strictly against the rules for shifters. How he'd ever ended up in the responsible position of alpha leader of the pack, I couldn't imagine.

He didn't look the least bit responsible.

He looked as if he wanted to forget all about the injured man on the ground so he could push me down in the ditch and do filthy, sexy things to me.

The hell of it was, I wasn't sure I'd even resist him if he did.

CHAPTER TWO

Cade

"Jessica?"

The beautiful naked shifter standing opposite me all smooth and lush and tempting was Jess MacLeish. The new chick in town whom I'd been picturing naked ever since I'd first laid eyes on her. And damn, she wasn't disappointing on the naked front, now that I had the full monty view.

She was curvy and voluptuous, just the way I like 'em. Fantastic breasts that I could hardly wait to stroke and squeeze. But given the way her green eyes were spitting fire, I didn't think I'd be lashing those hard, pink nipples with my tongue quite as quickly as I'd hoped.

I should have picked up on who she was sooner. I'd caught her scent. But it was fainter than it ought to be—elusive. Mysterious. But sweet, oh so sweet.

I must have been more muddled by the near-miss than I'd realized. I'd barely avoided a collision that probably would have killed me.

She hadn't stayed in her wolf form for long, but she'd had that sleek, golden-eyed appearance of a magnificent beast before her facial features settled back to human. I'd never seen her wolf before. Tom had told me she didn't like to shift. Which was weird. Almost unheard of, in fact.

Tom.

"Fuck my life!" I whirled back to the injured man on the ground. This wasn't some stranger; Tom was my neighbor and my friend.

"Dammit Tom, can you hear me?"

He stirred. His eyelids flickered. He was still out, but not deeply. His head and neck seemed unscathed, which was a good sign.

I sought his pulse again. Steady. Other internal injuries could probably be mended if we could get him quickly to a trauma center.

I wiped some of the dirt off his face as I turned him slightly. I didn't think there was a spine injury, but I didn't want to move him too much. Dammit. As if Tom didn't already have enough issues with his health.

"Grandpa has been trying to convince me that you'd grown up and left your wild ways behind," the naked girl said. Her tone was scathing. "Guess he was wrong. What were you doing? Joyriding?"

I couldn't deny it. There's always joy in riding for me. I'd been reveling in the night and the time alone and, yeah, the speed. I'd been reminiscing about a time when I'd had a lot fewer responsibilities and a lot more fun.

Still, this fuckup wasn't my fault, and I wasn't gonna let her put it on me. "Who was driving?" I barked at her. "You or Tom?"

"He was."

I guess I'd already known that. Jess had emerged from the passenger side. She'd been thrown or something…hell, it had looked like she was flying. "How the fuck could you be stupid enough to let Tom drive? Don't you know—" I stopped, cutting myself off as I realized what I'd been about to say: *Don't you know how sick he is?*

Because she didn't know. Stubborn old Tom had insisted on not telling his granddaughter that his cancer had spread. He hadn't wanted to ruin her homecoming.

"He assured me he was capable of driving." She sounded pissed. "He's been driving me around since I was a little girl, and he knows these roads far better than I do. I've been living out of the country for years, as I'm sure you know, Mr. Derringer. You know everything, since you're the pack alpha now."

Yep, she was pissed. It was cute on her. I liked a spirited lover. And her lover I fully intended to be. Well, not her *lover*, exactly. I wasn't interested in any kind of attachment. I just wanted to slide my dick into that prime mouth. That bound-to-be-juicy pussy.

She wasn't making it easy, though, and this crack-up would probably complicate things. I flashed back to what she'd said when we'd been introduced a couple of weeks ago. She hadn't been diplomatic, which had amused me at the time. She was sassy.

"Cade Derringer? You're the alpha now? *You?*"

I'd heard that before. The surprise. The incredulity. No one had ever expected Bad Boy Cade Derringer to grow up to be pack alpha. There were moments when I doubted it myself.

"What about your older brother?" Jess had asked. "Shouldn't Aaron be the alpha now that your father is gone?"

Well, that had been a knife in my heart. Most people weren't so blunt about it. They had more respect than to compare me to my brother right to my face. "Aaron's dead," I'd told her. Saying it kicked me deep inside. Goddamn, I missed him so much.

"I'm so sorry." She'd looked stricken, and she'd even put a soothing hand on my arm for a moment. It had been a kind gesture, but her touch had roared straight to my cock.

I'd known at that moment that I wanted her. Focusing on my lust helped distract me from thinking about the various other crap in my life, so I'd actually devoted quite a bit of time to planning my Jess MacLeish seduction strategy.

That was then. Now she looked as if she'd like to thrust a spear into me. This didn't help my mood. What the fuck was her problem? I hadn't been the one driving on the wrong side of the road.

On the other hand, it was possible that I'd been at least partially responsible for the damn accident.

Yeah, Tom might have been speeding, but I hadn't exactly been driving slowly, either.

In fact, up until a few hundred yards before that curve, I'd been racing. Not a smart way to behave on a foggy night like this.

Couple miles back, two guys had come up on me and challenged me. I'd figured they were members of one of the two rival motorcycle gangs in the region, the Tigerbears or the Rockets. But they weren't patched like those MC club dudes, and besides, they were shifters.

Their full helmets hid their identities. I didn't know if they were total strangers or a couple of guys from my own pack.

I shouldn't have raced. But knowing they might be members of my pack—the pack I'd led for less than two years—how could I refuse that challenge?

The two riders were good. They'd worked as a team, crowding me from either side. One had deliberately tried to wreck me on an earlier curve. I'd kept it together that time, but they'd pulled the same tactic again, nearly forcing me off the road, and sending my anger levels soaring.

While one came about two inches from skidding into me, the other pulled ahead and raised an arm in triumph. Won, yeah, but not exactly fair and square.

I might have laughed off the nasty tactics—I'd seen a lot worse—had the other dude not given me the finger as he rode off.

That was rude.

No alpha likes being dissed, and I'd been stewing about it when I'd rounded that curve and come upon Tom's headlights. I was pretty sure that the SUV had already been out of control. The other two bikers might have had something to do with that.

"Did you see a couple other bikers on the road before you entered that curve?"

Jess frowned as if trying to recall the details of the accident. "Bikers? Yes. I thought it was a car, but the headlights were too widely separated. They startled me and must have spooked my grandfather."

Bingo. Fuck those two assholes. Had they even realized they'd caused an accident? They hadn't stopped.

I glanced up at the granddaughter. The naked granddaughter. The very fuckable naked granddaughter.

"You might want to put some clothes on. The ambulance guys will be here soon, and they're ords."

Ords. Ordinary humans. Not shifters.

"Not that I wouldn't like to keep looking at you naked," I couldn't help adding. I threw in a smirk for good measure and loved it when she rolled her pretty green eyes at me.

"I'm not naked, I'm skyclad."

I chortled at the euphemism.

"Please don't pretend my nudity shocks you."

"Shocks me? Not likely. Affects me, though?" I dropped my hand to my groin in a gesture I ought to have been ashamed of, but wasn't. This had turned into one helluva fuckup already. I doubted there was much I could do to make it worse. "Color me affected."

The corners of her mouth turned down enough to tell me she thought me an ass. She had that right. I was supposed to have put the bad boy swagger shit behind me now that I was pack leader. I'd had to grow the fuck up.

And I had, too. Most of the time.

"God, you're just as crude as you were as a teenager, aren't you?"

"How the hell do you know what I was like as a teenager?"

"I spent a lot of my childhood here. You probably don't remember. You were a lot older, and you never paid any attention to me."

I tried the winning grin that always works with women. "Can't imagine why not, but I'd be glad to remedy that mistake."

She snorted. "You were too busy playing rebel without a cause, roaring through town with your motorcycle club friends. You were always in trouble. If one of the Derringer brothers was gonna die young, I'd have expected..." her voice trailed off. "Um, never mind. Sorry."

She'd been about to refer to Aaron again. My brother the golden boy, the prince, the heir. No one could forget Aaron, even though he'd been in his grave for years. I couldn't forget him, either. If one of us had had to go, it should've been me, not him.

I pushed the negativity away. Screw that. It hadn't happened the way the pack had expected, and now they just had to deal with it.

Flashing red lights and sirens warned me that the ambulance was approaching. Jess started toward the wreck, but I grabbed her by the arm to stop her. "Wait." I'd already taken off my jacket, so I unbuttoned my shirt and ripped it off. I had a T-shirt on underneath, so I was still covered, compared to her butt-naked self.

"Better not go poking around in the wreck. Might be twisted metal bits sticking up. Put this on instead."

She took it and, as she did, she gave me an absentminded smile. She had a great smile. It had been one of the first things I'd noticed about her when Tom had introduced us. When Jessica smiled, she was fucking radiant.

"Thanks." She pulled my ratty shirt on without making any comments about its dubious cleanliness. When she closed the front, it covered two absolutely perfect plump breasts and a kissable belly. I didn't even dare contemplate her pert mound or her shapely legs. I wanted those legs wrapped around my waist while I slammed into her.

My shirt fell to her thighs. Good. I didn't want the ambulance crew to look at her.

My cock throbbed as I realized I was saving that sight all for myself.

CHAPTER THREE

Jess

"Sorry, ma'am, but unless you're hurt, there's no room for you in the ambulance."

"I'm his granddaughter. Make room."

"She was in the crash," Cade said. "You guys haven't even examined her."

"I'm not hurt," I said when one of them turned to me, mumbling an apology.

"Sorry, I thought you were with him," he said, gesturing to Cade.

"She is with me. Now. You guys go; take care of Tom. I'll bring the girl on my bike."

I was about to protest, but I realized from the urgency of the two EMTs that they needed to devote their full attention to keeping my grandfather stable.

"Yes, go. Please take good care of him, okay?"

"We will, ma'am. And the officers will be right along. If you're unhurt, it's best to wait for them and not leave the scene of the accident until they take your statement."

Indeed, I could hear more sirens approaching. Cade nodded. "I'll bring you right along after him. Everything'll be okay. Here," he said, walking toward the wreck, "Let's find your things."

Some kind of adrenaline ebb must be hitting, because I felt trembly and exhausted. As the police car drew up and the ambulance pulled away, I was glad he was there, asshat though he was. He climbed over the twisted metal of the SUV and found my clothing. He even retrieved my backpack with my phone and my sketchpad.

I dressed behind a couple of trees while he spoke to the police. He clearly knew the officers, and he must have explained what had caused the accident because when I went over to where they were examining the wreck and taking pictures, they nodded to me and asked after my health.

"They'll ask us their routine questions tomorrow," Cade informed me, slinging one arm around my shoulders and pulling me close to his side. I was glad of that, too, because the wind had picked up and I felt chilly. He was big and tough and warm.

Alpha wolves were a pain in the ass in all sorts of ways, but they were leaders and protectors, and he seemed to have that role down solidly enough.

"C'mon. I'll take you to the hospital."

I went with him. I probably could have gotten a ride with the cops, but that would delay things since one of them was walking around the SUV and photographing it, and the other was making some kind of measurements on the road.

As Cade and I climbed the gentle hill to the pavement where he'd left his motorcycle, I studied him. He was tall, with broad shoulders and long, muscular arms and legs. His clothes consisted of a T-shirt and jeans, the lower ends pulled down over a pair of riding boots. His hair was dark brown, thick, and shaggy.

There was something appealing about his scent, too. It was hot, spicy and delicious. But that perception came from the part of me that I didn't want to acknowledge. The animal part. The beast within.

He was staring at me, so I returned the scrutiny. Regular features, clean lines and angles. Good eyes—large, expressive and blue-blue-blue. A strong blade of a nose over a generous, mobile mouth. A slight cleft in the chin. His cheeks were scruffy with dark whiskers, but it wasn't clear whether he was growing a beard or if he just hadn't bothered to shave today.

He gave a lazy smile, and I noticed his mouth again—full-lipped and sensuous. He was hot-damn sexy.

When he'd straightened up the motorcycle, he mounted and patted the leather seat behind him. Something about the way his hand caressed that leather sent sparks through me. I imagined his fingers on my breast. Between my thighs.

Damn. That was all I needed now—an attack of the lusties. No way in hell.

He had the kind of smokin' vibe that drew me against my will. Why did males like him always push my buttons? It was a flaw I hadn't been able to stamp out.

"At your service, ma'am," he drawled, smiling. He offered me his hand. "Climb on."

Such bullshit. This guy wasn't at anybody's service. He was the local alpha. He didn't serve. He commanded.

He was a cocky bastard, too. Oh, he knew how to be smooth. I had already seen that he was quick with a laugh or a grin, but he was also full of himself. He had that arrogant way of walking and talking that told me he knew he was valued, admired and even feared by the members of his wolf pack. And by most of the clueless human inhabitants of Whittier, too.

I took the hand he offered me, but I was quick to extricate my fingers from his too-firm grasp as soon as I was seated. I felt a bit unsteady after the crash, so the idea of nestling up to someone strong and capable didn't offend me.

Pressed against him, I could feel that Derringer was tough, hard and as ripped as a wrestler. Since he'd removed two layers of clothing, I'd seen some scars, probably from fights he'd been in, and tattoos that made him look like the leader of a biker gang. He'd walked around the wreck with the loose-hipped swagger of a cowboy. His steely blue eyes had glowed with the lingering wildness of his youth. I could sense his wolf lurking just beneath the façade of aw shucks Western courtesy.

I supposed you didn't get to be the alpha of a wolf pack without having a deep inbred ferocity. How had he snagged the job? Grandpa had told me something about it, but I hadn't paid a whole lot of attention at the time.

"I guess I should have mentioned," Cade said, "if you'd prefer to shift and run, you're welcome to do so. But shifting back in town is forbidden, unless you're in a private dwelling, unobserved by humans. Plus," he added with a smirk at my now-covered body, "You're kinda new here, so I doubt you know where the clothing stashes are kept."

It hadn't occurred to me to shift. In my current stressed-out state of mind, I wouldn't even consider it. If I couldn't control my shift...god, I didn't even want to think about that. I'd already gone through one spontaneous transformation tonight; I shuddered at the idea of falling into another.

"I'm not part of your pack." Nor likely to be. "But thanks for the ride. If you'll just drop me off outside the hospital, I'll be fine."

"I'll come in with you. I want to talk to a friend of mine who's on the staff there. He's one of us and he's familiar with your granddad's case. I don't want Tom to get stuck with some ord doc who doesn't know how to treat our race."

I'd always been healthy, so I'd never given much thought to what happened when a shifter was treated in an ordinary human hospital. Humans didn't know shifters existed, although there were plenty of legends, not to mention the occasional sighting. "There are shifter doctors?"

"Sure. You oughta know that. We're everywhere."

"I guess I do know that. I just...how do you know which doctors are familiar with my grandfather's case?"

He seemed to shut down when I asked that question. "I'm alpha leader. It's my job to know stuff about the members of the pack. You ready? Let's go."

When he kicked the engine, the bike jolted as if it were alive. "Have you done much riding?" Derringer yelled over the roar.

"Hardly any."

"Easy as pie. Just press yourself against me and hold on tight."

He gripped my wrists and pulled my arms around his waist. In some weird way, he felt familiar to me. No accounting for that. There was something surreal about this—the dark, the unplanned shift that had saved me from injury, the crash, Grandpa silent and hurt, this man I hardly knew whose body felt so right.

Frightened though I was for Grandpa, I couldn't deny how exciting it felt to be seated astride Mr. Sex Personified's motorcycle, my thighs locked around his and my belly hard against his back.

"Hang on tight. I wouldn't want you to fall off."

"I'm not worried about falling off. I'm worried about my grandfather. Can't we go any faster?"

He hit the gas and we sped up, the trees melting into a blur.

Cade

I was nothing more than a vehicle to her. But as soon as I'd touched her, I knew I was going to fuck her. Whatever it took to get her down on her back beneath me—or, even better, on her knees—I intended to do.

I considered everything I knew about her. We'd only met twice since she'd arrived, and not for more than a few minutes on either occasion, but Tom had talked about her enough. In fact, she'd been just about all he'd talked about, once she'd told him she was moving back to Whittier.

She was some kind of artist. Painter or graphic designer or something. She'd been born here in Montana, but she'd moved away after her father's death. At some point, she'd left the country for Scotland, where her mother's family resided.

I remembered something else: "She's wary around males," Tom had said. "Especially shifter males."

"What's she got against shifters? She's a shifter herself."

"Plus she's got this silly prejudice against hunting. I told Jess she was gonna have a rough time here in Montana, finding herself a man who doesn't hunt, but the girl's real stubborn."

"What the hell? She's a wolf. Show me a wolf who doesn't hunt."

"She doesn't shift much."

I'd wondered why not, but Tom declined to elaborate.

"She's independent," he'd claimed. "Probably thinks she doesn't need a man."

"What about a mate?" Most shifter females found a mate sooner or later; many sooner.

"You lookin' for your mate, Cade?"

"Me? Hell no. I don't believe in that crap, and besides, I got my pick."

Which was true. Jess was in my territory now and she was hardly likely to turn me down should my choice fall upon her.

Feeling her hanging onto me was intoxicating. Superhot. Her pelvis against my ass was delicious torture. Her hair, whipping forward over my shoulders, smelled fresh and clean and exotic. I'd fucking love to bury my face in that hair and wind its strands around my fingers, my limbs, my cock. Better still, I'd love to bury my face in her pussy.

I would, too. Soon enough.

Shame arrowed through me. Here I was, fixating on this woman, reveling in the lust and desire she'd aroused in me at the same time that Tom MacLeish, her grandfather and my friend, was fighting for his life in the ambulance.

What a horny bastard I am.

CHAPTER FOUR

Jess

I sat by my grandfather's bed in the hospital late that night, doodling on my sketchpad and chatting with him when he felt hearty enough to speak. The doctors had prescribed pain medication, which tired him out. He had a broken leg, a concussion, and some sort of unspecified internal injuries, but they'd assured me that he would probably survive this.

This.

The doctor Cade had told me about had found me in the emergency room. While Grandpa was being admitted, he'd taken me aside into a little conference room, where he'd revealed the critical information that Grandpa had neglected to tell me. His cancer was not in remission. It had never been in remission. He had lied to me.

Grandpa had always downplayed his bout with cancer. He probably hadn't wanted to worry me. Or maybe he couldn't face his own mortality yet.

I sure couldn't face it. Ever since Dr. Cartwright had explained the situation, I'd felt as though I couldn't get enough air into my lungs.

Cade's shifter doc had been kind and empathetic, but his explanation of the situation had left no room for doubt. "So you're telling me that he's going to die?" I'd asked, dreading the answer.

"Pretty soon, yes. I'm so sorry. He's already had treatment. Chemo, radiation. Unfortunately, by the time he was diagnosed, the cancer had already metastasized. The regimes we've tried were all unsuccessful."

"I didn't know. My God, if I'd known, I'd have come home months ago."

"He refused to permit anyone in his family to be contacted. But he hasn't been alone. Cade's been with him a lot, and he's had the support of other members of the pack as well."

So Cade Derringer had known my grandfather was dying, but I hadn't been informed? I must have looked on the verge of tears, because Dr. Cartwright added gently, "He didn't want to worry you. He said something about you having troubles of your own?"

Yeah, I'd had some troubles. But I'd have come for Grandpa.

Years ago when my dad had died, I'd been so deeply mired in grief that my own mother hadn't known what to do with me. Grandpa and Granma, who was gone now, had comforted and cared for me in the warm and loving way that had never come naturally to my mother.

I'd recovered with my grandparents' care, and maybe I'd helped them too. My dad had been their only son.

Anyway, I owed Grandpa. Not that he would ever think of it that way, but I wanted to give him back some of the love he'd always given me. When I decided to return to Montana, I'd envisioned spending the next few years living with him as his age caught up with him. I'd figured I could help him out with chores around the ranch.

I was fortunate in that, as a graphic artist whose clients were all on the web, I could work from any location. And as a landscape painter, I'd looked forward to painting the magnificent mountains and plains of Montana. And the wildlife.

"How long does he have?" I'd asked Dr. Cartwright.

"Hard to predict, but I fear not very long. This accident will weaken him. His injuries from the wreck are not that severe, but I doubt he'll bounce back the way a healthy person would." He'd paused, and then added, "You should prepare yourself."

Prepare myself. How could I possibly do that?

"Oh, Grandpa," I stroked his elderly fingers where they lay quietly in my hand, "I wish you'd told me. And I wish you'd let me drive."

"Thank the good Lord you weren't hurt," he said. "I would never have forgiven myself for that."

"Heya," said a gruff voice at the door. "How's the race car driver?"

The biker, the alpha wolf, was still hanging around. He seemed to swagger as he entered the room. His steamy sexiness had excited me while I'd been clinging to his back with the

Harley throbbing between my thighs, but now it annoyed me. He'd known about Grandpa. He'd been allowed to take care of him and I had not.

I could tell by the way he looked at me now, his eyes all taunty and his lips twisted up in a cocky smile, that he was remembering my bare-assed appearance. Jerk. Why was he here, anyway? Why was a former motorcycle gang bad boy acting so devoted to his eccentric elderly neighbor?

I didn't know what to make of Cade Derringer, whom I still remembered as a hellion and a fuckup.

When he'd been a senior in Whittier High, I'd had been starting junior high. Everybody knew the Derringer family. Cade's father had been the alpha.

My own parents hadn't been too involved with the pack in those days, maybe because my mother was, like me, a multiform shifter. It was something we didn't talk about. I guess my parents had hoped I'd take after my father instead of my mum.

But I'd certainly been aware of Cade, the rebellious hell-raiser with the killer grin, who was continually in trouble. The other girls my age had all been hot for him. I hadn't been immune. I'd dreamed and fantasized about him.

On a couple of occasions, I'd summoned up the courage to talk to him. He'd never paid much attention, beyond bestowing his melting smile on me and tugging at my braids when he passed me on the street.

Now his father and older brother were both dead, and Cade had somehow grown into the role of pack leader. I wondered if he was any good at the job, or if he was still the careless risk-taker he'd been as a teenager.

"Cade!" my grandfather said as soon as he saw the man crossing the threshold. His wan face shone with a grin and he tried to push himself up on his elbows. "Good to see you, my friend."

Cade leaned over the bed and gripped Grandpa's hand. I could see that there was affection on both sides. Grandpa was pleased as punch, but Cade seemed dismayed by the sight of the pale, weakened man straining to look perky.

He wasn't perky, though. His face was gray, his eyes were sunken, and his fingers shook as they toyed fretfully with the coverlet.

"You crazy devil," Cade said in that razzing tone males often used with one another. "What were you doing driving? Stubborn old coot. You coulda killed me and your gorgeous granddaughter."

Grandpa beamed as if he were being praised. "She is gorgeous, isn't she?" He nodded to me and then to Cade. "She tells me you got me to the hospital? Took care of me? Much obliged. Why they insist on keeping me here, though, I don't rightly know. Let's get that doctor friend of yours to break me out. I want to go home."

"You're not going anywhere until you get a little better. I talked to the doc and he says you're staying put for now."

I rose from my chair. "You can sit here for a while. Please don't tire him out."

Cade turned to me and gave me his devastating lady-catcher smile. To my chagrin, it worked. Sparks fizzled through me as his blue gaze seemed to sear my clothing off. Down between my legs, tiny muscles throbbed.

"I'm good standing."

He was good in any position.

"Please, I need a little stretch, anyhow."

We switched places and he made sure to brush the side of my breast with his arm as we did so.

"She's been taking such good care of me, Cade," Grandpa said, smiling at me. "I'm blessed to have such a devoted grand-daughter. She's a talented artist, too. She's been drawing me and the nurses and the docs, and she even did a lovely drawing of my sweet Annie, God rest her. Show him, Jess."

"Yeah, show me, Jess," Derringer said with a wicked intonation and an equally wicked gleam in his eye. He held out his hand for the sketchpad. I didn't want to give it to him, but Grandpa looked so eager that I acquiesced. When Cade flipped through the pages, making polite murmurings, Grandpa watched him and beamed.

"Will you be here for a few? I need to run down to the cafeteria to get a coffee, but I don't want to leave him alone."

"Sure, I can stay. Anything you need, babe." The way he emphasized the word "need" and the look on his face as he said it made it sound as if he was offering every dark variety of pleasure.

Asshole. "Want me to bring you back a cup of coffee?"

"No, thanks. I'm good."

"Bring me back some whiskey, girl," my grandfather said hoarsely after me as I headed for the door. He and Cade both laughed.

When I returned to the room fifteen minutes later, Grandpa was dozing and Cade was lounging in the chair beside him, his long legs stretched out. He looked as though he might be snatching a nap himself.

His eyes rolled open as I crossed the threshold. They were an intense electric blue.

He stood and ambled over to me. "He fell asleep. Would you like to go home, get some rest? You can come back in the morning. They sedated him, so he won't even know you're gone. I can offer you a ride."

Yeah, I'll bet. A ride on his dick, probably.

But I flashed for a moment to the feeling of sitting astride his motorcycle, my body plastered to his firm back.

No. That would not be smart. Anyway, how could I have such a thought when Grandpa was so ill? "Thanks, but they said I could stay. I want to be here when he wakes up."

"You were in the crash too. A little sleep might be just the thing."

I knew he was trying to be kind, but I felt prickly and vulnerable. "I'm fine. I appreciate the offer. But I'm staying."

I expected him to leave, then. Why would he hang around? I wasn't being nice to him and his dear friend Tom was floating on sedatives.

But Derringer made it clear that he wasn't in any hurry to take off. He stood at the foot of Grandpa's bed, watching him silently and not making any further attempt to chat me up. I could feel him staring at me, though.

I avoided his eyes and did some sketching. But I had the sense that he'd bound me with invisible cord and was waiting to reel me in. It was eerie and unaccountable. Some kind of chemistry, I guess.

My wolf felt it, too. She wanted to meet his wolf. Frolic with him. My wolf had even less sense about these things than I did.

My darkling self wanted out, too. She always wanted out. It was a constant struggle between us—I kept her damped down and hidden and she schemed to escape and wreak havoc in the world. Since I knew all too well what a disaster that would be, I blocked her as best I could.

Except when instinct took over, as it had at the moment of the accident. At times like that, my darkling demon ruled me. I hated that.

The truth was, I had a bit of a problem accepting myself. Who and what I was. A darkling shifter. One of the few alive on earth. A killer. An avenger, as my cousin Cam would say. If someone tried to harm me or anyone I loved, I would be their worst nightmare.

I'd convinced myself that my powers were stronger in Scotland, where my family originated. In the Highlands, where mystical powers for many shifters were enhanced, I shivered with bursts of both light and dark energy. Here, far away in Montana, I felt calmer and more in control.

Well, until now.

Now my darkling self had pushed up, nearer the surface. I shuddered to think what might happen if she gained the upper hand.

CHAPTER FIVE

Cade

I hung around for a while, wanting to talk to Tom's granddaughter but finding myself oddly at a loss for words. Probably because of Tom. He looked so helpless, lying there. Thinner and paler than usual, poor guy.

Jess wouldn't leave him. She was a stubborn damn chick.

So much for my fantasy of taking her home and comforting her. Best kind of comforting—the kind I could do with my tongue and my dick.

Shit. I really had to stop imagining how it would feel to slide my cock into Jessica MacLeish's plump, juicy pussy.

A little later, I was riding down the street, heading home, when I noticed two Harleys parked side by side on the road in front of the all-night café. I pulled over, examining the tags. One was mud covered and unreadable, but the other was clear.

Fuckin' hell. These bikes belonged to the guys I'd raced with, the ones who had tried to force me off the road. The guys who had so rattled Tom with their antics that he'd swerved into my lane and then rolled into a ditch. Had they stopped to help? Nope. Bastards.

I pulled in beside the two bikes, locked my own and stalked over to the door of the café.

Keep your cool, man, I warned myself. Easy does it.

Things got even worse when I checked out the occupants of the café. Besides the middle aged and weary-looking barista, there were only two. I knew them both. Hell, I'd fucked one of them. And I'd defeated the other for the position of dominant male of the Whittier wolf pack.

Brandon, the closest thing I had to a rival in the pack. And his mate Suzanne. Both clad in leather riding togs. Their closed helmets were sitting on one side of the table.

I strolled over and stood there, looking down on them. Brandon smiled. He smiled a lot. I thought about driving my fist into his perfect, shiny teeth. "Evening, folks."

Suzanne, who had been a hookup of mine a few years back, didn't look anywhere near as pleased to see me as Brandon was pretending to be. But she forced herself to be polite. I got the feeling she was forcing herself a lot lately. She'd supported Brandon as pack alpha, and she'd taken his loss to me a lot harder than Brandon had. 'Course it was hard to tell with Brandon—he was skillful at hiding his feelings, and I didn't trust him.

"Cade," Suzanne said coolly, bowing her head in acknowledgement of my rank.

Brandon made the same head bow. "Alpha. You're out late. Shouldn't you be resting up at home? Hard work, running the pack. Wouldn't want to see it slow you down."

Good one, I thought, half admiring his faint sneer. "Gonna give you two the benefit of the doubt. Gonna assume you didn't realize you left a crack-up in your wake on the road into town."

Brandon and Suzanne exchanged a quick glance. If I was reading them right, they were surprised. I could read Suzanne pretty well, but Brandon was opaque, as always.

"What kind of crack-up? Who was involved?"

"Tom MacLeish. Spooked by a couple of bikers. Careened off the road."

"Shit," Brandon said. "No, we didn't know. Would have stopped if we had."

"We saw an ambulance go by," Suzanne said. "Is he badly hurt?"

"He's alive. He's got some injuries, though, on top of his illness. His granddaughter was with him. Jessica. She saw you speeding in the opposite direction just before they nearly collided with me."

Suzanne looked me over. Her cool assessing gaze managed to be insulting. "You don't look damaged."

"They missed me. Went into the ditch. Their car turned over and rolled a couple times."

"I remember an SUV," Brandon said. "Driving a bit fast, for the conditions. Who was at the wheel? Tom or the granddaughter?"

"Tom. The girl shifted and dived out in time, but Tom got thrown. Broke his leg and might have internal injuries."

"Sorry to hear it. Can he have visitors? We'll stop by before heading home."

"No visitors. Not tonight."

"What about the girl?" Suzanne asked. "Did we know he had a granddaughter? First I've heard of her."

"She's not hurt. She moved back to town recently to take care of Tom. Tough way to begin her stay in Whittier."

Suzanne bristled. "Are you blaming us? We had nothing to do with the crash. We didn't even know there was one."

"You were going damn fast on a road not built for that kind of speed."

Brandon treated me to one of his most charming smiles. "And you were going a mite too slow."

"You tried to run me off the road."

"Bullshit. You're the guy who hung with the Rockets motor-cycle club for a while. I hardly think Suzanne and I would be capable of committing road aggression against a pro biker like yourself."

"I expect dirty tricks from the MC guys. Not from shifters in my own pack." I smiled as I said it. A fuck-you sort of smile. A don't let it happen again smile. A don't push me if you want to remain in my pack smile.

Brandon got it. He bowed his head a little lower. "Apologies, Cade. Just having a little fun."

"Accepted." I looked at Suzanne, whose brown eyes remained defiant. I stared harder, and she dropped her gaze.

"Suzanne?" her mate prodded.

"Sorry," she mumbled. "Hope Tom recovers. That sucks about the accident."

I knew I ought to be mollified, but I wasn't. I still wanted to kick Brandon's ass, but the guy had submitted, just as he had when I'd won the leadership election. As long as he accepted me as pack alpha, there was really nothing more to say.

"Have a cup of coffee with us," he offered. "You look tired."

"Sorry. Heading out." After one more hard stare, I left them.

CHAPTER SIX

Jess

I woke up naked and shivering in the woods outside my grand-father's ranch.

At first, I didn't even know where I was. I lay curled on the ground, my mind churning with images of bushes and stones, treetops and a brilliant sky ablaze with stars. A chase. Dizzying speed and predatory excitement. A lunge. Triumph. Hot blood erupting into my mouth and flowing down my throat.

As I pushed myself up to a sitting position, the images jumbled and became confused. It was dark all around me. My eyesight always took a while to adjust when I came back from sleep shifting. I recognized the gnarled oak tree where I had come to rest. I'd climbed it joyously in my childhood when I'd visited my grandparents. I leaned back against it now and tried to catalogue what I'd done.

I must have ventured outside to run as a wolf. Or fly as a darkling.

This time it seemed I'd done both. I had tangled memories of viewing the night-time world from above as well as from the ground.

I'd hunted and killed my prey. The metallic flavor of fresh blood still lingered in my throat.

A cool breeze shook the leaves of my tree. I folded my arms around myself and jerked to my feet. I had to get inside. Without fur or feathers to keep me warm, I was freezing.

As I jogged across the field and the back garden of my grandfather's ranch, I felt like even more of a freak than I was. It's unusual for a shifter not to retain full memory of the shifted experience. It was probably related to my assault. Supposedly, the problem would fade over time.

I'd been hoping it wouldn't happen here in Montana. I'd thought I'd feel safe and protected, living with my grandfather.

But there was no safety here.

It had been a rotten week. I'd spent several days and nights going back and forth from the hospital in Whittier to Grandpa's. His SUV was in the shop for repairs, but I had my own car, and I'd come to know every curve of that treacherous road where our accident had taken place.

Dr. Cartwright had given me more information this morning before ordering me to go home and rest. The news was even grimmer than we'd feared.

The latest scans had shown that the cancer was everywhere, and the accident had left Grandpa with broken bones and a stubborn infection that was getting worse instead of better.

It was beginning to look as if he might never leave the hospital.

I'd finally followed the doctor's orders about resting because some of the shifters from Grandpa's pack, Cade Derringer among them, had shown up around noon to sit with him. I'd come home and pulled all the curtains to shut out the sun. But I was so distressed by the bad news that I found sleep impossible.

I'd set up my easel in the living room of Grandpa's rambling old house, once the main building of a successful ranch. My work had always been a source of comfort in times of stress, but all I could do was stare at a blank canvas. Instead of soothing me, the smell of my oil paints irritated me so much that I'd finally packed them away. I'd stretched out on the sofa and tried to relax.

The rustic ranch house resembled a hunting lodge, with its rough-finished woodwork and dusty old fixtures that gave off little light. There was a stag's head over the fireplace—a magnificent animal with a huge rack of antlers. Another stag's head adorned the west wall. There were ducks—both stuffed and wooden—on the top shelf of a bookcase. Several trophy-sized trout had been mounted on the walls.

I found the trophies repellant, but I couldn't stop staring at them. Trophies from dead animals reminded me of Jonathan. Those were memories I did my best to suppress.

I must have dropped into a restless sleep because I began having nightmares about the Highland wolf pack we'd lived with in the years after my father's death. My mother and her fucked-up lover Martin. Jonathan's bullying of me. My anxiety as his violence escalated. The horror that had struck so unexpectedly when I'd thought I was safe.

I'd woken up sweating and shivering. I hated feeling that way. Hated myself for allowing my past to haunt me. It seemed weak, and I wanted to be strong.

I'd prowled the empty house. Driven by instincts I couldn't resist, I'd ventured outside to the old stables, the barnyard and beyond to the meadow and the woods. It had been evening by then. I'd lain down under my old oak tree and dozed off. I remembered the pain of shifting, but very little after that.

Until now. Waking up bare-assed in the woods.

Once inside, I headed directly for the shower. I was covered in dirt and grit, and there was blood under my fingernails. I must have shifted back to human while I was still reveling in the blood of whatever I had killed.

I turned the water on as hot as I could stand and scrubbed myself so hard that my skin was left raw. Then I called my cousin in the Highlands.

Cam Malloch, my darkling shifter cousin, was not thrilled to hear from me. "What the fuck are you doing calling me at this hour of the morning?" he'd growled when he'd answered his phone.

Right. Scotland was a few hours ahead. "I think I'm regressing," I told him. "I sleep-shifted again. I don't remember what I did, but I must have hunted because there's blood."

"Animal blood? Do you know what you killed?"

"I don't know." I had to squeeze my eye muscles tightly to keep from crying. Cam had zero tolerance for women who cried. "There are woods behind the ranch and that's where I was, so animal blood, I guess. I don't think I attacked a person or anything."

"You're fucked if you do, Jess. I warned you about this. Are you under some kind of stress or something? Having flashbacks?"

"We were in an accident and my grandfather's dying."

"Shit. That isn't good. Tell me."

I spilled the whole story, probably in more detail than he would have liked. He wasn't the most patient man in the world. Nor was he particularly empathetic. I wasn't even sure I liked him much, but he was the only person I knew who shared my curse of darkling shifting.

He'd been teaching me how to control my demon side, but his methods had been harsh and I wasn't sure they'd worked on me. He'd also tried to recruit me into his secret spy organization or whatever it was. I didn't know too much about it. I didn't want to know and I certainly didn't want to participate. Cam scared me sometimes.

"You still have the collar I gave you?" he asked.

"Yes, but—"

"You haven't found anyone you can trust to put it on you and remove it?"

"I thought Grandpa would be able to do that, but now that he's sick, he can't." *Now that he's dying.*

"You'll have to find someone else. No boyfriends yet? Are you having sex?"

"Jeez, getting personal? Are *you*?"

He snorted. "Of course. You should be too. It lets off steam. Relieves some of the pressure. Go fuck some American cowboy and you'll start to regain your balance."

"I don't have time for romantic relationships. Didn't you hear me? My grandfather is *dying*."

"I'm not talking about romance, I'm talking about fucking. Go to a pub and pick up a guy. Or use one of those hookup apps. You're hot enough. All the guys around will be swiping to get you. Find one and fuck him."

"That's the advice you're giving me, Cam? Go fuck someone?"

"Works for me."

That was the trouble with my cousin—he tried, but he wasn't all that helpful. He was the first to admit this. "I'm not a god-damn therapist, Jess," he'd said to me over and over. "All I am is a few years older than you. If I can figure this thing out, so can you."

We hung up and I'd tried to settle myself down to get some actual sleep, since it was now after eleven and there was no point in returning to the hospital tonight. I called the nursing station near Grandpa's room and found out that he was resting comfortably. His condition was the same. I hoped he'd have a good day tomorrow. Maybe he would even feel a little better?

I was planning to settle down and try bed again when the doorbell rang. The members of Grandpa's pack had been rallying round, both here at the ranch and at the hospital, bringing food, sympathy, and encouragement. I didn't know any of them very well yet, but I was grateful. I went downstairs, wondering who would stop by so late.

I found Cade Derringer on our front porch, looking just as big and tall and hot as ever.

CHAPTER SEVEN

Jess

"Hey. Did I wake you? You said you'd come back to the hospital tonight. When you didn't show, I figured I should check on you."

"Did something happen?" I unhooked the screen door and he took it as an invitation. In he came, crowding me back into the front hall.

"No. He's doing okay. Mostly sleeping. Jake says he has some fever, but he's not worse."

I knew that from my call to the hospital, but I was glad to hear it. I'd panicked for a second when I'd seen him, afraid he'd come to break more bad news to me.

He followed me into the living room and sprawled on the leather couch. He seemed right at home in the place. I guess he'd been here many times before to visit Grandpa.

I knew they were friends and all, but wasn't he carrying this bromance thing a little far? Coming to check on me? That wasn't much of an excuse for dropping in at this time of night.

My grandfather hadn't stopped talking about Cade. He'd told me several rambling stories about him while lying in his hospital bed. I'd heard what a good companion he was—he took Grandpa fishing. What a loyal friend—he lent Grandpa money. What an entertaining raconteur—he knew a lot of dirty jokes. What a prodigious intellect—he beat Grandpa at chess. What an all-around stand-up guy.

But from what I'd gathered over the past couple of days, it sounded as though Derringer had been as casual about the cancer as Grandpa. He must have known he was sick, but it hadn't stopped Cade from dragging my grandfather out fly-fishing in the early hours of the morning.

"Fishing is good therapy," Grandpa had told me yesterday. "I need to get out of this damn hospital so I can pull on my waders and get out in a fast-flowing stream again. I'll fish with Cade. That'll fix me up a whole lot better than these damn needles. Or maybe we should go hunting. Cade is a crack shot with a rifle."

Given how much I hated hunting, Derringer's skill with firearms was hardly likely to endear him to me. "Sounds like Cade Derringer has even less sense than you," I'd said. "You need to rest and get better, Grandpa."

"I feel fine when I'm with him. Cade's a good man. How are you two getting on? He's a great guy, isn't he? You be nice to him, OK?"

Was he matchmaking? No way I was having any of that. If I'd wanted to be paired up with a man my relatives thought was right for me, I'd have stayed in Scotland. I'd thought Montana would be a refuge from that kind of romantic interference.

Besides, a freak like me with an ordinary shifter? That would never work.

If Grandpa hadn't been lying in a hospital bed he might never get up from, I'd have put him straight.

Anyway, I didn't even like Cade. He'd spent his teenage years drinking, joyriding, fucking every female in town, and generally raising hell. Good for him for straightening himself out enough to take over leadership of the pack, but I doubted that the improvements in his behavior carried over to his sex life. With that big, handsome body and that insolent masculine grace, he probably used his cock a lot harder than he used his brain.

On the other hand, Cam's words slammed back into me: Go fuck some guy.

A guy had conveniently turned up on my doorstep. A mouth-watering, thong-melting, rugged hunk of a guy.

I wouldn't ever want a relationship with a man like Cade, but that didn't mean I couldn't enjoy a quick one-night stand.

If I offered, I doubted he'd refuse. You didn't get to be pack alpha without having some mad skills with females. It was kind of a job requirement. So how bad could it be?

And just like that, I made up my mind.

"I don't know why you're here, but since you are, there's something you can do for me."

He gave a quizzical shrug. "Sure. What do you need?"

I let my gaze drift down over his body. He was wearing tight jeans that did little to disguise that he was packing large. My core tightened at the thought of it. Damn, how long had it been? Too damn long!

"I need an orgasm."

His eyes gleamed and he started to laugh. I hadn't expected the laugh, but it was a good one—husky and pleasant. Not nasty at all. I like a man who can laugh. My cousin Cam was darkly serious all the time.

"Yeah? That'd be my pleasure. Is this a one-way thing you're proposing or do I get to come, too?"

"I'll return the favor of course, but this is strictly one night only. I need some stress relief. That's all it is. I was going to pull out my vibrator, but here you are."

He grimaced, but his eyes still looked amused. "Not the best offer I've ever had, but I'll take it. On one condition."

It figured there would be a condition. As the alpha, he was probably used to initiating these things, but I'd made the first move. "What's your condition?"

"Simple—you obey me."

"Obey you? As in…?"

"As in you do everything I tell you to do. Sexually."

I must have hesitated, but in truth, his words caused another curl of excitement deep down in the pit of my belly.

"Nothing too weird," he added, grinning at me. "Just give up control and leave everything to me. I'll take good care of you. You'll get your orgasm, but you'll get it my way."

"I'm not in any mood to play games. I just want…I need—"

"I know what you need," he said, exuding confidence. "And I think it's cool that you don't hesitate to ask for it." He leaned back and stretched out his legs. "I want to see you naked again. Or should I say skyclad?"

He winked at me as he drawled the word. I rolled my eyes. Jerk.

"So start stripping."

Whatever. I could do that. I gave a little nod and shed my clothes, not even bothering to do it seductively. He'd seen me naked before anyway.

Still, his hot eyes studying each part of me wound me up even higher. At least I wasn't ashamed of my body. I was a few pounds overweight, but I'd never yet met a man who minded my generous boobs and curvy hips.

He crooked his fingers and beckoned me. "Very nice. Come closer."

I put some swing into my hips as I approached him. When I got within touching distance, he put up his hand to stop me. I obeyed, since he seemed to want it that way.

He stood up. He was tall; he towered over me. He reached out to caress my breasts. Slow and calculated. No hurry. Damn him for that. I wanted swift and sure with no time to think. I'd figured him for the hungry cock type who would seize what he wanted and get on with it. Probably selfish as all hell, but he'd make sure I got the orgasm I needed because seeing me come for him would be a sop to his ego.

He ran his index finger over my nipple. When it turned button-hard, he did the same to the other breast. Then he took his hands away so I was left with two tingling nubs that were telegraphing wild quivers to my crotch. He fisted my hair, which is too damn long. He got a real good handful of it and jerked my face to his. He kissed me roughly.

I dug my fingers into the sweet muscles on his back and returned the kiss. I moved closer and pressed my pelvis against his. His cock was massive. He was ready to rock.

So was I. I rolled my hips against his. His breath huffed out of him. The flat of his free hand came down hard on my ass. Ow! He squeezed.

"Get down on your knees."

I dropped to the floor. No hesitation.

"Take me out."

I unbuckled his smooth leather belt, my pussy tightening as I wondered if he would find a use for that. It only took a second to undo his jeans. His dick was practically busting out of them. I liked the look of it—thick and hard and long.

He let go of my hair and dropped that hand to his own cock, which he stroked for a moment. He ran his middle finger over the tip and then put that finger to my mouth. I sucked it in, tasting him. It made me hungrier. He pulled my hair again, forcing my head back. His eyes glittered into mine as he finger-fucked my mouth, holding my chin still with his thumb. So hot! My pussy was already clenching in mini-spasms.

He withdrew his hand and nodded toward his dick, which was twitching a couple of inches from my face. "Blow me. Do it nicely and I'll let you come."

He was crazy turning me on. I hadn't really gotten the dominant/submissive vibe from him before this. His alpha temperament was clear, but it was more the confident, natural leader thing than the arrogant kowtow-to-me sort of thing.

What he was doing now felt more like a sex game than like his everyday personality. If so, that worked for me. I hated the thought of actually being dominated by some male. But in a sexual context, it was thrilling.

I sucked on his cock the way I had just sucked on his finger—drawing him in slowly and swirling my tongue as I hollowed my cheeks. He let me go at my own pace at first, for which I was grateful, because he filled me up. I was afraid I might gag if he pushed me too hard, and I didn't want to show that kind of weakness. Showing any weakness is something I learned at a young age never to do.

He moved in closer until his hips were jammed up against my face. He held my head again with one hand, pulling on my hair a bit. He was still mostly dressed and I was naked. He was standing and I was on my knees. Now he shoved harder into my mouth, tilting my head back so my throat was elongated. I felt his knuckles brush my bare neck.

"I could get used to this, babe."

Yeah, well don't. I couldn't say it, obviously. Find someone to fuck, Cam had said. That's all this was.

I started fondling his balls, hoping to bring him off faster. I tongued the rim of his dick every time he pulled back. I sucked hard on the shaft. I caressed him with all the skill I possessed, but he maintained the same steady rhythm, making me feel every inch.

"Your mouth is amazing. Bet your pussy's even hotter. Bet your muscles down there can clench me tight while I fuck the daylights out of you. I want you on your back, squirming. I want you begging for my cock. I want you desperate, girl."

I pulled my mouth off him and looked up. "You want a lot, alpha. Maybe I'll kick you out and go for the electric boyfriend option, after all."

He started to laugh. His merry laugh swept the tension away. I felt my own face cracking a smile. Damn.

He had blue eyes—a vivid cornflower blue—and around the edges were tiny lines that suggested he laughed a lot. I felt a wave of—I don't know—liking for him? An alpha had to have some people skills along with the leadership potential. I think I saw that in him now for the first time.

He bent over, scooped me up in his strong arms and carried me to the sofa, where he laid me down. Pressing me back against the cool leather cushions, he parted my legs and dropped to his knees between them. He kissed the insides of my thighs, moving up toward my crotch. I could hear my breathing turn to panting.

His fingers found me. He explored. "So hot, so wet." A finger slid inside me. His thumb discovered my clit and brushed it gently. A little harder. Then rhythmically, driving me crazy. My ass came off the sofa as my spine arched.

"That's good, ah wow, that's really good."

"I need to taste you."

Who was I to deny him?

"Spread a little wider, hon. I love to see that pussy, sweet and melting, all ready for me."

I parted my legs even more, hooking one foot up over the back of the sofa. The feel of the leather cushions under me was a further turn-on. I was spread out nude and licentious as a porn star, lying on leather with a gorgeous man I hardly knew poised between my thighs.

"Show me your tits."

I giggled. "They're right there; can't you see them?"

He lowered his head and nipped my inner thighs. Punishment?

"Hold them for me. Present them to my lustful gaze." He was laughing a bit, too. "And pinch your nipples for me while I do this." His tongue swiped across my clit, making me jerk and moan. "Imagine there's a taut line between your nips and your clit. Imagine I'm tugging on it while I suck on you."

Holy shit. He was going to sex talk me into a climax. I cupped my breasts and obeyed his instructions. As I started squeezing the wildly sensitive tips of my breasts, his tongue stroked over my slit and slowly pushed its way inside. His tongue was big. He was a wolf shifter and it seemed to me now that he had a wolf's large and agile tongue.

"Ride my tongue."

I didn't need commands on how to do that. I was so damn excited my limbs were thrashing. He had to hold me down with one hand while he used the other to stimulate my clit as he fucked me with his tongue.

I lost all self-consciousness, all awareness of anything except the need to climb this mountain and throw myself off the top. My fears for Grandpa, my anxieties over my own sleep walking or sleep shifting or whatever it was, my past in Scotland, all of it disappeared. There was just the primal me and this wild, handsome alpha wolf who lapped me into the joyful here and now.

I came hard. The noises issuing from my throat weren't even recognizable to me. I felt as if I'd shifted into my wolfish self, seizing pleasure with my wolfish mate, all caught up in his lovely smell and taste and strength and dominance.

He was kissing my mouth, quite tenderly, when I regained some awareness of where I was and what I was doing.

"You're beautiful, Jess," he murmured when my eyes popped open to see his face suspended just above mine. "I could watch you climax all night long."

Mmm. That sounded fine to me.

But it didn't happen that way. Just as I started tugging at his shirt to get him as bare as I was, a cell phone started ringing. I wasn't sure if it was his or mine, but it jerked me right out of the warm, fuzzy place where my mind had gone.

Grandpa? I sat up in a panic.

CHAPTER EIGHT

Cade

Shit!

My damn phone chimed, and the sound freaked Jess out. She was probably worried about her grandfather.

I pushed myself off her as she started scrambling away from me. I was still wearing pants, so I tugged the phone out of my back pocket, cursing myself for not switching it off. I saw on the screen that it was Jake Cartwright calling.

Jake and I were good friends. He was my second in the pack—my beta, despite his own alpha tendencies. Fortunately, unlike Brandon, Jake had no desire to take on leadership of the pack, so rank wasn't an issue between us. We'd grown up together and trusted each other implicitly.

He rarely called at this time of night. Maybe it was bad news about Tom? I knew he worked some night shifts at the hospital. He was probably there now.

I decided to take the phone outside where Jess wouldn't hear the conversation. I tossed her a smile before heading out. She was searching among her discarded clothes, probably looking for her own phone. "Sorry, got to take this. Back in a few."

"What's up?" I asked Jake. I was out on the porch, the front door closed behind me. I wasn't eager to hear any more bad news myself. I'd been pack leader for almost two years, but I still hadn't gotten used to all the shit I had to deal with.

My dad had been the pack's alpha for most of my life. It wasn't an inherited job, but in our pack that was the way things usually worked. My brother Aaron would be in my position now, if he hadn't gotten himself killed in a shoot-out between two human motorcycle gangs. Random killing, all because Aaron had stopped in to meet an old friend for a beer at a bar. It had gone down so unexpectedly that he hadn't had time to get the hell out before a bullet had shattered his skull. He'd died instantly.

And, fuck, I still missed him. His death had hit me like an avalanche of boulders. To make things a whole lot worse, I used to hang with one of the MCs—a really dumb move for a shifter. I hadn't been in that bar on the night it went down. I'd wished many times that I had, but I'd been miles away, fucking some biker chick whose name I could barely remember.

I'd still been young then, all kinds of stupid. I'd been acting out for years, probably to rebel against my otherwise perfect family. Motorcycle clubs were one of my asshole ways of bucking the traditions of my pack.

After Aaron died, I'd wised up. Mostly. Dad's aspirations for the pack's future had fallen on my shoulders, and I'd taken on the gargantuan task of trying to fill my older brother's boots.

In the waning months of my father's life, I'd had to contend with Brandon. He wasn't of the Derringer family line, but I knew he was a worthy adversary. Because of my wild youth, Brandon had the support of a sizable number of people in the pack. I'd had to campaign hard to beat him, and my victory had been narrow.

Brandon had been gracious in the aftermath. There had been no challenge, no duel between us. He'd bowed to my leadership. Suzanne hadn't been too happy about it, and she'd made her feelings clear, but Brandon was an alpha and he had his mate under control. Although that motorcycle stunt the other night made me wonder.

I didn't think it was paranoid on my part to keep a close eye on the two of them. I got the sense that they were waiting, watching, and hoping I'd screw something up.

Until my leadership was absolutely secure, I had to be damn careful. So every problem felt like a crisis.

Jake got right to the point. "Sorry to bother you so late, but I thought you should know about this right away."

"Is it Tom?"

"No, not Tom. That is, he's not doing too well, but that's not why I'm calling. This is something else. We had an emergency case brought into the hospital tonight. Human. He was clawed to death by a wolf."

"Fuck. By a shifter wolf?"

"Yes. Cops won't be able to tell that, but I can. Our guy down in the morgue confirmed it."

"Who's the stiff?"

"Small-time thug. Got a long record of offenses, including drug dealing and grand larceny. Seems he may have been one of those motorcycle dudes you rode with for a while."

Shit. "Name?"

"Jock Nichols. Age 25. Know him?"

"I don't recognize it. But he'd have been known by whatever name his club had given him. It's been a while since I was involved with any of those guys."

"Know anybody in the pack who might be mixed up with the MCs? The cops are probably gonna write this off as an animal attack, but it was homicide."

If so, it was up to me to find out if the killing involved anyone in my pack. It was against long-established shifter law to kill humans.

"There are often a couple of young guys who hang with the MCs. Wild and stupid like I was. Plus the bikers are the pipeline to illegal drugs."

"You didn't do it, right?"

"Me? What the fuck, Jake?"

"Sorry, bro. Had to ask. Just wondering if this Nichols dude could be one of the creeps who shot your brother."

I felt part of me close down. "You mean did I kill him as some kind of revenge thing? I don't even know who shot my brother." Caught in the crossfire was what the cops had claimed. Wrong place, wrong time. "No, I didn't kill a fucking human. How can you even ask that?"

"Dude, take it easy. I'd kill the bastards myself if I knew who shot Aaron, despite my ancient oath to do no harm. Don't tell me you've never wondered if Aaron was targeted on purpose that night. He was your dad's successor, and, at the time, you sure weren't looking like a possibility for the post you hold now."

"It's occurred to me, yeah. You know that; we've talked about it."

"Not lately."

"Lately I've been busy with all this pack business crap. Trying to manage our resources, herds and lands and shit so we don't all starve to death. Still trying to learn everything I didn't bother to learn growing up because I was too busy being a wiseass. You know the drill."

"Yeah, I know, Cade."

"Anyway, the cops couldn't pin it on anyone and neither could my father. He and Mom exhausted every possible line of inquiry. Dad told me before he died that he was pretty sure it had been a random thing."

"I don't think the latest death is random. Some shifter wanted Jock Nichols deleted, and now we got his body down in the morgue."

"I fucking hope it wasn't someone in the pack. Does anyone else know about this?"

"Nope. We'll have to notify the cops that the guy's dead, but they'll think it was a wild animal attack."

"Great. Last thing we need is a panic among the ords. They'll all take their shotguns and hunt down every wolf they can find, not to mention every stray dog." I thought for a moment then added. "I'd better contact Marta." Marta was a shifter police officer, one of our pack. "She'll have to know the truth, of course. Maybe she can investigate discreetly and find out if there's any connection with our pack."

"Good idea. I'm hoping it's a lone wolf type."

The news jarred me enough that when I headed back inside, my plans for finishing up what I'd started with Jess had to be set aside. Even though I didn't doubt Jake's conclusion, I wanted to see that body with my own eyes.

In my absence, Jess had pulled on a paint-stained smock. Her legs were bare and she looked adorable. But worried.

"Who was that?"

"Pack business." I was preoccupied, trying to work it all through in my head. "I have to go, babe."

"Wait." Her hand on my arm stopped me. Her touch felt fine, even when I was stressed out. "You look upset. What's going on? It's nothing to do with my grandfather, is it?"

I stroked her thick, tangled hair. "Nope. I'd tell you if it were."

"Okay, thanks." A grin skittered across her pretty face. "Sorry you have to leave before I could return the favor."

"Yeah. Fuck. Me too."

CHAPTER NINE

Jess

For the next two days, while Grandpa got weaker instead of stronger, Cade kept returning to the hospital. I was glad for my grandfather's sake. For my own, not so much.

Every time I saw him, the violent passion I'd felt when he'd catapulted me into paradise with his magic tongue came roaring back. My very bones seemed to burn when he was around.

But I didn't want to dwell on that. Especially considering how abruptly he had left that night.

Anyway, it seemed wrong to be thinking about sex when Grandpa was dying.

This didn't seem to bother the alpha. Even though I believed he was coming to visit his friend—no one could fake the caring and devotion he showed to the sick man—he still made the most of every opportunity to brush against me, pat my ass or stroke my hair.

Today Cade was seated in the armchair next to Grandpa's bed, speaking to him in a deep, mesmerizing voice.

They were talking about hunting. Or rather, Cade was talking and Grandpa was listening, his frail fingers tight on the hospital sheet, his eyes intent on his friend's face. I pretended to be unaffected, but I knew I wasn't fooling the cocky bastard. It is hard to fool a wolf about something as basic as biological attraction. Our scents, imperceptible to humans, give us away.

And his scent drove me into a frenzy.

"There's nothing like it. Rising before dawn to dress in the dark, dragging on those heavy socks and long undies to keep warm even though you're toasting in your country kitchen with the bacon frying on the stove and the coffee bubbling in the pot. But you know it'll be cold outside, with that bone-stiffening chill in the autumn air."

He paused for a moment in his narration and glanced at me. He smiled. Something about his smile warmed me. Against my will, I was picturing the scene. I wanted to grab a pencil and start drawing. I was opposed to hunting except when the hunter needed to feed himself and his family. But even so, Cade's vivid words brought images into my head that I itched to paint.

"You've got your dogs, rushing about underfoot, eager to go. You've got your orange cap and comfy old shooting vest and your shell boxes and shotguns—the new double you bought last winter, as well as the trusty single-shot your dad gave you on your tenth birthday.

"That old gun takes you back to the days when you were young and short of leg, too new-hatched to drink the coffee the men gulped to keep warm, too shy and too dumb to have an opinion on whether that thorny blowdown over there might be sheltering grouse.

"Those golden mornings were magical. Remember when the leaves crunched underfoot and the skeleton limbs of the trees scratched the pale blue November sky? The woods went on forever. That was when we learned to love the land and all its creatures."

"Used to hunt with my dad," Grandpa whispered. "Down near Yellowstone. Wilderness all around then, but now it's ski lodges and time-shares."

"Same everywhere," Cade said. "Construction where the woods used to be, rivers and streams that are losing fish, dying of pollution. Real shame."

"The world's changed." Grandpa's voice was low; the words came hard. "Don't like what it's becoming. Guess I won't mind leaving it."

"That's enough of that kind of talk."

My heart gave a pang at the thought of Grandpa leaving this world. It was happening, I knew, and probably very soon. A serious infection had set in. His immune system was so worn down by trying to fight the cancer that the antibiotics they were flooding into him weren't doing their job. He was feverish and he seemed much weaker than he'd been just an hour ago. I should probably ask Cade to leave and let him sleep.

Looking at Cade's dark, handsome face inclined toward Grandpa's pathetically thin visage, I noted that there was something primal about him. Hot. Ferocious. Hungry.

As if he felt my gaze, Cade looked up. Grandpa's eyes had closed; he seemed asleep. But Cade was alert and wary. The corners of his mouth stiffened as our eyes met. In that moment, he seemed to see into me. I felt naked. Which, knowing him, was probably exactly how he was imagining me.

Chapter Ten

Cade

Jess' scent kept wafting through my nostrils, making me forget Tom, forget the pack, and just about forget my own name.

I wanted her naked again. Right now. I wanted her down on her knees, sucking me off.

Someone ought to put up an easel and paint her. Because, damn, she was fine. Her midnight-black hair flowed loose and wavy down to the middle of her back. Her face was pure of form and line, its classic beauty marred only by a whimsically upturned nose and the hint of stubbornness in her chin. She was lush and curvy. A gleaming gold belt that resembled a serpent was cinched around her waist, and she wore a bracelet of similar design high on her arm.

I couldn't stop staring at her intent face, her full lips, her large, luminous eyes. Not to mention those generous tits and that tasty ass. My cock was so hard it was about to bust out of my jeans. One time only, she'd told me the other night. Fuck that.

Tom groaned, sending a stab of shame through me. Thoughts of fucking Jess had been distracting me ever since I'd gotten here. She didn't seem to suffer from the same affliction. Jess was focused on her grandfather. Rightly so. Only a miserable, heartless, hormone-drenched wretch like me would be calculating my next move on Tom's granddaughter while Tom was lying here in front of me, dying.

He and I had been good friends, especially considering the age difference. There was something sweet and calm about Tom's personality that had given me an anchor during the hellish months after I'd lost my brother and my dad. Tom had been someone to talk to, someone to fret about, someone who was there to relieve the worst crush of responsibility after I'd taken over as head of the pack.

He was a man's man, a hunting partner, a fishing buddy. He'd understood my occasional desire for solitude; he'd never come too close nor demanded too much. He'd known and respected the boundaries of intimacy.

Women couldn't do that. At least not the ones I knew. They just couldn't back off, leave you alone. They didn't seem to understand the basic premise of masculine friendship— you were there for your friend when he needed you. But you never pressured him or asked him to talk about shit that was private.

When a man was dying, he counted on his buddies to do whatever had to be done. I was willing. It's a point of honor that you stand up for your friends. And especially for your pack brothers.

You also stand up for their granddaughters, if they need you. Even if all they need from you is an orgasm.

Tom shifted in bed. He opened his eyes. "Jess?"

My throat ached when I saw Jess' face brighten. She was still hoping he was going to make it. Losing him was going to be tough on her.

"Love you, lassie," Tom whispered. His breathing was more labored. Jess must have noticed it, too, because the spark of hope in her eyes faded and tears sparkled behind her lashes.

"I love you, Grandpa," she said, taking a tight grip of his fragile fingers. I knew she was holding on to more than just his hands. She was trying to stay the flight of his soul.

Tom's expression changed from peaceful to frantic. "Jess? Promise me."

"What, Grandpa? Promise you what?"

"That you'll abide by my wishes. That you won't—" he broke off to cough "—challenge my will."

"We won't need your will for a long time. Please keep hanging on."

Why should she challenge his will? I couldn't imagine that there would be much to challenge. Tom owned a ranch, some grazing lands, and hundreds of acres of rugged back country—some of which I'd hoped to acquire for myself since it adjoined my family's property and would be good hunting grounds for the pack. But there wasn't much money. I knew this because Tom had hit me up for several substantial loans.

Which reminded me, I'd better remember to tear up the paperwork. I didn't want Jess to get stuck with repaying me. She would have little enough as it was.

"Everything I've done, I've done for you. You won't like it, but one day you'll understand."

"I know that," She leaned over to kiss Tom's brow. "You've been so good to me, always, and I love you very much."

"Promise you'll abide by my wishes as stated in my letter. That you won't challenge my will."

"Uh, what letter?"

He coughed, badly this time. When he could speak, he whispered, "Say it, Jess. Please."

Jess looked over at me with raised eyebrows, apparently seeking advice. I wished I could give it to her, but I had no clue what Tom was talking about. I shrugged my shoulders and showed her my hands, palms up.

"Jess?"

Leaning over, she kissed his sunken cheek. "I promise I'll abide by your wishes and I won't challenge your will," she stated in a firm, clear voice.

Tom sank back. He looked relieved. "You're a good girl. Always were." His eyes wandered. "Is Derringer there? I need to talk to him, too."

I joined her by the side of the bed. "I'm here, Tom. Shoot."

"You, too, lad. Promise me."

"Sure. What?"

"The same."

"You want me to make sure everything's in order with your will? I can check with your lawyer to be certain your wishes are respected."

Tom was shaking his head. "Promise me," he said in a stronger voice. "You can make a vow, right? One you'll honor as a pack brother?"

I nodded, wondering what was up. Was the old man's mind wandering?

"Swear you'll abide by the wishes stated in my letter. And you won't challenge my will."

"Tom, your will isn't my concern."

"It *is* your concern," Tom insisted. "Promise."

"Okay," I said. Jess nodded, encouraging me. "I'll abide by your wishes. I won't challenge your will. You have my word as your pack brother and leader. And as your friend. Rest easy now, Tom. I'll take care of everything. And I'll watch out for your granddaughter, too, so don't worry about that."

He smiled and relaxed visibly. "Love you. Love you both."

It was as if the effort to extract the promises had been the last thing that kept him animated, and there was nothing further to be said or done. Closing his eyes, he nodded once and slipped into sleep.

Or what looked liked sleep.

Jess sensed it a moment before I did. She jerked forward, leaning over the bed. "Grandpa? Grandpa!"

Nothing. As the breath slowly left his lungs, Tom's face settled imperceptibly into an expression of peacefulness so deep and pure that I was awed. I'd seen death too often to fear it, and I guessed it held no terror for Jess, either. Shifters lived close to nature, close to the earth. Like me, she probably regarded death as a natural process, part of the inevitable cycle of life.

Not that this made mortality any easier to accept. I saw her shudder and knew how fiercely she must resent death's power to separate her from the people she loved.

"He's gone." She whispered the words as if that would make them less real.

I moved closer, allowing my hands to settle onto her shoulders. As soon as I touched her, she crumpled. I caught her, turned her, supported her, felt the mettle inside her gather and reform. She regained her balance but remained in my arms, shivering, the tears chasing each other down her cheeks.

"I'm sorry, Jess. He was a good man."

Her face was pressed against my neck; I could feel the warmth of her breath. "He gave me refuge, always. I loved him so much."

"He loved you, too." Refuge? What the fuck did that mean?

I stroked her shoulders and back, feeling the subtle musculature under her skin. She was strong. Her body was beautiful. I tried to ignore the stirring in my dick. Getting a hard-on by the deathbed of an old friend was not cool.

Somewhere an alarm was sounding—the cardiac monitor must have touched it off. I noted the commotion in the hallway, saw the hurried entrance of a doctor and a nurse. Not a damn thing they could do now.

We stood together, frozen in our sad embrace. She twitched, and I felt her mouth brush my throat. Fuck. My cock was rock hard now. Hard and hungry. I needed to stroke her, soothe her, slide my mouth all over her and drive my aching dick deep inside her. I'd been cheated of that the other night.

She moved against me, angling her hips in such a way that her pelvis was pressed right into mine. Shit, I couldn't help myself. Before I could control my body, I was grinding up against her, pressing my dick into the cradle of her thighs, yearning to strip away the cloth that separated us. Aching to ram myself into her. I guess it was as much an expression of life and a defiance of death as anything else.

Her head tilted back and her eyes cleared long enough to show some scorn breaking through. With a jerk, she pulled free. For a moment, I thought she was going to scream at me for my crudeness. I almost wanted her to. Face it: I *was* crude. Rough, unpolished, and so sex obsessed that I wanted to throw her down and fuck her right next to her grandfather's body.

It's a wolf thing, I tried to tell myself.

That was the usual excuse for bad behavior. Blame it on the beast within.

Jess didn't yell at me, though. She turned back to the bed and stroked Tom's chiseled face. Ignoring the doctors and nurses who were crowding around, she bent and touched her lips to his closed eyes. "Goodbye. I love you."

If I'd been capable of embarrassment, I'd probably have felt it. But hell, I'd done a lot worse shit in my life than getting an inappropriate hard-on.

Under my breath I said again, "I'll watch out for her, Tom, so don't you have any worries about that, buddy."

'Course I'd fuck her while watching out for her. Bring her into the pack, where she'd be under my protection and at my beck and call, whenever I wanted her.

She had no mate and no other male relatives, now that Tom was gone. I would just have to take her under my wing.

CHAPTER ELEVEN

Jess

"This is not happening," I said.

I was sitting in the Bozeman office of Meyer, Bolton and Brannen, my grandfather's attorneys, listening to the reading of his will. Cade Derringer was beside me, having been asked to attend by the lawyers. I'd thought it odd, but now I understood.

"You're telling me my grandfather divided the property? Left all the land to Cade Derringer and only the house to me?"

Looking uncomfortable, Geoffrey Bolton, a dour, middle-aged shifter attorney in an ill-fitting suit, met my eyes. "The house and all its furnishings and personal items, yes. And the barn. In addition to the acre of land the buildings sit on. The remainder of the real estate goes to Mr. Derringer."

"That can't be right. I saw a copy of my grandfather's will. Cade Derringer was not named. Why would he be? He's not a member of the family."

"This is a new will, dated less than a month ago."

Less than a month ago? That was around the time I'd moved back to Whittier.

Cade was on his feet, also. "If Tom made a new will in my favor, he must have been mentally impaired or something. It'll never stand up."

"I executed the will myself," said Bolton. "I've known Tom for years. He knew what he was doing."

"But he never said anything. Why would he do something like this without telling me?"

"If you will just be patient, Ms. MacLeish, you will hear that there are some conditions attached to the will. But before getting to those, I'd like to read a letter that will explain Tom's intentions. The matter is complicated, not to mention highly unusual."

"Look, Bolton, I'm not taking land away from his only grandchild." Derringer was stalking back and forth. "No way I'm doing that."

"I love the land," I said. "My grandfather knew that."

"Jess will challenge the will, of course, and I won't stand in her way. As a matter of fact—" He stopped.

As our eyes met, I knew what he was thinking. The realization had struck me, too. I envisioned Grandpa, struggling for breath, insisting that we make him a solemn promise. "We told him we wouldn't challenge."

"Yeah, I know, but—"

"We also promised to abide by the wishes in his letter, whatever they are."

"We were humoring a dying man, for fuck's sake."

Stunned, I shook my head. I believed in keeping my word. You didn't deliberately hurt someone, you didn't betray a friend, and you didn't break your promises.

"Blast him, the old son of a gun." He slammed one fist into his other palm. "So this is what he was up to?"

"But I don't understand. I can't see why—"

"Let's hear the damn letter."

The attorney cleared his throat noisily before beginning. "I'd appreciate it if you would both refrain from further outbursts until I get to the end."

"That bad, huh?" Cade said.

His expression determinedly neutral, Geoffrey Bolton began to read.

"My Dears,

"By now you will have heard about my will. You're probably confused and defiant, wondering what the hell that crazy old man is thinking of. Bear with me. I have a plan.

"Jess, you're my only living relation and I love you more than I can express. But I haven't done well by you. All the money I've ever had has slipped right through my fingers. Even worse, since I've been sick, other people's money has also slipped away. If it were not for the friend who's lent me far more than I could ever hope to repay, I'd have been tossed out of house, home and hospital long ago.

"Jess, my benefactor is Cade. He's a good man, and I owe him. I can't die without repaying my debt. It would be a betrayal of friendship and honor.

"That's why I'm leaving him the land. He wants it, he loves it, and the good Lord knows, he's lent me more than it's worth. It's all I have to give.

"I know you love it, too, Jess. And I know you were hoping to settle here to find the serenity to paint and do your artwork in the most beautiful spot on God's green Earth. I want that for you. But I worry that if left to your own devices, you'll lose yourself in your art and your memories and never let a single member of the opposite sex invade your sanctuary.

"You're not getting any younger, and, as far as I can tell, there's no man in your life. You and I both know why. But this can't continue, sweetheart. You can't judge the whole male sex by the viciousness of one of its members.

"As for you, Cade, much though you might deny it, I suspect what you really want is to put an end to your wild ways, find your roots, and establish a family. I know you're cynical about the possibilities, but hell, you're pack leader and you need a mate.

"The two of you have a lot in common. You'll thank me one day.

"That's all I've got to say. Bolton will explain the conditions of my will. I charge you both to respect the wishes of a dying man."

"That's how the letter ends," Bolton said. "He signs it with his love."

I said nothing. Anger had risen up at several points in the letter, but even more powerful was the sorrow that choked me at hearing the familiar cadences of my grandfather's words and phrases. During the years I'd lived elsewhere, Grandpa had written and emailed me often. I'd loved receiving his rambling missives. It was impossible to believe that he'd never write to me again.

As for the "not getting any younger thing, jeez. I was only twenty-four.

"This sounds ominous to me," Cade said. "You'd better explain the conditions, Bolton."

The lawyer coughed. His eyes darted about, seemingly eager to fix on anything other than our faces. "You get the land, Cade, but only if you agree to, uh, marry Ms. MacLeish immediately and maintain a joint residence in the house for a minimum of six months."

"Marry me?!"

"What the fuck?" Cade yelled.

"The marriage must be a true union in every sense of the word," Bolton said, keeping his head down. "It can be dissolved only in the case of irreconcilable differences. If, in other words, you and Ms. MacLeish find that you cannot tolerate each other's company, you may divorce after the six-month cohabitation, at which point the property, house and land, will be equally divided between you."

"Forget it! There's no way I'm marrying him."

"We agree on that. Fuck my life. I'm not getting hitched. And I've got no interest in Tom's estate."

"Oh, no?" I whirled on him. My heart was leaping all over the place. "Grandpa was talking about selling some of our land to a friend just before the accident. Was that you? How do I know you and Grandpa didn't set this up between you?"

"We did discuss it, but only because his lands adjoin my own. It was his idea, but nothing was agreed upon. If you think I had anything to do with this will, you're dead wrong."

"Please, I haven't finished," the lawyer said. "If you refuse to marry, the house, the barn and all the land are to be sold to whichever real-estate developer is willing to pay the highest amount. Apparently Whittier, Montana, has the potential to become the next fashionable retreat from the city. Instead of fields, woods, mountains and grazing land, we'll have condos, ski resorts and dude ranches."

"No way. Grandpa would never have allowed that."

"What's more, if you decline to marry and the property is sold, you will receive no proceeds from the sale. The money is to be donated to—" Bolton paused and cleared his throat again "—the National Rifle Association."

"Oh, my God!"

This was too much for Cade. He sank down into a chair opposite the lawyer's desk, put his face into his laced fingers and howled.

"How can you laugh? This isn't funny."

"Sure it is," he said when he could speak. "It's about as fucked-up, ass-kicking, gut-punching funny as anything I've ever heard."

"I am *so* not marrying you."

"Think of all the poor, helpless critters who'll die if you don't."

"That's the most ridiculous—"

"Hell, Tom was no fool. He knew which of us would be more reluctant to go through with this preposterous scheme."

"Are you saying you're *willing* to marry me?"

He put his head to the side, considering. He gave my body a thorough head-to-toe inspection. "Marriage isn't exactly what I had in mind. How 'bout we fuck for a while first? Hate to buy before I've thoroughly tested the merchandise."

I tipped my head back. "Why are you always so crude?"

Cade laughed again. "I'm no gentleman, babe, that's for damn sure. Wouldn't want to wed the lady under false pretenses. You marry me, you marry the local alpha hellhound." He nodded toward the lawyer, who was also a shifter. "Ain't that right, Geoff?"

Bolton cleared his throat nervously. "You're the alpha, Cade."

"So we have ourselves a temporary match to meet the terms of the will and I get you naked in my bed for six months. That's a bit longer than I usually stick with the same woman, but I guess I could live with it."

He was loving this, I could tell. Mocking and humiliating me seemed to get him all fired up. And just when I had been starting to think that he wasn't quite as much of a jerk as he had seemed when we met. He'd been kind during Grandpa's hospitalization. But now his inner assholery was showing again.

"You're clearly amused by this whole thing. But we made a solemn promise. A deathbed vow. I don't take something like that lightly."

Our eyes met and clashed. There was a pause; then Cade broke contact. He looked abashed. "Neither do I."

Geoffrey Bolton rose and headed for the door. "I'm going to excuse myself for a few minutes and allow you two to discuss this matter in private."

"That's not necessary," I said, but the door was already closing behind him, leaving me alone with Cade. Had he grown larger over the past few minutes? He seemed taller, and his shoulders were too damn broad. I wished he didn't look so lip-licking good. I had an urge to put my fingers into that thick, dark hair and smooth it away from his rugged face.

He would just *love* that. Dude had an ego as big as Mt. Everest.

"It's difficult to believe you're not somehow responsible for this. How do I know you and my grandfather didn't cook it up together? You probably thought I'd go for marrying a stranger because of what happened to me in Scotland. As if I need a man's protection—an *alpha's* protection—or some chauvinistic crap like that. Well, I don't. I don't need you or your pack or anybody else."

He had gone still. "What happened to you in Scotland?"

I blinked. Dammit. I'd assumed my grandfather had told him. He'd told him everything else.

"Does this have something to do with the vicious male Tom mentioned in his letter?"

"I'm not discussing that with you." Reliving the assault and its aftermath was still difficult for me. Not to mention everything else about me that he didn't know. "Anyway, that's not the problem. My grandfather playing Cupid from beyond the grave is the problem."

"Look, babe, I swear to you I didn't cook anything up with Tom. This is the first I've heard of his lame-ass scheme."

"Don't call me babe."

He rolled his eyes.

"You'd probably love to get your hands on our land. It's a hunter's paradise. We've got pheasants, we've got ruffed grouse, we've got deer and elk and bear and maybe even some antelope. All living and feeding and propagating. All beautiful. All waiting for you to kill."

He sighed. "It's the joy of the hunt that I love, not the killing."

"Hunting's a blood sport. And you're a wolf."

"For fuck's sake, so are you! What is this obsession with hunting? I've never met a shifter who didn't hunt. Are you trying to deny your animal self?"

I flushed and looked away. "That's my own business, so don't you dare mock."

"Hunting is not the issue here."

That was true enough. The real issue was that *I* was a hunter. And a much more vicious one that he could even imagine. Even a strong alpha wolf would have trouble handling me in my predatory darkling form. If I sleep shifted and lost control of myself, I might even kill him.

Damn him, anyway. And damn Grandpa for landing me in this mess.

CHAPTER TWELVE

Jess

I was deep in my work, lost in color and imagery as I tried to reproduce on canvas the beauty I could see in my head. It was always difficult—not so much to translate what I saw and felt inside to canvas, but to do it precisely and well.

Sometimes the brushstrokes flowed with startling perfection, as if my fingers were being guided by some greater power. Sometimes I would mix exactly the right color and apply it with the right flow and texture, getting lost in the physical act of painting. That was happening again, finally, and it felt good.

This was the first time I'd really worked since the accident. My grief for Grandpa had been so deep that for a few days, I'd thought I might never paint again.

Many members of Grandpa's pack had been visiting, and I'd tried to be gracious to them all for his sake. They'd left me with tears, hugs, blessings, and enough casseroles to last me a month.

When I emerged from my creative trance, the first thing I usually felt was pain. Cramped muscles, stiff fingers and wrists, an aching back. The second thing was hunger. Or thirst. But I noticed none of these now. Instead, I heard an unusual sound—very soft, very low. The hair on the back of my neck rose.

I quickly laid down my brush, shaking the fingers of my right hand and wiping paint off with my left. The urge to shift roared through me, which typically meant that danger was nearby. I beat it down.

I opened one of the windows just a smidgen and, with my wolf sense of smell, sniffed the air. A familiar spicy odor filled my nostrils.

Not danger, then. Lust.

It was amazing that a simple scent carried on the air could set my body alight with desire.

Face it. During the only moments over the past few days when I hadn't been sunk in grief for Grandpa, I'd been thinking of Cade. His lusty grin. His impudent eyes. His hard, fit body. His dirty-talking sexiness.

His smooth, delicious dick.

Damn. I didn't even like the man. Now I was supposed to marry him?

This would not end well.

I glanced back at the canvas I'd been furiously painting for several hours. I blinked at it, for it seemed to go out of focus. I realized that I didn't even know what I'd been painting.

It was a wolf. A large white wolf, probably a shifter, with blazing blue eyes that reminded me of Cade's eyes. He was standing against a green hillock with the peaks of the Rockies rising in the distance. He dominated the center of the piece just as Cade dominated the wolf pack.

But there were swirls of color around him that distanced him somehow. I wasn't even sure how I had achieved that effect. And deep in the darkest part of the canvas I could see an abstract representation of a face—those were eyes, surely? The curve of a brow? Lips that seemed to smile and snarl simultaneously. The flare of nostrils, the jut of a chin.

Was that a human face? Or a darkling's? Was it me? Why was she hovering so threateningly over the white wolf?

There was a sharp rap on my front door.

Pull yourself together, girl.

"Who is it?" I called, quickly rubbing paint smears off my fingers. But I knew.

"Open up, Jess, it's me," drawled the voice that was becoming so familiar.

"What the hell do you want?" I knew I must sound hostile, but please. What else could he expect?

"We need to talk."

I rolled my eyes. I'd put down money that he hadn't come here to talk.

At least I wasn't afraid of him. I wasn't afraid of anything, except myself.

I unlocked the door. Why the hell not? He thought he could take me on? Fine. Let him try.

He was there on the porch, all six foot two of him, clad in a blue denim jacket tossed carelessly over a black work shirt and a disreputable pair of jeans. He filled the narrow doorway with his broad shoulders and his uncompromisingly masculine air. His eyes were fathomless and mysterious. There was something carnal about his mouth, especially when tipped up in a smile.

Why not marry him? an imp inside me suggested. For the sex, if for no other reason. He was good at that.

He entered, glanced around and said, "Has everybody left?"

"Yes." I led him into the darkened living room, where I was certain he would feel right at home. He'd probably shot one of those stuffed ducks himself. "I'm going to have to get used to being alone."

He grinned. "Not necessarily."

I rolled my eyes. Was he going to be difficult? Of course he was.

He headed straight for my easel. I wanted to tell him not to look. I hated showing anyone my work until it was finished. But I contained myself. I had more important things to worry about.

"This is remarkable," he said, staring at my canvas. "That wolf looks like me, but I didn't think you'd ever seen me in that form."

"It's not you. I just portray what's in my imagination."

His grin was arrogant. "Looks like you're fantasizing about me, then."

I scoffed. "In your dreams."

"I love your use of color. So vivid. Not that I know anything about art. Did you study painting?"

"I studied art in college, yes."

"Can you make a living painting?"

I laughed. "I wish. No. I make my living doing graphic design. Websites, advertising, business logos, book covers, that sort of thing. Digital art mostly. I paint for pleasure. It's a kind of meditation, I guess. It helps me—" I paused "—not dwell on painful things."

Like Grandpa's death and his crazy will.

He sat down in an easy chair opposite the fire, stretching out his endlessly long legs. He was wearing scuffed Western boots. He always had a rustic air about him, but if my grandfather's information had been correct, Cade had made a nice pile of money somehow or other.

I thought about the money my grandfather had borrowed from Cade. It had never occurred to me to wonder how rich he was. Or how he had acquired his wealth.

Most shifter wolf packs had ways of making money in the human world. As far as I knew, they lived among humans without revealing their dual nature.

Shifters could always identify another shifter, even if the species of shifter was different. They didn't tend to mix socially too much, though. Bears hung with bears, cats with other cats. I'd heard there were higher ups in every species who interacted with each other to settle disputes and avert conflicts, but I didn't really know much about shifter politics.

People like me didn't have a social circle. Freaks like me were rare. The only other darkling shifter I knew was far away in Scotland.

I focused on Cade instead. Those boots. Did he own horses? Probably. Grandpa didn't just want me to wed an alpha, he'd hooked me up with a freaking cowboy.

"What do you do, exactly? I mean, for your work? I know you're the leader of the wolf pack. Is that a fulltime job?

"It's time-consuming, yeah. And there's the ranching and resource management side of things. My dad brought back the bison herd a few decades ago. No one was raising the animals much in those days, but they produce good meat, tasty and lower in fat than many other varieties of beef."

"Do you sell the beef or feed the pack on it?"

"Both. My father expanded our ranching and he also put some money into other ventures. When he started doing well, he invested in technology and software. He was clever at figuring out what was likely to succeed. I seem to have inherited that ability."

"You're an investor?"

"Part-time only. I'm careful about it, researching everything up the wazoo, and generally being conservative. I don't mind a little risk myself, but when it comes to the pack, I'm Mr. Responsibility."

Wow. Who'd ever have thought I'd hear Bad Boy Cade Derringer say that?

"I've made a few bad investments, but I've been lucky, too. I've increased the family's wealth over the last couple of years, and I'm good at managing the ranch, too. Or at least supervising the folks who know even more about that end of things than I do."

"So you're a man of many talents, huh?"

He shrugged.

I moved away from the canvas and gestured to the sofa. He followed. "Please sit down. I presume you've come to discuss our ridiculous situation?"

"Yeah. We need to figure out how to resolve things." He seemed to fill the room with his broad shoulders and long legs. I was used to being in this room with Grandpa, who was so much smaller and more fragile.

My heart throbbed. I was still thinking of Grandpa in the present tense.

Focus, Jess.

"There's nothing to resolve. I mean we certainly aren't getting married."

"Figured that was what you were going to say. Why not? What are you afraid of?"

"I'm not afraid of anything."

He was the one who ought to be afraid. He probably would be, too, if he ever saw my demon emerge. Damn, it was tempting to marry him just to scare the shit out of the fucker.

"I want to be left in peace. There must be another way to meet the terms of the will without our getting stuck with each other."

I had tried to rehearse this conversation, but I wasn't going to tell him the truth. How could I? Maybe if we were in Scotland, I could have been more candid. There were other multiform shifters there, and he might have been able to understand.

Here in Montana, I was an anomaly. People knew less here about the complexities of the shifter world. And as far as I could tell, they knew nothing about darklings.

"The way I figure it," he said, "we've got no choice. It's that damn deathbed promise. He trapped us neatly, the clever old fox."

"People can't be trapped into marriage."

"Still happens all over the world. There are a lot of cultures where folks believe young people are too foolish to choose their mates. Maybe they're right. The divorce rate in this country exposes our bad decisions."

"Maybe so, but you and I aren't that young. And my grandfather wasn't that wise."

"No?"

"I adored him and I miss him terribly, but he was a romantic. God knows why he continued to believe in happy endings, given all the screw-ups in his life."

"He knew he was dying. He faced and accepted it. I'd like to think I could be as brave, someday."

This struck me as a masculine reaction. An alpha shifter reaction. They were all warriors. Fighters tied up with their ideals about the courage a man needs to face death. An alpha might encounter it many times, while leading his pack. Didn't hunting have something to do with that ethic, as well? Ernest Hemingway and all that standing tall in the path of a charging rhino stuff?

"Sometimes I think it was life he couldn't face. Reality. He couldn't deal with the practical, the mundane. This house, this life, hunting, fishing...they were an escape. He was hopeless at finances. He had no idea how to live in this world."

I knew I sounded tetchy, but I couldn't seem to help it. He probably thought I was a real bitch. I was angry, I realized. Angry at Grandpa for dying.

"And you? Do you know how to live in this world?"

I shot him a glance. The question made me nervous. "What's that supposed to mean?"

"I was curious. So I did some checking up on you."

I felt snakes twist in my belly. "As in?"

"I know you and your mother ran into some troubles after your dad died. We, the pack I mean, have contacts with various shifters in other countries. Especially Scotland, since so many of us seem to be able to trace our lineage back to the Highlands."

How much did he know? How much *could* he know? Not much, probably. My family wasn't going to talk candidly to a stranger just because he was the alpha of an American wolf pack.

The real question was, how much should I tell him?

If I was going to marry him, even for a short time, was I obligated to tell him the truth?

I imagined it: oh, sorry, I can't marry you. Why? Because I'm different. Not your species of shifter, dude. What am I? Well, I'm a darkling. What's a darkling? You know—slow heartbeat, pale skin, insane thirst for blood? Humans call us vampires, but that's only because they don't really understand....

He went right on talking: "I know you had a psycho stalking you. I know he kidnapped and assaulted you. Dude was a shifter, wasn't he?"

Well, he clearly had some sources. "Who told you that?"

"I'm not asking to embarrass you, Jess. But it does seem relevant. Tom was worried about you. If he couldn't be around to take care of you, I guess he wanted to make sure the task fell to someone who could."

"And that would be you?" I said, trying not to snarl. "Because I'm only a female and thus not able to take care of myself?"

He held up a hand and gave me an impudent grin. "Whoa. Wasn't me who drew up the will. We got plenty of strong women in the pack. Have you ever met my mother?"

I had, of course. Not only did I remember Lorna Derringer from the old days when her husband had been Grandpa's pack leader, but I'd also recently renewed my acquaintance with the woman who was still the pack's alpha female. Lorna had been to the hospital to visit Grandpa and she, along with most of the other members of the pack, had come to the funeral. She was kind, warm, and iron-willed.

"I know and respect your mom, but there are packs where the females are relegated to a subservient position."

"Yeah? Well, not in my pack. I thought you didn't go much for communal life, so how would you even know about these male-dominated packs?"

"I lived in one, that's how."

Shit. I shouldn't have told him that. He wasted no time in jumping on the information. "Did you now? And didn't like it much, huh? Was that where you met your stalker?"

He was too damn quick. I rose from the sofa and walked over to the fireplace, turning my back on him.

"Where's the fucker now?" He spoke these words in an aggressively proprietary tone. As if it was up to him now to take care of any such problem.

"Look, I really don't want to talk about this. It's over. In the past. I left Scotland and I'm planning to live here."

"So he's back in Scotland?"

Was I chilled or was the fire dying down? I opened the grate to throw on another log. It flared up immediately, casting tall shadows on the walls.

He came up behind me far too swiftly to anticipate. He touched my shoulders; I whirled around.

"Don't touch me."

"I like touching you. I plan to be doing it a lot."

I jerked away.

"I want to know if the creep who stalked and assaulted you is still after you. If you're here because you're hiding out, I'm entitled to know what to be on the lookout for."

"I told you, I don't need protection. I can handle myself. Anyway, no one is coming after me."

"How do you know? These creeps don't give up easily."

Exasperated, I blurted, "I know because the man who attacked me is dead."

"So they got him? Good."

They didn't get him. I did.

I turned back to the fireplace and stared into the flames. I hoped he couldn't see the way my body was quivering.

"Look, I get that you're grieving and I understand if you're feeling overwhelmed by shit from your past. But cut me a break, okay? I've done my damnedest to help you out during the past few days, but you've received my efforts with very little grace."

I bit my lower lip, feeling guilty. He'd helped with the funeral arrangements. He'd contacted friends of my grandfather whom I didn't know. He'd even brought food.

"You're right. I apologize."

He was still pissed off. "I know you're upset about Tom's will. I feel as manipulated as you do. Do you think I want a wife thrust upon me?"

I sneaked a look at him. He was frowning, his generous mouth thinned and hard. I liked the slight scruffiness of his cheeks. Shit. I wanted him again. It shot through me, leaving me breathless. If he ordered me down on my knees, I'd gladly crawl.

"How much did my grandfather borrow from you?"

He shook his head. "It's not important."

"To me, it is. I want to repay you."

"He's dead, and I consider the matter closed."

"How much, Cade?"

"Look, it doesn't matter. I can afford it. You can't."

"The land he's left you must be worth close to a million dollars. Surely he didn't borrow that much?"

Cade said nothing. But before he averted his eyes, I read the silent confirmation there.

"Holy shit."

"It was the cancer treatments. His insurance wasn't great. It didn't cover everything. In some ways, you're right, he was unwise."

"He told me he had decent health insurance!"

"He didn't want to alarm you. He knew you had a lot on your mind."

I sat back down on the sofa. "He owed you a debt, and this is the only way he could think of to repay it." I took a pillow and hugged it to my middle. "I hate to admit it, but the will is fair."

"The will is nuts. I've got some lawyer friends. We'll break the damn will and that'll be the end of it."

"No." I drew a deep, determined breath and said, "We should honor our promise. I'll marry you. For six months. That's all we have to commit to. After that, we'll be free to split the property in a way that seems reasonable to both of us. Your half'll be worth more than he owed you, so you'll finally be repaid."

He was leaning back against the near wall, his arms folded across his chest. I couldn't tell if he was pleased or dismayed.

"Maybe it won't be so bad. I suppose I can tolerate anything if I know it'll only last six months." I hesitated, and then blurted, "We should probably skip the sex, though. Nothing personal, but the marriage'll be a lot easier to break at the end if there's no emotional involvement."

"The sex would be physical, not emotional," he said dryly. "And we're not skipping it."

CHAPTER THIRTEEN

Cade

Skip the sex? Oh no. That's not the way things were gonna work.

Time to do a little dickering. Maybe she didn't feel anything for me, but since the moment I'd first seen her standing naked on the side of the road, I'd been hot for her.

At first, it was pure chemistry, but now it seemed to be building into something with more potential. She might be prickly and independent, with crazy ideas about the evils of hunting, but she was also an honorable woman who believed in paying her debts and keeping her promises. I liked her for that. Hell, I was beginning to like a lot of things about her.

Starting with the magnificent way she sucked cock.

Damn. I was going to do it, wasn't I? I was going to marry her.

How bad could it be? Six months wasn't long. I could stand anything for six months, right? Having this woman all to myself, her delectable bare body under mine every night…hell, I could think of a lot worse ways to spend the next half-year.

Now that I knew she'd been assaulted, I figured I could understand her prickliness better. Even if her attacker was dead, she clearly had some residual anxiety. That was normal in crime victims. Maybe I couldn't give her much, but I could give her some safety and security. If some other nut decided to come after her, he'd have to deal with a fucking alpha wolf.

I pushed off the wall and moved to stand in front of her, conscious that remaining on my feet while she sat gave me a psychological advantage. "If we wed, it'll be real. The will calls for a true union in every sense of the word."

"I don't think that means—"

"Yeah, it does. It means we fuck."

"I'm not familiar with *your* personal habits, but *mine* do not include climbing into bed with strangers."

I patted myself in the pelvis and grinned. "We're not exactly strangers, babe."

"Kindly stop reminding me that I had a moment of weakness. One time only was what we agreed."

"No, that was what you proposed. I didn't agree to anything. And you're far too luscious for me to settle for that. So here's what I propose. We marry as quickly as possible, to start the six months ticking. We live here together, as the will demands. This place is big, so we'll be able to give each other space. We'll get to know each other better." Yeah, like maybe for a day or two. "I'll court you."

She looked away and stared into the fire. She said nothing. At least she wasn't arguing.

"I'm not going to force myself on you just because we have a piece of paper saying you're mine. But I do want you. No point in denying that."

I could see color come up in her throat, even though she was turned away from me. I was 99 percent sure she wanted me just as much. A she-wolf couldn't really hide it. Bitch was in heat for me.

"I know you're grieving, and I respect that. I'm not going to hound you." Well, not much. "But sooner or later, I'll wear you down."

Sooner. Not later. I sure as hell didn't want to wait.

"Think about it. Think about how it would feel to have my dick inside you. How good it would be. Think about my mouth on your breast, my tongue on your clit. The way you'd moan and writhe and clench your pussy muscles around me. Think about the ache in your belly and the burst of pleasure you'll feel when you come."

The flush on her neck grew deeper. She was just as excited by the prospect of surrendering as I was of mastering her.

But she remained still and silent. She didn't even snipe at me for being crude.

The firelight cast her shadow—stiff yet supple—on the wall. "Are you listening?"

She turned her head. I was startled to see that her huge green eyes were shiny with unshed tears. "I hear you."

"Jess—"

"It's a bad idea, Cade. You don't know me. I'm not who you think I am."

I shrugged. "Who ever is? We'll learn each other, just like other folks do."

Wordlessly, she shook her head. There was more to this, I realized. It was deeper, darker, more complicated.

I wished she'd been more willing to discuss the assault she'd endured in Scotland. I hadn't been able to get much information. How bad had it been? Maybe she was dealing with some sort of post-traumatic distress thing?

I felt a wave of fury toward the creep who'd tried to harm Jess. Good thing the fucker was already dead or I'd have gone to the Highlands to take him out. I'd have torn out the bastard's throat.

She's mine, I thought savagely. No one else is going to have her now that I've got my claws in.

Fuck. I wished I could stop thinking about how much I wanted to nail her.

"Jess. Can I ask you one thing? There was no mention of rape in the police report, but sometimes the police don't know everything."

She sighed. "If you're asking if that was what he intended, the answer is yes." She was hugging herself. "If you're also asking if it's affected my ability to enjoy sex, the answer is no. Obviously. I love sex."

"Well, it sure seemed that way, but—"

"I'm not damaged. Not in that way. But that doesn't mean I want to just coldly fuck some guy whom my grandfather owes close to a million dollars to as a payoff or something."

"You and I will never coldly fuck."

She rose and faced me. "There are things about me you don't know, Cade. Dark things. If we get married, my darkness might reach out and grab you. I wouldn't want that for you. Or for anyone."

For some reason this touched me more than anything else she'd said. She didn't want to bring her own problems down on my head and shoulders?

But hell, I could take it. I could take just about anything.

The impulse to jerk her into my arms and offer her physical, sexual shelter was almost too strong to resist. I did resist it, though. I didn't want her to think that fucking her was the only thing on my mind.

Even though it kinda was.

"There's shit in me, too, babe. I'll match my darkness with anyone's. But together maybe we can lift a lantern, shine a light."

She smiled at me, but her eyes remained doubtful. Her skin was silk, her hair the color of a blackbird's wings. She stood there straight and tall, her shoulders squared, her gaze steady, but there was such a softness to her bottom lip, such vulnerability in the curve of her throat.

I wanted to scoop her into my arms and carry her upstairs, kicking down doors until I found a cozy bedroom. Lay her down and strip her. Soothe her fears and smother whatever evil she had seen.

I could do it, too. I didn't think she'd fight me. The pull between us was powerful, and desire can heal as well as burn.

"Fine," she said. "I'm willing to risk it if you are. Let's go into Whittier and start the process. Get a license or whatever we need. There's a justice of the peace who can marry us, right? You can move in as soon as it's done."

I felt myself grinning.

Yes! She was mine.

CHAPTER FOURTEEN

Cade

I held a pack council meeting the next day at my place, inviting the members of the small group I'd appointed to advise me early on. The existence of an advisory council was not mandatory—my father had not had one—but it had seemed like a good idea.

Jake showed up early, and we hung out for a while. We agreed that we should consult the group about the thug who'd been killed by a shifter wolf. So far, there'd been no developments in that case.

The rest of the crew arrived shortly.

Grizzly Pete, so named because his wolf had once defeated not one but two grizzly bears, was arguing with Lorna, my mother, about the future selling price of bison on the pack's largest cattle ranch.

I didn't think that Pete knew all that much about the economy of bison herds, although he was a damn fine wrangler. My mother, on the other hand, had been instrumental in acquiring and growing the herd at a time when buffalo and bison ranching was still rare. She knew far more about the enterprise than Pete did, but Pete was an old school wolf who'd never accepted that a female could play a strong role in the pack.

I disagreed.

I'd always been close to my mother. Not in a sentimental way, but with acceptance and mutual respect. During the years when I'd been in one kind of trouble after another, she'd never given up on me. "Let the boy sow his wild oats," I had once overheard her saying to my angry father. "He'll learn a lesson or two and come around in time."

Her support hadn't saved me from a whipping on that particular occasion, but my father had backed off in the succeeding months. And I had come around, although it had taken more than oat-sowing to knock some sense into my head. It had taken my brother's death and my father's fatal illness.

My mother dealt with Pete in her usual calm, informed manner, and he finally backed down without me interfering. Good. I preferred it when they settled their own disputes.

When Jake reported on the mauling death, the tension in the room shot back up again. Hector Campbell, who'd been a trusted advisor of my father, questioned Jake closely. Jake shared what he'd told me the other night at the hospital. His information was even more solid now. The results of the autopsy had confirmed that a shifted wolf had killed the motorcycle club thug.

Marta, our Council member who was also on the Whittier police force, chimed in, "We have filed it as a wild animal attack. The force suspects a sick or hungry wolf."

"How can you tell it was a shifter wolf as opposed to an ordinary wolf?" Brandon asked.

Jake was evasive, probably because the process involved DNA shit or something.

"Surely no one in our pack would be capable of an attack on a human," said Suzanne.

I hadn't wanted Suzanne on the Council, but Brandon had made it a condition of his own membership. He could have made trouble for me if he'd declined to accept my leadership. When he'd run against me, he'd had a lot of support.

I shrugged. "Folks are capable of pretty much anything, in my experience."

Brandon nodded thoughtfully. At one point after Aaron's death, Brandon might have even been my father's choice for the role I held now, although I was sure he had never been my mother's. "I don't trust that man," Ma had told me more than once. "He smiles too much."

I didn't trust him, either, but Brandon was smart and he always had something sensible to say. He didn't seem to resent not having won the election, and he hadn't tried to enforce his own dominance among other members of the pack.

He and Suzanne now seemed to be a permanent thing. Supposedly, their mating had been a true one, complete with the sevmelle, the mystical fire that confirmed a fated mating.

I had my doubts about the sevmelle nonsense. I'd never seen it during any of my own erotic encounters. Thank God.

I'd always dreaded some female moaning out in the heat of the moment, "Oh Cade! I see the light! You're my forever mate... you have to marry me."

Yeah, well.

I'd been trapped into marriage by another method entirely.

"Any recent trouble with MC members?" Hector asked. He was a big man, strong, with graying hair and well-defined muscles. There had been a time when I'd wondered whether Heck might challenge me for pack leadership upon my father's death. If he'd been a bit younger, he'd have made a fine leader.

"Nope. But you know how it is with the youngsters. Like me, not so long ago. The clubs have a certain forbidden allure. And they're the local drug pipelines. Even if none of the kids are riding with the gang, they might be buying drugs off 'em, and the dead guy was a dealer. If he pissed someone off, or tried to cheat him, not knowing what he was dealing with, well..." I let my voice trail off.

Back in the day, there'd been a few guys in the MCs I'd come to blows with myself. Fortunately, I'd had the sense to do so in my human form. I'm stronger than any human; just about all shifters are. There's no need to go wolfish for a fight.

I'd been hoping to keep my personal life quiet, but Brandon brought it up toward the end of the meeting. He'd always sniffed around for news and rumors about people and he was damn good at nailing these correctly. Bastard.

"I was talking to the justice of the peace in Whittier this afternoon. He tells me you're getting married tomorrow, Cade? Who's the lucky woman? I presume you're planning to hold a pack mating ceremony?"

My mother's head turned sharply; I could read the shock in her expression. "You're getting married and you didn't *tell* me?"

"It's not really pack business. The marriage is a formality."

"A formality?" That was Suzanne. "You found a mate and you're calling it a formality?"

"Who is she?" my mother demanded.

I looked around the conference table. All eyes were on me. Expressions ranged from amusement to bald curiosity. In the case of my mother, I couldn't decipher what she was thinking, but it didn't look good.

"Tom MacLeish's granddaughter Jess. But it's not a real marriage. Well, it's real enough, I guess, but it's not permanent. It's a small matter of Tom's will."

And then of course I had to explain. Upon hearing the whole story, Jake, my closest friend, could barely suppress his laughter. Dick. My mother seemed doubtful and concerned. Brandon looked thoughtful. Suzanne looked annoyed. Grizzly Pete was the only congratulatory one of the bunch.

s

Jake lost it and started to laugh.

My mother, however, was not amused. "You can't get married, no matter how informally, without a pack ceremony."

It was true that on the rare occasions when I'd envisioned myself marrying, I'd figured it would be a pack ceremony, with a big celebration afterwards. But that was for marrying one's acknowledged mate. It was special. My marriage to Jess wasn't happening for any of the usual reasons. It was a technicality.

Hopefully I'd get some good sexing out of it, at least.

My mother looked as if she was winding up for a debate. She could be a powerhouse once she got running. Time to assert my nature and make damn sure she didn't spring into action.

"No pack ceremony," I said in my alpha voice. "This is no wedding, not by our standards. It's a marriage of convenience, and it'll be dissolved at the end of six months. If and when I ever get married for real, you can have your fun, Ma, doing all sorts of ceremonious shit. But not this time. Jess just lost her grandfather and she's not in any mood for celebrating. Besides, I'm not having her think this is something special. Because it's not."

Looks were exchanged, but nobody argued.

I wasn't sure what I'd done with my gavel, so I rapped my fist on the tabletop. "If there's no other business, meeting's over."

My mother stopped me after the meeting and insisted on taking me aside. Uh-oh. I loved my mom and I respected her, but I really wasn't in the mood for any discussion about the wedding.

Mom had recently turned fifty, but she didn't look it. I noticed absently that her dark brown hair had turned considerably grayer since my father's death. But her face was still unlined and her blue eyes were as sharp as ever.

Dad had been ten years older. He'd died young, especially when you considered that shifters usually outlived humans. My mom had only recently begun to smile again, but I was pretty sure she would never get over James Derringer's death.

"What's all this about a marriage, Cade?" she demanded once she had me in private. "Are you telling me that this girl, Tom's granddaughter, is your mate? Have you slept with her? Did you see the sevmelle?"

"Shit, Ma, privacy invasion much?" She had never questioned me about my sex life. Much less about the sevmelle.

She didn't back down. She rarely did. "You're the alpha now. You can't trivialize your mating. The rest of the pack will be watching everything you do."

And you still haven't proved yourself, was the underlying message.

"It's not a real mating. Tom left me all the lands of the ranch, and you know we need those lands, those field, those streams, the grazing, the woodlands, the resources for the pack. But he left the ranch buildings to Jess and demanded we marry to keep the two together. If it ends in divorce—which it will—we're free to settle it amicably."

"Shit," my mother said. Whoa. She rarely cursed. "Tom MacLeish," she said, rolling her eyes. "That man always had the oddest ways of behaving."

"Yeah, well, he was my friend. I miss him."

Her expression softened. "I know you do. I miss him, too. But we don't know the granddaughter at all. That is, I remember her when she was a child, but that was a long time ago. Her father was a good man, but he died young. Her mother, on the other hand..." her voice trailed off.

"I don't remember anything about the mother."

"And Jess hasn't told you about her?"

"Jess hasn't told me much about anything. The woman is grieving."

"Is it true that she was recently living in Scotland with her mother?"

I shrugged. "I guess. Why? So what?"

"If I remember correctly, Fiona comes from a powerful family of Highland shifters."

"Yeah, well, we all come from somewhere." I wondered what she was hinting at.

"Have you ever seen her wolf?"

I had a flash of the night of the accident. Jess had flown—no, that was impossible—she must have leapt out of the SUV as it rolled over into the ditch. The fog had cloaked her, but soon afterwards, I'd seen the gold-glowing eyes of her wolf close to the ground, moving, sniffing for her grandfather, whining. Then she'd shifted to her naked human self.

My cock stirred at that memory. Her lush and beautiful nude human self.

"Yeah, I've seen her. She's sable-colored with gold eyes. Magnificent."

My mother seemed to relax a bit. "Well. That's good then. And you're attracted to her?"

"Look, Ma, enough. I'm marrying the girl and that's the end of it. Six months from now, I'll get divorced and the whole thing'll be done. Let's not make a bigger deal of it than it is."

"Fine, Cade. I just wanted to make sure you'd thought this thing through. You don't always act sensibly where women are concerned."

That was an understatement.

CHAPTER FIFTEEN

Jess

As I contemplated my wedding, I felt like Persephone in the underworld. Cade Derringer had swept down on me one night and carried me off on his iron horse, and now I was honor bound to live with him for six months as the big sky closed over Montana, the plants withered in their fields, and the chill of autumn set in.

I'll be free, I mused, before the end of March. With the coming of spring. As the wildflowers ventured to poke their heads through the thawing earth, I'd be independent once more.

If I didn't kill anybody first.

The day before the wedding, Cade moved his stuff in, bringing the first load over in a pickup truck. He was accompanied by his friend Jake Cartwright.

I smiled as Cartwright tipped his hat in the manner of polite wranglers everywhere. The doctor was a tall, chestnut-haired man who, with his broad shoulders, slim hips and sulky mouth, was almost as sexy as Cade.

There sure were some hotties lurking up here in the Montana highlands.

"Sorry once again about your grandfather. Liked him enormously. My condolences."

"Thanks. You've come to help Cade move his things?"

"Yup. I have to admit, I never thought I'd see the day. Old Cade, roped and tied."

"You're not married yourself, Dr. Cartwright?"

"Just Jake is fine. And no. Cade and me, we're the holdouts. We just can't seem to hang on to a woman for long. Shame."

What he really meant was that women had been unsuccessful at hanging on to *them*.

I looked in the back of the pickup truck. "Lots of stuff."

"Not really," said Cade. "I'm leaving most of it at the compound. The family home, that is. I ought to be taking my bride to live there, but for the ridiculous terms of Tom's will."

I was glad I wouldn't be forced to move into Cade's home. I'd been uprooted enough. My grandparents' ranch had been a refuge for me since my childhood. It felt like home. While I wasn't thrilled about having a stranger move in, that was better than me having to live at his place.

I watched as Cade and Jake began unloading a comfy maroon leather recliner, several cartons of books and assorted odds and ends, sporting equipment of every variety, an office table, a desktop computer, a laptop, a printer/copy machine, multiple video screens, and various other electronic items. Cade asked if it was okay if they set this all up in what had been my grandfather's den.

But the biggest surprise was the frisky golden retriever who leaped down from the cab of the truck.

"I didn't know you had a dog." I squatted to welcome the excited animal, who promptly slobbered all over me and offered me his paw.

"You like dogs, I hope."

"Love them. He's okay around shifters?"

"Yep. I play with him sometimes in my wolf form."

Some animals were spooked by shifters, whom they seemed to be able to sense. "What's his name?"

"Barney. Uh-oh," he added as I continued to scratch Barney's ears and offer my face to be licked, "you're gonna spoil him, I can tell. Cut it out, Barney. Come!"

I laughed when the dog ignored him. "Well trained, I see."

"He's still young. I've got to do some field training with him during the next few weeks. Toughen him up."

I stopped smiling. "You're training him to hunt?"

"Hell, Jess. He's a retriever. That's what he's for."

I offered to help them bring in the rest of his things, but he and Jake refused. "Stuff's too heavy. You might hurt yourself," Cade told me with typical masculine arrogance.

"Not likely," I snorted. "But fine with me. I'll just stand back and supervise, shall I?"

Cade didn't look entirely pleased with this suggestion, but Jake gave me an amused wink.

The second load contained Cade's personal items and clothes. There was even a suit covered in plastic, looking as if it had never been worn. Jeans and leather seemed so perfect for him that I had trouble imagining him in anything else.

It was after the second trip that we had our first disagreement. He'd returned alone now that the heavy items had been moved. I watched in silence as he unloaded a quantity of fishing equipment—fly rods and reels; waders and vests and nets and all sorts of little gadgets.

"You really need all this stuff to catch a bunch of placid, unsuspecting fish?"

"Nah. I need it to catch the smart, wily ones." He grinned. "Actually, I don't use most of this junk. Anglers always have a lot of equipment they don't need. Just in case. You'd kick yourself if you lost a twenty-three-inch rainbow because you lacked a net to land him."

"It seems unfair to the fish."

"If that were true, trout would be easy to catch. Truth is, they're not. I'll take you fishing one of these days. Maybe down east to the Big Horn. I know a great fishing guide there. You'd like her—she's very cool. Name's Molly Tyler."

He began unloading several long, narrow objects in cases. At first, I thought they were more fishing rods, but then I realized they were rifles. Or shotguns. Probably both.

Hands on hips, I blocked his entrance to the house. "You can take those back where you got them. No guns."

"They're mostly for hunting."

"That's what I figured. Please get rid of them. They can stay at your place for six months."

"Well, darlin', problem is, this is the wrong six months. Fine if it were spring. But it's autumn. Hunting season's upon us, and I'm not giving up hunting, marriage or no marriage."

"If I can give up my freedom and my privacy, you can give up murdering birds and animals, for one season at least."

"Nope. Not negotiable. I'm a wolf. So are you. We hunt. It's part of me, rooted in childhood. It's who I am."

"I don't want guns in my home."

"Then we got ourselves an impasse. What do we do, call off the wedding?"

"Stop calling it that. The word implies celebration, lots of friends and relatives, love and hope and joy. What it's going to be is a short, sterile ceremony in front of a justice of the peace. That's not my idea of a wedding."

"I'm sorry I can't give you the sort of celebration you deserve. If it's any consolation, I feel cheated, too. This isn't happening the way I'd imagined it, either."

Hmm. He had a point. Wolf pack weddings were a big deal.

"Come to think of it, what we've really got here," he added with a wry glance down at the lethal object in his hands, "is a shotgun wedding."

In spite of myself, I started to laugh.

He pressed his advantage. "Don't worry about the guns. They're always unloaded, and I'll store them out of your sight."

I stood aside and allowed his guns entrance.

Cade didn't hang around. After asking if I would mind watching his dog for the night, he went off to party with Jake and his other friends. "One last chance to do some serious male bonding," he told me with a grin.

So while he went to his bachelor party, I spent a solitary afternoon playing a computer game on my own machine. It was geeky, but the game allowed me to socialize in a limited way with the other people in my MMO guild. I'd never met them in person, but they were good online friends—there when I wanted to hang out.

The humans I gamed with in Hunt the Night City played vampires and other supernatural avatars. They had no idea that one of their fellow gamers was a werewolf/darkling. Or that I was getting married on the morrow to a man I hardly knew.

I passed the rest of the evening before my wedding playing with Barney—petting him, throwing balls and sticks for him, even grooming his thick golden coat with an old hairbrush. He was a large, sweet dog who communicated by the changing expression in his brown eyes. I quickly learned when he wanted to play, eat, sleep and go outside.

Barney had an oval dog bed with a red plaid cover that Cade had tossed on the floor of the room where I'd told him to put his personal things. When it was time to retire, I led the dog down to the room and showed him his bed. He sniffed it appreciatively and stepped onto it, circling three times before lying down and curling up.

"Good boy. You have a nice sleep now."

With his head on his front paws, Barney watched as I pulled the shades and drew the curtains. But as soon as I shut off the light and left the room, he leapt up to follow me, his eyes injured, as if to say, "Aren't you sleeping here, too?"

"I suppose this is exactly the way your master's going to behave," I said as Cade's dog trotted confidently into my bedroom. He explored briefly, sniffing everything.

"No," I said in a tone that tried—and failed miserably—to be severe. But the truth was, I liked the company, and I raised no further objections when Barney lay down on the braided rug beside my bed and closed his eyes.

I fell asleep, listening to the soft breathing of the animal beside me. It was the first night since my grandfather had died that I didn't feel bereft.

Chapter Sixteen

Jess

"By the authority vested in me by the state of Montana, I now pronounce you husband and wife."

Even though the words were uttered in the confines of a dingy registry office instead of ringing out over the entire congregation in a church, they seemed momentous to me. It was done. Standing beside me, his hands firmly clasping mine, was Cade Derringer. Stranger. Alpha. Husband.

"You may kiss the bride."

I'd forgotten that part. I felt him lean toward me. I tilted my face up to meet his. Our kiss was brief, but when his firm mouth pressed against mine, my body came alive. I think because I'd been grieving, my sex drive had been suppressed for the past few days, but it roared back to life there in the registry office.

I couldn't wait to get my new husband home.

I saw it in his expression too: an intense flare of desire. The tingling inside me increased. He must have read my response in the way my body softened for him, because the look in those cocky blue eyes of his turned smug.

Damn him! He'd already won, and he knew it. He'd be giving me orders again soon.

I stepped back. The wedding had seemed so cold-blooded—marrying because of a condition in a dead man's will. There were no real feelings involved, or so I'd been trying to convince myself.

But that wasn't true. There was lust beating between us, and it wasn't just his. We stared at each other, a silent duel of wills, until the justice of the peace cleared his throat. Cade backed off, grinning. I guess he considered me easy prey.

When we left the registry office, exiting into the bright sunshine, my emotions took another flip. "I wish Grandpa could have been here on my wedding day," I explained as he helped me into his Jeep. At least he hadn't shown up on his motorbike. "My mother too, if she weren't living in Scotland now."

"My mom wanted to have a big shifter wedding ceremony, but I managed to talk her down."

"I'm sorry…should we have invited her today?" I felt a stab of guilt. I hadn't been in much of a state for socializing at the funeral, but his mother Lorna and I had chatted a bit and I'd liked her.

I remembered when his family had been bigger. His dad, the pack alpha, his mom, the alpha's tough and beautiful mate, his brother Aaron, the golden boy of the family, and Cade, the youthful trouble-maker. He had lost a lot over the years, too.

"Where are we going?" I asked as he put the engine into gear.

"Back to your place to change into something more comfortable. After that, a surprise."

"What sort of surprise? I really ought to work today."

"No way, babe. This is our wedding day. It's a lovely September morning, and we're going to enjoy it. Winter comes early in the high country of Montana. Are you game for an adventure?"

His voice was so vibrant that I got caught up in spite of myself. "Sure, why not?"

His right hand moved from the gearshift to briefly squeeze my left thigh. It was gone before I could outwardly react, but the afterglow from his kiss flared again.

After we'd both changed into jeans, he took me for a motorcycle ride into the wilderness. He drove us up a narrow dirt-packed, pine-scented road that led into the hills that stretched away beyond Grandpa's ranch.

The countryside was lovely—wooded hillsides rising in the distance toward the majesty of the Rocky Mountains. There was a rolling quality to the land all over Montana that was unlike anything I'd seen elsewhere. It was even more dramatic than the Highlands. The vast blue dome seemed to hover close to the ground in a true melding of earth and sky.

The air was clean and fragrant with the scents of autumn. The trees were bursting into the color that would glorify their last few weeks in leaf before the starkness of winter set in. All around us, I could hear the sounds of small animals scurrying to stock their nests with enough food to last them through the long, harsh winter that loomed ahead.

Because I was hanging on behind him, I could enjoy the feel of his body while he had to concentrate on the road.

He shed his leather jacket as the day grew warmer, revealing a thin T-shirt that molded over the smooth planes and valleys of his shoulders. The straddling position of his thighs pulled his jeans tight over hind-quarters that were definitely worthy of appreciation.

"We're near the top," he said a little later. "Let's take a break."

We'd been climbing steadily for half an hour or so, zigzagging up the steep side of a hill on a road that had grown increasingly narrow. I'd been looking askance at the ground falling away beside us. Rounding a rocky crag, we broke out of the woods onto a high, spacious plateau. "Oh, wow, how lovely."

We had a magnificent view of the surrounding countryside. Behind us stretched forest and scrub land, and ahead the mountains jutted toward the sky. The sun was at its zenith, its light brilliant and golden, and the air was clear and dry, with just the slightest edge that hinted of the coming fall. The plateau itself was a gigantic meadow, dotted with wildflowers.

"This is amazing. I'd love to come up here with my easel and my paints."

"I thought you'd like it," he agreed as we both dismounted.

I bent over to jerk off my boots and socks. Barefoot, I walked into the field of flowers.

"Careful. Wouldn't want you to cut up those pretty feet of yours."

"The soles of my feet are tough." I tossed him a smile over my shoulder. "Just like the rest of me."

He chuckled. "So you paint landscapes, right?"

"Yup." He'd been moving closer to me, and he was at my side now, our shoulders nearly touching.

"I'm not very good at portraits. I paint nature."

"Yeah?" There was a slight smile on his mouth—it gave an expression to his face that I found appealing. "And imaginary wolves?"

A low tangle of weeds caught my foot and I stumbled. Cade's hand shot out, gripping my upper arm. His fingers were full of sunlight.

"I'd like you to paint me." He turned me around to face him. He was so close.

I could feel the wildflowers tickling my bare feet and ankles. "As you pointed out the other day, I've never even seen your wolf."

Damn. Why had I said that?

"My wolf wants to meet yours, too." His arms slid around me, imprisoning me. His mouth came down on mine. Unlike the brief kiss in the registry office, this one was deep and rough.

I remembered the feeling of his cock in my mouth. I wanted it again.

As he jerked me closer, I felt that lovely dick through his denim jeans. My own clothing seemed paper-thin as one of his arms tightened around my waist. His other hand cradled the nape of my neck, slipping beneath the long fall of my hair to caress my bare skin.

I squirmed, needing to feel his flesh against mine. My spine arched as he pulled me closer and tongued me deeper.

He lifted his head and raised his palms to my face, cupping my cheeks. "You good?"

"Yes." As usual when he was around, my body had responded instantly and powerfully. Must be chemical attraction. Or maybe it was simply deprivation. As Cam had put it so crudely, I needed to get fucked more often.

"Not trying to rush you. Well," he laughed low in his throat, "That's a lie. I want to get inside you, woman."

He said the words clearly, with an edge to his voice that made my belly flip.

"But first, how 'bout you get to know my wolf? And me yours? This is a great place for it. Shift with me, Jess."

I felt the old anxiety rise up and grip me. "I don't shift often."

"You must have shifted the night we met. Or you'd never have escaped that car in time."

What had he seen that night? He'd never said anything. Never indicated by his treatment of me that he wondered what I was. Or that he knew.

I'd never meant to shift that night. It had been a survival reflex. I didn't think he'd seen my darkling because it had been foggy. Besides, it was a property of darklings that we carried our own aura of shadow, which helped to hide us, even from other shifters like Cade.

"Why don't you shift?"

The question was out there. Bald and clear. He was my husband now. We'd be living together. How long could I keep this secret from him?

He was the alpha. The leader. What would he do to me if he ever found out?

"These Americans, they don't understand us," my mother always said. "They are related to us. Descended from us. But when shifters dispersed all over the world, they lost something. Our wisdom, culture, and traditions. So many of them don't even know the old ways."

Even so, my mother had married an American. She'd rebelled against her traditional family in Scotland and lived in Montana with my dad. It hadn't been until after his death that she had taken me back with her to Scotland.

I'd tried to live there. A beautiful country, full of intriguing people. There were lots of shifters in Scotland. In the Highlands in particular. I'd spent time with my cousins at Mallochbirn. Ross Malloch, the current laird, was married to an American woman, Kate. She wasn't even a shifter, but she was the wife and mother of shifters. If that wasn't defiance of tradition, what was?

I thought of Cam, Ross's identical twin. I hadn't told him I was getting married. My mother didn't know yet, either.

It was so ironic that I'd fled Scotland in part to escape my mother's machinations about an arranged marriage. Yet here I was, trapped in one.

There ought to be a Greek chorus singing in the shadows about the impossibility of escaping my fate.

"I prefer to live my life in human form."

"Don't you feel the need to leave your human form sometimes? I know I do."

"You're the alpha."

"Yeah, but that's not why. It has nothing to do with that. That role was kinda thrust upon me. My father had it. My grandfather. My older brother would have taken on the job, if he hadn't died young."

"I never figured you'd end up being the one in charge of things."

He laughed. "I don't think anybody did. There are still folks who think the pack made a serious error when they chose me."

"Like who?"

But he shrugged off my question. "We were speaking of shifting, which is something I need on a regular basis. Like food. Or sex. Surely you need it, too. Come with me now. Shift. We're in the wilderness. Let's run together as the wolves we are."

He rose to his feet and started stripping.

CHAPTER SEVENTEEN

Jess

I'd looked at naked shifters all my life. But I didn't think I'd ever seen one who was so freaking gorgeous.

He was my husband. Which meant that, officially, I had every right to stroke my fingers over that lovely firm, ridged flesh.

He stood in front of me for several seconds, his merry blue eyes daring me to imitate him. I clamped my fingers together, resisting. Damn the man! He knew he was getting to me.

"Are you shifting or exposing yourself?"

He laughed. "Whatever works, sweetheart." But his flesh swelled and twisted and I heard the crack of bone as his body began to distort. I knew what that meant. I felt it far too often, and on occasions when I didn't even remember what I had done.

I didn't like the feelings involved in shifting—the pain, the crack of bones changing, the reorganizing of the shape that resulted in four legged rather than two legged locomotion. The disorienting changes in perception—vision, hearing, sense of smell. The loss of human language. Some shifters were adept at telepathy, but that was something I'd never been able to learn. Not that I had ever spent much time trying.

The wolf that took shape before me was beautiful. His coat was white, with only a few scattered accents of gray. His eyes, like Cade's, were blue.

I had painted him. How had I known?

He stood poised there near me, his head high and proud, his tail pointed upward in the vertical position that signified an alpha male. He trotted over and nudged my hand with his muzzle. He was so silky soft that I couldn't resist petting his head and stroking his perked-up ears. He preened for me as I patted him, and I sensed...knew...that if I were in my wolf form also, he would mount me.

I flushed to think of it. For several moments I indulged in a fantasy of the things I'd love him to do to me. Thank goodness I couldn't engage in telepathy! I didn't want him knowing my thoughts.

He danced away from me, his tail wagging stiffly. Maybe we couldn't speak, but I understood. He wanted me to shift too and play with him. Run over the meadow, among the wildflowers. Sniff the air for prey and hunt. Stalk, chase, attack, kill. Tear at flesh, swallow raw meat and drink hot blood.

My head began to pound. Inside me, something dark insistently rose. She was coming. Not my wolf but my darkling self. I could feel her pushing from the inside, trying to get out into the world.

And she was very interested in Cade.

Shit.

I can't, I can't. I can't let him see, can't allow him to know.

My top and bra already lay in a puddle at my feet. I unsnapped my jeans. The wolf—Cade—my husband and an alpha—was watching me intently from a short distance away. Even as a wolf, he would enjoy the sight of my human body naked. I knew it.

I used it.

Ripping off my jeans and sliding out of my thong, I let the sunshine pour over my naked flesh. I posed for him. My blood was beating at my temples and it took every ounce of my control to prevent the bones that wanted to melt and reform, the dark wings that wanted to sprout from my back and shoulders. If I shifted, it would be to my darkling. I could feel that self struggling to break the bonds of humanity and spring forth.

No.

No!

I figured I only had a few seconds before things escalated. Cade must be made to shift back. Because if he didn't…if he continued to tempt me to run with him, to play, to mate…I wouldn't be able to prevent my wild side from emerging.

I arched my back, thrusting out my breasts. My human breasts. I looked directly into the wolf's eyes and beckoned with my fingers.

Come and take me. I'm yours.

He got the message. The wolf looked crestfallen, but only for a second. The loud cracking sounds of his shift began and, lightning-swift this time, he reverted to his naked human form.

Complete with the biggest erection I'd seen in a long time.

"Jess?" he said, moving toward me, coming fast.

I forced myself to smile. It wasn't difficult. He was absolutely all that.

"I can think of things I'd rather do on my wedding day than run through the meadows sniffing the ground for deer or whatever you eat around here." I winked at him. "Besides, I owe you one."

And I beckoned him again.

CHAPTER EIGHTEEN

Cade

Well, I'd had a little run in mind, and I'd thought when she started stripping that she was down for it. But my senses did not lie. Jess was offering me sex again. Can't fool an alpha wolf about something like that. A human male might not be able to smell the pheromones, but I didn't suffer from the same limitations.

I stalked over to her. The little minx gave me her sultry smile. Okay with me! She wasn't the only one who could think of other things to do.

I stroked her hair, which wound around my eager fingers. She had petted my muzzle when I'd wolfed in front of her. I'd seen the admiration in her eyes. She liked me as a wolf. Maybe even better than she liked me as a man?

I ran my thumb over the soft plumpness of her lower lip. Her mouth parted, revealing a hint of her tongue and teeth. I envisioned that mouth on my dick again, those lips kissing me and that tongue stroking me. I remembered tightening my hands in her hair and holding her face steady as I drove my cock inside her.

It felt as though we were connecting at some primal level. When she dropped to her knees in front of me, my heart started to pound with exultation. She ran her palms up my legs, making a soft sound of pleasure as she caressed my quads. I was rigid with lust. One of her hands slipped around to knead my ass and pull me closer. The other moved up between my thighs to explore my balls.

Holy fucking shit. She had magic hands.

"You're a beautiful man," she said, giving a quick glance up at my face. She smiled and tossed her hair back over her shoulder with a jerk of her head. Her hands grasped my cock and stroked gently over me, making me twitch and burn. She glanced up again. "No rules this time?"

I laughed harshly. "You're doing fine so far. If I have orders for you, I'll state them."

Her smile was mischievous now. "Anything you say, sir."

Yeah, she was just my type. Damn. The woman had hidden depths, and I liked them. This beautiful chick—my wife, for fuck's sake—was kneeling naked in the grass at my feet. Even after the other night at her place, I hadn't expected it to be this easy.

She didn't waste another moment before bobbing her head forward and sliding her gorgeous lips around my cock. As her tongue probed at me, her mouth sucked, and she drew me deep.

She pulled back and brought her hands into the mix. She stroked me with her fingertips. She was so gentle and tender that I almost ordered her to do it harder. But then I saw the worshipful look on her face. She enjoyed this. That was a relief! I'd thought maybe, because of what she'd said about her attacker, that she might have some hesitancy. It had been hard to read her mood the first time we'd been together.

Her touch roughened. She tightened her fingers and slid her fist up and down my dick, increasing her speed as she leaned forward and teased the head with her tongue.

It felt so damn good. So hot to have her on her knees again.

Her tongue swirled around my girth and then she sucked me deep.

My entire pelvis just about melted as she moved back and forth, her mouth working me expertly while her fingers curled into the muscles of my ass. I'd been hoping to run as wolves and court her the way the alpha courts his mate. Soften her up a little when her animal instincts were closer to the surface.

But now that plan was forgotten. Now all I wanted to do was pump ferociously into her willing mouth until I found my pleasure. Because this woman, Jess, my sexy wife, gave head better than anyone I could ever remember face-fucking before.

It was something about the way she made the tip of her tongue hard and rigid as I thrust. Her mouth formed a tight spool of delicious suction, warm and liquid and smooth as hell except for that tantalizing ever-active tongue that kept stimulating my most sensitive spots. She found tiny collections of nerve endings that I'd never even known were there.

As lust ripped through me, I forced myself harder and deeper, seizing and jerking at her hair as I rode that stroking tongue toward completion. She didn't seem to mind. She pressed her voluptuous breasts against my bare legs and tilted her head back to take me deeper. She moaned as loudly as I did. Her sounds, her scent, and the crazy wild feel of her mouth working miracles sent me plunging into some alternate universe of erotic delight.

"Fuck," I muttered, thinking I should stop, pull out, offer her something in return, but how could I when she was not only sucking me but using her hands on my balls, pressing into that spot behind my scrotum where she could finger my prostate and just about kill me with pleasure.

Shit, I was gonna come. Too late to stop it now. But I didn't want this to be over.

I squeezed my eyes shut and gave myself up to the final drive. She was gripping the base of my cock, tonguing the tip and pumping me somehow, all while sucking the hell out of me. She was killing me. I groaned, delighting in her lips, her tongue, her bare breasts pressed up against my thighs. She found the tender spot behind my balls again and pressed, sending waves of pleasure to all corners of my body.

She was...ah fuck...I was spinning, swimming in shards of pleasure as I arched my hips and shot into her, spasming endlessly while her fingers dug into my buttocks and her own body arched against my legs.

It went on and on. She took it all and swallowed, continuing a much milder tonguing of my dick as the clenches of my orgasm slowed and died away.

I fell to my knees in the grass beside her. My arms wrapped around her, pulling her bare body against my torso. She was still kneeling, and her face was now pressed to my chest. I tangled a hand in her hair and tipped her head back. She arched against me, her body moving as if we were intended to fit together.

Hell, maybe we were.

I lowered my mouth to hers and kissed her. Her arms slid around my shoulders as she kissed me back.

"That was amazing. I don't even know how to tell you. You give one helluva blowjob, baby. You're fucking sexy as hell."

"So crude," she teased me.

CHAPTER NINETEEN

Jess

We were both quiet that evening on the way home. Night had fallen in the swift, surprising way it does in the autumn.

When Cade stopped the bike in front of what had been Grandpa's place, I felt shy. We had both withdrawn after our moment out in the high country meadow. This was our wedding night, and I still wasn't sure how to deal with that. All I knew for certain was that his touch made my body sing.

Meeting his eyes, I could see the quizzical look on his face—his eyebrows arched, that sexy mouth angled up in a cautious smile. My core clenched to the memory of that mouth on mine, those strong arms around me. It had been lovely, that passion in the sea of wildflowers.

From the way he was looking at me, I knew what he wanted and expected. No simple orgasms for either of us this time. We were about to have an entire night together. Very likely a sleepless night, with sex in every possible position.

I wanted that.

But I had to be careful. Very careful. I had almost lost control in the meadow when he'd wanted me to shift.

"Jess? What are you brooding about?"

I tossed him a smile. "Nothing. I'm just a little stiff from the bike riding. It was lovely, though. Thank you."

"My pleasure," he drawled.

Together we climbed the four steps that led to the front porch. Outside the door to the house, I fumbled in my pocket for my keys. "We'll have to have a set made for you," I said when I found the correct one, inserted it into the lock and twisted. As I pulled it out, the key ring slipped from my fingers and fell to the porch. Cade and I bumped heads as we stooped to retrieve it.

His blue eyes glinted at me. "Don't tell me you're nervous after what happened out in the meadow."

"Who me?" I moved to enter the house, but his hand on my shoulder prevented me.

"Wait. Let's do this properly."

He bent and slipped one arm under my knees and lifted me. I automatically reached an arm around his neck, which brought his head down close to my face. I could feel his breath on my lips.

I giggled as he carried me across the threshold. Barney greeted us with his tail thumping.

He kept carrying me until we were well within the house, kneeing the excited Barney out of his way and finally setting me down near the foot of the staircase that led up to the bedrooms.

He stretched and arched his back to loosen it, then reached down to stroke the dog.

"So, let me go upstairs and get ready."

Groaning, he ran a hand through his hair. "Don't take too long. I want to fuck you until your teeth rattle."

Turning, I fled up the stairs, leaving Cade at the bottom. "Come up in ten minutes."

"Don't think you're gonna start giving the orders around here," he growled. But he stayed put at the bottom of the stairs.

Cade

Well, hell. Ten minutes sounded like forever.

For the first time in my life, I had a legal right to be with a woman. Never thought I'd care, but now that it was done, I didn't relish any delays. I didn't want to wait one minute, much less ten.

Sitting on the bottom step, I made a fuss over Barney, patting and playing with him, throwing a soggy tennis ball that he delightedly retrieved. "What's up with her, boy?"

Barney's intelligent brown eyes focused on the ball in my fist. *Thump, thump, thump* went his tail on the hardwood floor.

I decided I'd better take him for a quick walk so I wouldn't have to worry about it later. He was overjoyed when I got the leash.

"I know there's something scary in her past, but I'm not going to let that stop me," I told Barney as we walked. "I'm gonna figure it out and help get rid of it, whatever it is. Hero to the rescue. Right, boy?" Even Barney seemed to understand that I was mocking myself. As if I'd ever rescued anybody? Mostly what I did was mess people up.

Barney gave a little whine of agreement and found a spot to do his business.

"Good dog. I sure wish my life was as simple as yours."

We were back inside in a few minutes, but it seemed like an age before she called down to tell me she was ready.

I took the stairs two at a time.

Her bedroom was down at the end of the hall. Not Tom's old room, but something more feminine. A good, large space, with its own bathroom. It had a queen size bed with brass trimmings. I approved.

She was waiting for me, looking great as always. Her long, dark hair was loose on her shoulders and she had put on some sort of flimsy nightgown that I intended to strip right off. Why did women bother with nightgowns or pajamas? Or sexy underwear, for that matter? While I can appreciate the aesthetics of such attire, I prefer my women naked.

I lunged into the room and grabbed her. I pushed her toward the bed.

"Wait."

Shit, was she going to try to stop me now? I felt ragged and frayed, at the edge of my control. This chick was going to kill me. "Do *not* tell me you've changed your mind. I need you, Jess."

"No, I haven't changed my mind." Her voice was ragged, too. "But there's something you don't know about me. And there's something I need first. I'll be right back. I have to get it."

Jeez, she'd had ten minutes to get things. What had she been doing?

I sat down on the bed while she walked quickly to the other side of the room. I figured she was going into the bathroom. Some kind of birth control? We hadn't discussed it. Maybe she wasn't on the pill? Maybe she used something else?

"I've got condoms, if that's what you're looking for," I said as she opened a drawer in her dresser. "Don't worry; I'll take care of it."

"This isn't something you can take care of." She returned to the bed with an object in her hands. She sat down beside me and handed it to me. It was a circular piece of metal. I wasn't sure what it was. A necklace? A collar?

The thing was heavy, wrought metal that looked like a combination of silver and some other metal. Iron? Steel? Maybe even bone? As I slowly turned it, trying to categorize it, I realized that it was old and beautiful in a savage sort of way. It also had a presence to it. Power. Where it was touching me, I felt a warm sensation.

"What the hell is this?"

"It's a Highland Choker."

"So it's some kind of Scottish thing?"

"Yes." She caught up her hair in one hand and lifted it away from her shoulders and throat. "Will you put it on me? You have to do it. That is, I could put it on, but you'd have to take it off. I can't remove it myself."

I wondered why. Did it lock automatically? The choker was closed and I didn't see a way to open it. It looked small. Would it even fit around her neck? "How does it open?"

"Just pull it apart. When you apply pressure, it will open."

I twisted the metal and sure enough, the two ends parted easily. She bent her head toward me. I spread the metal enough to slip it around her slender throat. It seemed to close almost of its own accord, snapping shut with a click that, for some reason, echoed in my dick.

Whoa. Was it some kind of dominance collar? Was she signaling her interest in erotic submission? Offering herself to me as my slave? The idea sent my already-heated body into overdrive. I could barely prevent myself from toppling her flat and driving my cock into her with no more preparation than this collaring thing.

"If this is some kind of sex game?" I bent to kiss her throat where the metal bound it, "I like it."

"Not exactly. You don't have these chokers in Montana? You don't use them in your pack?"

"Nope." I ran my fingers over the metal, so smooth and warm. I kissed her mouth and stroked the choker. Surely she must be burdened by the weight of it. It definitely had an aura. It felt to me like it was imbued with magic.

I didn't even believe in magic. Except that, hell, I was a shifter, so how could I deny that some type of magic existed?

"It's to prevent me shifting during sex. When you're wearing a Highland Choker, it's impossible to shift."

Yeah, right. I didn't know of any foolproof way to prevent shifting, so I was dubious. "Do you like to shift during sex?" Shifters did that sometimes. It was not unusual. But I preferred sex in my human form.

"No. On the contrary, I want to feel free to enjoy sex and be a little bit wild without worrying that I might lose control and shift. With the choker on, I know I'll stay human."

There it was again. For some reason she was afraid of shifting. That was something I needed to probe. Find out why she felt that way.

Not now, though. That could wait.

Now, if there were no more delays, I was going to fuck her silly.

CHAPTER TWENTY

Jess

Now that we were finally together in a bedroom, Cade didn't waste any time. He pulled me close. He brought the sexy with him. Something about him aroused me deep inside.

When he leaned down to kiss me, my fire caught and spread. My nipples pebbled and I grew wet and slick between my legs.

His fingers ran down my backbone, investigating each vertebra. I arched and rubbed my cheek against his, feeling the roughness of his unshaven whiskers. I imagined that roughness rubbing me in between my legs. My pussy rippled.

"You have no idea how many times I've pictured this." He tipped my head back. One of his fingers feathered across my upper lip, and then dropped to attack my lower lip. He slid his index finger into my mouth. I sucked on it avidly. As he drew it back, I nipped his fingertip, and he laughed softly.

"I've pictured it a few times myself," I confessed.

"I love your mouth." He planted a slow hot kiss on me. His tongue advanced, touched mine lightly, and then withdrew, leaving me panting for more. I grabbed his head in both hands and pulled his face to mine. He fisted a hunk of my hair. He scattered kisses over my cheeks and chin, nose and eyelids. When I began to laugh, he sealed my mouth with his. His fingers gripped my jaw and held me still while he plundered me.

As our kiss broke, he teased my lips with the tip of his tongue. "I want this mouth around my cock again. Your tongue licking me. But first I need to feel the inside of your pussy."

I loved the sexy things he said to me. During sex, I didn't mind the crude. It turned me on.

I felt confident now that I was wearing the Choker. My worst fear was that I would shift to my darkling self spontaneously and either shock Cade into a state of dismay over the creature he had married or, even worse, attack him.

Now shifting was impossible. I planned to wear the device at night when we were together to prevent sleep shifting. If it turned him on to think of it as a slave collar, all the better. I could get into that.

I dropped my hands to his trousers while he stripped off my nightgown. He was wearing that sexy leather belt again, the one that smelled so good and felt so soft and smooth to the touch. I jerked it out of his waistband and dropped it on the floor. His mouth took mine again, hard, demanding. He held my head still so he could control the kiss. He liked to hold my head still for his cock, too.

I rubbed my belly against his partially open pants. His ripped, hard body was harder still, his erection straining at his jeans. I twisted my face away long enough to smile at him and say, "Too many clothes,"

"Easily fixed." He let me go long enough to tear off everything he was wearing and toss his garments over his shoulder, not caring where they landed. "You didn't answer me about birth control."

"It's okay. Pill. And clean checkups. You?"

"I get tested regularly, so I'm good. But I've got condoms." He tossed a few on the bedside table and then dived back into kissing me again. A bit more of that, flesh to flesh, and I could barely contain myself. I lay down and opened my arms for him.

He fell atop me. His strong legs forced mine apart. "Arch your back. I want to feel your breasts rubbing against my chest."

I obeyed. My nipples were hard little buds full of jangling nerves. He rubbed them in a manner that seemed to set each nerve ending aflame.

He raised himself on one arm and used his free hand to explore, beginning with the Highland choker. "I like this thing. Looks way hot on you, especially when you're naked. You say it's not a slave collar, but I say it is."

"Whatever you say, Master."

His blue eyes glinted. "I'm going to fuck you 'til you beg me to stop."

"That's what they all say," I sassed him.

He laughed in that unexpected manner that made me like him. I'd been hearing about what a player Cade Derringer was since I'd turned thirteen, but he didn't seem to have much of an ego about it. Maybe I'd been wrong about his arrogance?

Don't start liking him too much, I warned myself. You don't know much about him yet and he sure as hell knows nothing about you.

We both explored each other, kissing, stroking, rubbing, finding sensitive spots and bundles of erogenous zones on each other's bodies. My climb to orgasm was usually slow, but with him it happened quickly. "Open your mouth," he ordered, saying it in such a low, sexy manner that it felt as though the simple opening of my mouth was a licentious act.

"Spread your legs. Grab my dick and position me between your pussy lips."

Holy shit…why did that sound so decadent?

As he forged his way inside me, I began to pant. It felt so amazing, but I needed more. I shoved back, rocking on his thick shaft.

"Clench your pussy."

No one had ever talked so dirty to me before. It got me hotter than I could ever remember feeling.

His cock plunged deep inside me, still huge, still spreading me wider than I'd ever been stretched before. I forced myself down on him, pulling back when he withdrew and slamming into him when he speared me anew. I wrapped my legs around his driving thighs and rocked, gasping as the pleasure suffused my clit.

"Talk to me, babe. Tell me what you want me to do to you."

"Um, you're doing fine. Don't stop."

"Not planning on stopping anytime soon. But you're gonna have to ask. Maybe even beg me. Think you can do that, babe? Try it."

"Fuck me, then," I said, trying the dirty on for size. It felt good. I rolled my hips against him and added a little rocking action of my own. "Fuck me harder."

Now he moaned. Good. He might pretend he had everything under control, but my own animal senses knew better.

The pleasure built until it was deep and rich and crazy. I reached the plateau and hung there for a splendid moment or two feeling the bliss as everything let go. Pleasure radiated along my spine and into every nerve center in my body. I screamed as I exploded, milking his thrusting cock.

My eyes must have come open because I saw him looking down, watching me, smiling in satisfaction as I climaxed. Almost at once, his expression hardened, his own eyes closed and he pounded into me in the last few seconds of his own surge. He pushed himself up on his hands, bringing his pelvis harder against mine. I could feel his body as it erupted—the shudder and pulse of the entire length of him as he ground into me one final time.

When his body stiffened atop me, I moaned some more to the sound of his hoarse shout.

It was almost like having a second orgasm myself.

As we lay there in the afterglow, he raised his head and grinned at me. One of his hands lightly caressed my breasts, and that's when I saw it. His drifting fingers gave off tiny glimmers of light. I blinked, wondering if I was seeing things.

"What?" he asked, noting where I was staring.

"Did you see that?" He looked down at my breasts. And stiffened. "What the fuck is that?" He tore his hand away.

"Maybe static electricity?" But even as I said it, I knew. From the startled expression on his face, he knew, too. The sevmelle was a sparkling light that was said to shine between two lovers who were fated to meet and fall in love.

But that was fable, surely?

My mother had believed in it, though. She had once told me that the sevmelle had burned between her and my dad. When he'd died, she said, he'd taken her soul with him.

That would certainly explain a thing or two, I'd thought at the time.

"Yeah, static," said Cade, looking relieved at the idea. "Must be."

"You don't believe that legend about—"

"Of course not! Only fools believe that love light crap."

"Agreed. We do seem to have some sort of physical chemistry, though. Atoms and molecules and that sort of thing."

"Pheromones, I guess. That's possible. That pheromone shit is even scientific."

I pressed my hands to his bare skin beneath his collar bone. I didn't see any lights now, but touching his skin felt so good. From the way he groaned and jerked me closer, I knew it was the same for him.

"Something in our DNA," I murmured, kissing his earlobe. I caught it between my teeth and nipped him.

"Hey," he laughed. "No chewing on the alpha."

CHAPTER TWENTY-ONE

Cade

Sometime much later, after we'd dozed and fucked and dozed and fucked some more, I fingered Jess' ornate collar and asked her if she wanted to take it off.

"I can't take it off myself. You have to do it. But not now. I'll sleep in it."

She had said something before about needing me to remove it. "It must be heavy and not very comfortable to sleep in."

She shrugged. "It's fine."

"Why can't you remove it yourself?"

"Some kind of magic. Once it's on, the wearer can't take it off."

"You're kidding." I wasn't a big believer in magical artifacts. "I can see why it might be difficult for you to get a good grip on it, but surely you can pull the ends apart the way I did. You're pretty strong, for a girl."

"Thank you so much." She sat up and reached behind her neck. She pulled on the two ends of the collar where they joined. Nothing happened. Was she really trying? I replaced her hands with mine. The metal halves parted smoothly with hardly any force at all.

I let it snap back. "Like that. You try."

She rolled her eyes. "I can't. Really. You must be able to sense its power." She tried again, and I could see by the way her muscles tightened that she was really pulling on the two ends. They stayed firmly closed.

"And it prevents shifting?" I wasn't convinced.

"If you don't believe me, take it off me and I'll put it on you. Then you can try to shift."

I reached under her hair again and opened the collar. Easy. I removed it and held it in my hand. It had already re-closed.

"It's too small for me."

"One size fits all." Jess took it from me and opened it without any trouble this time. She reached toward my neck. "Is it okay if I put it on you? You won't be able to remove it. But I promise I'll take it off you again."

She was fucking serious. But I was curious, so I nodded. She snapped the thing around my throat and it closed. I jerked. It felt tight but it had clearly rearranged itself, because my neck was much thicker than hers. It also felt weird in a way that's hard to describe.

"You want to try to take it off?"

"First I'm going to shift. Move back against the headboard."

She scooted out of my way and I focused my mind on bringing out my wolf. It rarely took more than a couple of seconds.

But damn, she was right. I couldn't feel him at all. I closed my eyes and went inside, where he was always frisking around, waiting for me to summon him. Sometimes he burst out of me all by himself, but that rarely happened anymore. Shifters learned how to control our shift some time during our teenage years.

Nothing happened. This was so strange and alien that I actually reached for the damn collar to claw the thing off me. I didn't like the way it made me feel.

I grasped the metal sides and yanked, but the Highland Choker stayed firmly attached to my neck.

"Believe me now?"

"Fuck. What is this thing?"

She placed her cool hands on my throat and removed it before I freaked out. As soon as she did, my wolf roared inside me. I could feel him now, and he was pissed. I pushed him down. I could feel my adrenaline racing through my blood vessels. Wow. I did *not* like that thing.

"Why would you wear something like that?"

She didn't meet my eyes. "Sometimes I sleep shift. I wear it to prevent that from happening."

"Sleep shift?" I had never heard the term, but it didn't take a genius IQ to understand what she meant. "Like walking in your sleep?"

"I shift in my sleep and go out and wander. It's a dream-like state and I often don't remember what happens during those times. I'd rather wear the choker than walk in my sleep.

Especially here, in a strange place. Well, it's not entirely strange, of course, but it's been years since I lived in Whittier."

Okay. I guessed that made sense. I got the feeling there was more to the story, though. Did it have something to do with that creep who had attacked her? I wanted to know more about that, too. But I sensed I was going to have to gain her trust before she told me.

Chapter Twenty-Two

Jess

"I knew your mother," Lorna Derringer said. "A beautiful woman, and you look so much like her."

I blushed and thanked Cade's mother, who smiled warmly and seemed sincere in the compliment.

"I remember you, too, when you were little," she went on. "You used to wear your lovely dark hair in braids." The tall, curvy, but extremely fit for her age woman slanted a glance at her son, who stood beside me near the entrance to the "compound," as the pack called the Derringer ranch. "I believe my dreadful son used to tease you by pulling your hair."

"I'm sure I'd have remembered if I'd ever done that," the dreadful son protested.

His mom and I both laughed at him. "I remember." I rubbed my head while tossing him a teasing smile. "I think my scalp's still sore."

Cade looked discomfited. "I know I was a hell-raiser as a kid, but please don't tell me I was a bully, too."

His mom patted him on the arm. "Not a bully, no. Just a mischief-maker. Come on in, you two. I hope you don't mind, Jess, but everybody is eager to meet you. I know you saw a lot of us at Tom's funeral, but that was such a sad way to welcome Cade's new mate."

I couldn't help but respond to Lorna's affability and kindness, but I shivered at the term "Cade's new mate." What had Cade told his mother and his friends about the marriage? Did they think it was a true mating? Didn't they know it was simply a marriage of convenience that would be dissolved in a few months?

A true mating. I didn't want to remember the sparks that had flashed around us when we'd touched on our wedding night. Surely that had been some kind of illusion? I'd felt the heat and the fizziness—like the best champagne—but if it was some sort of sign, it was elusive. It couldn't actually be a true mating, could it? I still wasn't even sure how much I liked the man!

But he was growing on me.

Cade's mother led us into a sunny living room that was much more tastefully decorated than my grandfather's place. Not a single rack of antlers in sight. I had some childhood memories of the Derringer ranch house. When Cade's father had been the alpha leader, pack gatherings were held here.

The house seemed much bigger now. Since that was the opposite of what usually happened when one returned to a childhood haunt,

I'd asked Cade about it. He explained that he'd built a new wing for his own use.

Cade had had to attend a pack Council meeting and his mom had invited us, along with a bunch of others from the pack, to come for snacks afterwards. I'd met many members of the wolf pack during Grandpa's illness, but my head hadn't been too clear at the time. I knew Dr. Jake Cartwright, of course, and Hector, whom everyone called Heck. He'd visited Grandpa multiple times.

Cade had filled me in last night about the others. Grizzly Pete, like Heck and Lorna, was a member of the old guard who had been Cade's father's lieutenants. Jake, Brandon, Suzanne and Marta, were of the younger generation. Marta was elegant but not overly feminine. She was a police officer in Whittier.

Suzanne was tall for a woman, several inches taller than me. She was thin and attractive, with long blond hair. She dressed down in jeans, flannel, and cowboy boots, but I noticed that she wore a lot of jewelry, including elaborate gold earrings and a large diamond on her ring finger. She and Brandon, her mate, were engaged. I'd learned that Brandon had been Cade's chief rival for the role of pack alpha.

It was already clear that Suzanne didn't like me. At the funeral, she had been polite but cool. I'd noticed her assessing me more than once, and shifting her gaze when I caught her eye.

When I'd asked Cade about her, he admitted that he and Suzanne had been together for a while: "I first hooked up with

her in high school. Then—this was fucked up—she started seeing my brother. That was serious, I guess, but it didn't work out.
After Aaron died, I was lonely and depressed and shit, and so was
she. We had another brief thing."

"You dated her twice?"

"Yeah. Second time was even more casual than the first. I
was in no mood to get serious and besides, it was clear she had
feelings for Brandon. They got together and have been steady
ever since."

"So Suzanne slept with you, your brother, and Brandon?"

He shrugged. "It's a small town."

It sounded to me as if Suzanne had been after the alpha male
of the pack. When neither Aaron nor his younger brother had
worked out for her, she turned to Brandon and campaigned for
him. But he'd lost out to Cade.

Since I was now married to the alpha, Suzanne was predis-
posed to resent me.

Whatever. I wasn't going to be married to him for long, so
she'd get over it.

I don't usually have trouble making friends, but I guess I'd
been more subdued than usual with Cade's pack members when
I'd first met them all. Grandpa's death had left me numb. Now
that I'd relaxed and started to feel more like my old self, it was
easier to socialize. Having Cade hovering at my side, with his
possessive hand touching my body, didn't hurt, either. And his
mom had gone out of her way to make me feel as if I belonged.

I joined in on several conversations and listened to several more. I was eager to learn as much as possible about Cade's pack.

"Is that a British accent?" Suzanne asked me at one point. "Or Scottish? You're Scottish, right?"

"Half Scottish." Did I really have an accent? If so, it wasn't strong. I'd spent some time in Scotland, but not long enough to acquire an accent like my mother's. "My father was Tom MacLeish's son." Surely she must know that. "After he died, we went to my mother's family in the Highlands, but I spent my childhood here."

"Really? I don't remember you."

"You probably wouldn't. Cade didn't either."

I didn't remember Suzanne, either, but I thought she might have been part of the cliquey "mean girl" group at the high school when I'd been in junior high. High school and junior high were on the same campus, and the older girls had tormented the younger ones whenever they had the chance. I'd been awkward and shy at the time, so I didn't have pleasant memories of those bitches. "I'm a few years younger."

She must have taken offense at that because she gave me a haughty once-over and shot back, "And a few pounds heavier."

I almost laughed. Did she think I could be embarrassed by the reminder that I didn't have a stick-skinny figure like hers? On the contrary. My darkling form, which I so disliked, was tall and bony. I'd take my curvy self over that aspect any day.

I was happy with the way I looked and I knew Cade was happy too.

Suzanne's mate smoothly filled the silence that followed her remark. "I love a Scottish brogue," he said. "How long did you live in the Highlands?"

I really didn't want to discuss that. "Not that long. I went to college here in the U.S. You have a faint accent, too," I said to Brandon. "Are you from somewhere down south?"

"That's my Texas drawl you're hearing."

"He moved here when he was a teenager. He was the new kid in town, but he quickly made friends." Suzanne touched his hand and gazed at him adoringly, but she was the type of woman who would gaze at any man if she wanted to flatter him. I was willing to bet that her adoring gaze had charmed many a man.

"It can be difficult to find one's place in a new pack," Brandon said. "So many traditions in local packs are carried down from one generation to the next." He assessed me with cool gray eyes. "You must have found that when you moved to Scotland."

I shrugged. I couldn't tell if he was hinting at something or just making conversation. I didn't think it likely that Brandon knew anything about my time in Scotland, but I could be wrong. Cade had managed to find out that I'd been kidnapped.

I wasn't sure what to make of Brandon. He seemed friendly on the surface, but there was a relentless expression in his eyes. The only time I saw his guard relax was when he and Suzanne were together in a corner of the room, talking animatedly. When he smiled at his mate, the smile seemed genuine.

"I've never been to the British Isles," Suzanne said. "I'd love to go if only to take part in a traditional fox hunt. Do you hunt, Jessica?"

"Please call me Jess. Everyone else does. And no, I don't hunt."

"But you must! You're the alpha's mate now, and Cade is a fine hunter. He and Brandon and I frequently hunt together. You could join us."

I kept trying to be courteous. "Thanks, but I'm really no good at hunting."

"We'll just have to teach you, then." Suzanne had a sly gleam in her eyes. Did she think she'd found a weakness she could exploit? "Here in Whittier, everybody hunts. In fact, why don't we ask Cade if he'd like to lead us on a short hunt, since we're all here together? We could shift and race into the woods for some feasting and exercise."

I felt myself go stiff. There were certain things I was willing to do in terms of socializing with his friends now that Cade and I were together, but shifting and running into the woods with them was not one.

"Great idea," Brandon said. I could feel him staring at me, taking my measure. He would be searching for my weaknesses, too. They all were. They were gauging where in the pack hierarchy I would fit. "What a good way to help our new member feel part of the pack."

Others must have heard Suzanne's suggestion because within moments everyone was agreeing that a run in the nearby woods would be just the thing. Marta, the cop, smiled pleasantly at me and said, "I can't wait to meet your wolf."

Cade, who was discussing weekend football scores with Heck and Jake, got the word and shot me a glance over the heads of several of his pack mates who were starting to move toward the back door. He must have been able to tell that I was panicking, because he made his way to my side and slid one arm around me. "Sorry. A group run wasn't on the agenda," he said low. "I'd love you to join us, though."

"You go. I'll stay here."

A flash of irritation crossed his face. We'd been married for a couple of weeks, but Cade still hadn't seen me shift. He'd asked me several times to tell him why I was reluctant to do so, but I'd always put him off.

Now I was cursing myself. I hadn't figured on Suzanne, but I ought to have realized that the other people in the wolf pack would expect me, as Cade's wife, to hang out with them in my animal form.

I needed to practice shifting to my wolf. I felt fine as a wolf, and in truth I missed running with a pack, but I didn't trust myself to be able to bring out the wolf without awakening the darkling.

"You should be the alpha female," Cade reminded me. "Come with me and show them all what you've got."

I didn't want to embarrass him in front of his pack, but I was also damned if I was going to let Suzanne manipulate me. So I smiled brightly and improvised, loudly enough for everyone to hear, "I'd love to, but one of our Scottish customs is to abstain from shifting while we're in mourning. I hope you'll all allow me to limit my social activities for a few more weeks."

"Of course we will," said the cheerful voice of Cade's mother, who had come up behind us. She put a friendly arm around my shoulders. "Come, my dear." She led me back toward the large, airy kitchen. "I'm not in the mood for a run now, either. Let's sit down and relax."

"Thanks."

"That Suzanne is a troublemaker," she said in a no-nonsense tone. "She hides her claws around all the men in the pack, but has no qualms about scratching the women. Cade'll have to go, though, as pack leader. But I'm sure he'll keep the run short."

The kitchen windows were open, and from the table where we were sitting, I could see the members of the pack milling around in the back garden. They shed their shoes and clothing in that casual manner of shifters everywhere.

Cade was among them, looking more relaxed and carefree than he seemed when he was stuck at his desk, running numbers and analyzing stock market fluctuations. As he stripped down, revealing his magnificent naked form, he looked truly happy and at home.

I felt a pang. The sight and sound of many people shifting at once was startling to me, since I'd rarely witnessed it. The air seemed to coalesce around them. Bones cracked and magic hummed.

In unison, the pack mates lost their human forms and reshaped themselves into large shifter wolves—long and sleek, strong and agile. They were mostly grey or brown or mottled in color, but they were all beautiful. And Cade, the only white wolf among them, was the biggest and strongest of them all.

They dodged playfully around one another, growling and giving low friendly barks. I noted the position of their tails, which varied according to their rank in the pack. Cade with his stiff, erect tail was clearly the dominant, but Jake, Heck and Brandon exhibited some alpha-type behavior, too. Among the women, Suzanne appeared to have the dominant edge. But of course, Lorna was in here with me.

You should be out there with him.

For the first time in a long while, I yearned to shift. I must have revealed that to Lorna, since she reached over the table and patted my hand.

"You could set aside your Scottish mourning custom. Tom wouldn't have minded. Go with Cade if that is your desire. He needs a strong woman by his side."

I snapped out of it. I smiled at her and shook my head. "Maybe so, but he doesn't need me."

She was wise enough not to ask me any questions.

When Cade returned, he found me in the kitchen where his mother was sharing some of her recipes. He had shifted back, but he was only half dressed—wearing trousers, but barefoot and bare-chested. He stroked my shoulders and, as usual, his touch was electric. My body bent toward him as if magnetized. "Gonna steal my bride away from you, Ma. I wanna show her my part of the house."

I said goodbye and thanked her as my husband clamped a hand around my wrist and led me down a hallway and through a door leading to another part of the building.

Another short hallway led into an area of newer construction. The aged wood of the original house was replaced with a newer, fresher scent, and the oils of more recent paints. It wasn't something a human would notice, but it was obvious to me.

A human *would* notice the cathedral ceilings and the two-story windows that let in vibrant light. Because the addition was on the west side of the house, the view through those windows was of woodland and hills rising up toward the Rocky Mountains. The other side of the house looked out on plains, fields and grazing lands for the family's herd of bison.

"This is great!" The huge open space was comfortable, elegant and tasteful all at the same time. "Did you decorate it yourself?"

"Nah. I hired someone." His voice was clipped and there was an edge to him that I hadn't seen before. Was he angry about my refusal to shift with the pack? "I did tell the architect what I wanted, though. I usually know what I want. I usually get it, too."

I didn't doubt that.

He walked over to a huge empty wall. "I'd love some art in here. My decorator made suggestions, but none of them appealed to me. Now that I've seen your work, I'm considering giving you a commission."

Whoa, I hadn't expected that. I could almost see it, though. Something about the space was already making my creative juices flow. I'd love to paint a piece to hang in this magnificent room. Maybe I could do a mural.

He didn't let me dwell on it, though. "There's more to see." He tugged me along through the rest of the wing. All the rooms were on one floor, but the area stretched out so much that I guessed he had more than doubled the square footage of the original ranch house.

"Where're we going?"

He laughed. "There's only one place I'm interested in showing you now." He swooped down and swept me off my feet. One of my fancy shoes fell off as he carried me down to the end of the hall and shouldered open the last door. We entered a huge, modern bedroom. He tossed me down in the middle of his king-size bed. "Slide out of those clothes, babe. I don't see you naked anywhere near as often as I'd like."

I laughed. "You see me naked every night." But I obliged, tearing off my top and unzipping my jeans while watching him subject his own clothing to the same treatment. Just being near him made me want him inside me.

"Yeah, well, that ain't often enough for me."

It didn't take long for us both to be naked. As I lay back among the thick pillows, he crawled up over me, holding his weight on his outstretched arms in a way that made his biceps flex beautifully.

"So," he said, as I stroked his sculpted chest, "I think it's time you explained to me why you keep refusing to shift."

CHAPTER TWENTY-THREE

Cade

"Mmm," she said. Then she pulled my head down and kissed me, sliding her tongue into my mouth. Which made my already-hard dick ache to take solace in her body.

But it was getting to be a pattern. Bring up the subject of shifting, and my lovely wife turned into a seductress whom I couldn't resist. It was ironic. Usually I was the one who resorted to sex as a way to distance a lover who talked too much or prodded me to "express my feelings." Now she was pulling the same old routine on me.

And who was I to turn down the delights of sex? But seriously, she was getting too damn good at this.

Usually a weekend run with my pack calms any violence or aggression I've built up during the mundane and often irritating daily grind. Although I hadn't planned on doing it today, when the suggestion had come, it had seemed natural to me and to everyone else in the pack.

Except to Jess.

I'd been wed to this woman for a little more than two weeks now, and seen her human body from every side and angle. I'd fucked her countless times. I'd felt her come on my tongue, my finger, my cock. I'd conquered her and mastered her body in just about every way. But despite all that, she still wasn't letting me in. She remained elusive. Mysterious. Silent with her secrets.

It was starting to piss me off.

I'd cut her some slack because, as she'd told my pack mates, she was grieving for her grandfather. Hell, I'd been grieving for him, too. I knew you couldn't put a time limit on grief, but that crap about Scottish mourning customs preventing her from shifting? I knew it was bullshit.

Not a bad excuse to come up with on the spur of the moment. I think even my mom believed it.

I didn't blame her for declining Suzanne's suggestion. I'm not sure how Suzanne had hit on that as a way to snipe at Jess, but she was an old pro at sniffing out vulnerability. She hadn't been fooled by Jess' excuse, either, and if I knew Suzanne, she'd find a way to exploit the matter again. Or Brandon would. I didn't trust either one of them.

Before that happened, dammit, I wanted to know what was going on with my wife.

I needed to know why a shifter wouldn't shift.

So while I explored her curves and valleys with my fingertips, I plotted. She curled and arched beneath my hands. When I arrowed down to the soft, dense curls at the apex of her thighs, I found her wet and yielding. I parted the folds and teased her a bit, approaching and retreating, enjoying the way her pelvis tilted up and strained, seeking my touch.

She was always so passionate. I loved it. Given that I was hard for her most of the time, I reveled in her responsiveness. The way she sighed and arched her hips made my dick throb with the anticipation of ramming her.

I slid my index finger into her pussy. Feeling the way her sheath closed around my flesh almost sent me over the edge. She was so hot, so tight. I added my middle finger and scissored them inside her until she gasped and shuddered. She lifted her hips up to invite me deeper. I obliged.

I kept my thumb on the surface, teasing her clit while she ground her body against my hand. Bucking, she cried out as I increased the stimulation. I wanted her to come, but I also wanted to control her orgasm. Make her beg for it. I knew myself well—I could be cruel that way.

Just thinking about it turned me even harder.

I moved down so I could add some tongue action. When the tip of my tongue circled her clit, she squirmed delightfully. I licked and sucked until she was thrashing violently.

"Not yet," I commanded.

She made a strangled sound that sounded like a combination of a gasp and a laugh. "Why not?"

I used my fingers to drive her even higher. "I'm the alpha, remember? Your alpha. I want your obedience in this, if in nothing else in our lives."

"Damn," she said, squirming.

My cock was rigid now. I needed to fuck her.

"I could tell you to ask nicely, my wife, and to say please."

"Please!"

I brushed her clit gently and watched her thrash. Then I rubbed it more firmly while my fingers drove roughly inside her. "But there's something else I want you to do before I let you come."

Her eyes snapped open and her writhing ceased. "Don't you dare."

Yeah, I was getting to know her—despite herself—and she was getting to know me. "You think you know what I'm going to say?"

"You're going to use this moment to demand answers to your stupid questions." Her voice was rough from her own churning desire. "We've talked about it before. I'm not comfortable shifting. Can't we just leave it at that?"

"Not anymore." I lifted my hand away from her. "You're the alpha's mate. When we're with the pack, it's not just you and me anymore. It's a larger entity, and I have a responsibility to them."

Her legs thrashed in frustration. "I'm your wife, not your mate. Your forced marriage bride. Your soon to be ex-wife."

I ran my fingers along her leg from her knee to her thigh bone. Tiny sparks of light burned along the path of my finger. "This says you're my mate."

She scoffed. "The static electricity? I thought you didn't believe in that sevmelle nonsense?"

I'd thought I didn't either.

"Anyway, you don't need me to shift. There was nothing in my grandfather's will that said I had to be your wolfish mate as well as your human mate. That's not what I agreed to."

I growled, feeling my wolf itching to emerge and prove her wrong. I liked that she was strong and sassy and that she took no shit from me. I also liked that when we were in bed together, I could make her set aside that sass and submit to me. She was delicious in that sense—all spit and fire until she got caught in her own flames. In the fever of desire, she'd do just about anything I asked of her.

But not this?

I didn't really care about what the pack thought. That was my excuse, just as her Scottish mourning period had been hers. What I cared about was breaking down the walls she'd erected to keep me out.

"It's not enough, babe."

"What's not enough?"

"What you're giving me. I need more. I want to be inside you. I'll crack you open if that's what it takes. Like this."

I rolled atop her and slid between her thighs. I thrust into her as smoothly as I could. I felt the walls of her pussy clamp down on me. She tried to resist, but tightening her body against me just heightened her desire. I could feel it happen. She melted around me and sighed. Then her hips rocked and she thrust back to meet me.

"You're such a jerk," she said as she matched me grind for grind. "I thought you were stopping, just to torture me."

I laughed low. "I love torturing you. Erotically, that is." I pulled on her hair and positioned her jaw. My mouth sealed hers and my tongue echoed my cock in syncopated rhythm. Her mouth melted, too. Holding her was like trying to harness a flame.

I drove harder into her. "You feel so good. So wet and smooth." My fingers played more roughly on her nipples and she mewed softly in pleasure. My cock began a steady thrusting motion. She circled her hips and clenched me, drawing me deeper.

"I knew you would feel perfect. I knew my cock inside you would feel like coming home. Especially here, in my own bedroom."

She giggled and said, "To me it feels like you're filling me up."

"I am. Always." I pinched her gorgeous breasts a little harder. "Does it hurt, baby?"

She moaned and dug her fingernails into my ass. "Hurts so good."

That was pretty much all it took. She stiffened and cried out, bursting for me. Her pussy pulsed violently, squeezing me so hard my cock jerked nearly to the point of exploding. I needed the same thing she was experiencing, so I sped up my rhythm until my body snatched control from my mind.

I was so hot for her that I exploded in climax after only a few more pumps.

She fell back on the pillows, breathing hard and letting out little gasps as the contractions rolled through her entire body.

I leaned over and kissed her mouth. "You're beautiful when you come, Jess. Actually, you're beautiful all the time."

Her fingers trailed down my spine and settled on my ass. Her touch felt warm. It gave me tiny shocks on the surface of my skin. Good shocks, though. If I could see her hand, I knew it would be glowing with light.

That static electricity thing was getting stronger between us every day.

"But?" she asked lazily.

"But what?"

"It sounds as if there was more. Something about cracking me open?"

"Yeah, well."

I meant to do that, all right. I just had to be smart about it.

CHAPTER TWENTY-FOUR

Cade

Jess dozed off in my arms. Perfect. I slid away from her and got a few things from my bedside table. A little while later, she opened her eyes, looking puzzled. She tugged at her limbs and found herself helpless and vulnerable. Just the way I liked it.

"What the fuck?" She thrashed as much as she could, which wasn't much, given she was cuffed and tied to the four bedposts.

I leaned up on one elbow and ran my hand over her stretched-out body. She twitched in her bondage and my cock twitched in appreciation.

Her green eyes flashed. "I knew you were kinky, but aren't you supposed to get consent before you tie up your partner?"

I stroked down, gently, from her throat to her breasts. As I circled her nipples, slowly closing in on the point, both nubs grew hard and her breathing escalated. "D'you want me to release you?"

She hesitated. I let my finger drift lower. She moaned instead of answering.

"Sounds like consent to me."

"Bastard," she muttered. But I didn't hear a safeword.

I was tempted to play with her a bit. Get her way up there again, where she couldn't easily turn away from the pleasure I was giving her. I also wanted to indulge myself. My dick was painfully hard again. The sight of her spread out for me was delectable.

"I know what you're trying to do. You think that if you make me really frustrated and angry, my wolf will get so aggressive that she'll spring out of me, whether I like it or not."

She was probably right. "Why won't you talk to me?"

"Why do you even care?"

I realized I didn't know the answer to that. Why the hell was it so important to me that I know all her secrets?

As she'd said, she was my soon-to-be-ex.

A year from now, I'd be sharing my bed with other women, other conquests. Just as I'd done for years. No strings, no commitments. You got secrets, honey? Keep 'em because I'm not interested.

"You keep secrets from *me*. If I'm not sharing, maybe it's because you're just as elusive."

That surprised me. "I don't know what you're referring to since I don't have any secrets. When have I ever hidden anything about myself? Everyone knows what a fuckup I used to be. The various ways I've messed up. I'm a goddamn open book to the whole shifter community."

"Still, there's a lot I don't know about you. It's not as if we've talked much these past few weeks. We have a lot of sex, but we don't talk."

"I admit I can think of better things to do with that sweet mouth of yours than chat."

"All right, then."

"So I'll trade you. If you want the info on me, you have to give me the info on you. I give a little, you give a little. How about it?"

"Fine, if it's fair. I am not going to tell you my whole autobiography in exchange for your favorite movie or something."

"Truth or Dare."

"You're fucking kidding me. What is this, high school?"

"Come on. Let's try it. Give me a question that I have to answer truthfully. If I don't wanna answer it, give me a dare."

"Fine. Untie me first."

"Prove you're really going to play and I'll untie you. I'm going to ask you a question. Truth or Dare."

She rolled her eyes. "Ask."

I'd already decided not to go in for the kill on the first question. That would just piss her off. So I said, "Okay, this shouldn't be too hard for you. When you were a kid in Montana, before your dad died, did you used to shift?"

She frowned, but she answered, "Ok, I'll tell you the truth on that. Yes. I started around the same age as most of the other kids." She added, although I hadn't asked it, "Everything was fine then. It was only after we went to Scotland and got involved with the other pack that shifting became a problem."

As gently as possible, I untied the ropes binding her wrists and ankles. "What pack was that?"

I thought she wasn't going to answer. She said nothing at all for several seconds. I busied myself with the ropes, winding them up into neat coils. Pretending I wasn't that eager to hear the answer.

"After my dad died, my mum fell apart. Well, we both did, really."

I lay back down beside her and put my arm around her.

"I was crushed by Dad's death, but my grandparents and I comforted each other. Mum felt alone, I think. Montana wasn't her home. She wanted to go back to Scotland. I was only 13 and had no choice in the matter. So we went.

"But it turned out that Mum's parents, my other grandparents, were still angry over her marriage to my father. She had defied them by marrying a man they didn't approve of."

"Whoa."

"Yeah. They'd planned an arranged marriage for her. Ironic, isn't it? A few years later, she tried the same scheme on me. She wanted me to marry Cameron Malloch, my second cousin. That's part of the reason I returned to the States—so I wouldn't have to marry a man I didn't love."

"Oops."

She laughed, which was reassuring. "Life is strange, isn't it? Anyway, for about a year we wandered around the Highlands, visiting family, being vagabonds. Then something unfortunate happened. My mother got mixed up with a man. An alpha wolf named Martin."

This was the first I'd heard of Martin. Or Cameron Malloch, although that name sounded familiar. I could swear I'd heard it before.

"She joined his pack and dragged me along. Martin was the alpha. His son Jonathan was a year younger than me." She paused. I could feel the way her body had tensed. "Jonathan was the shifter who kidnapped and assaulted me. Years later, when we were both adults."

"So," I hesitated as I tried to process this without leaping out of bed and going out to kill Jonathan, wherever he was. Or—maybe not. She'd told me before the wedding that her attacker was dead.

"This Jonathan guy was your stepbrother?"

"Not officially. My mum never married Martin. He was a strange kid who tried to bully me. But I was a tomboy—tough, strong, and scrappy. I think he hated me for that. As we got older and he gained height and muscle, he grew more dangerous. He was a psychopath. Narcissistic. Incapable of empathy. Sadistic. I was his favorite target."

"Fuck."

"Yeah."

"His father must have known. It was his responsibility to see that everyone in the pack was safe. "

"This pack was different. Women were subservient to the males. Martin was almost as bad as his son. Before she realized what she'd signed up for, my mother was in too deep. She admitted later that she'd gone into a dark place and didn't know how to extricate herself. Or me.

"The pack lived deep in an isolated part of the Highlands. But we didn't live as wolves. You've wondered why I don't shift more. We weren't allowed to shift, except on the alpha's orders. At first, I did it anyway. Rebelliously." She stopped again before adding in a low voice, "They punished me for shifting."

I could feel my hot blood pounding. I was furious on her behalf. What kind of a pack punished anyone for shifting? I wanted to fly over to Scotland and rip out their throats.

"Punished you how?"

It was too much. I could see by the look on her face that she was done. She wasn't going to tell me the rest of the story. Not now, anyway. She took a deep breath and said, "I've answered more than one question. It's your turn to be interrogated."

"Fair enough," I said quickly before she could withdraw. But I was trying to process what she had told me. It was worse than I'd guessed. She'd been abused and it had apparently gone on for several years. I was surprised that she was as together emotionally as she was. She must be really strong inside. And resilient.

"Ask away."

She had her question all ready to go: "Why did a kid like you, who grew up in a nice family with great parents, turn into such a messed-up dick as a teenager?"

I should have known she wouldn't hesitate to pull out the big guns. I guess it was only fair. It was spill your guts time. "I can answer that. Truth."

She pushed herself up on the pillows. "Okay, let's hear it."

"I was always a fucked-up kid. My father and I clashed a lot. He was stubborn as all hell and I'm the same.

"Then there was Aaron, the golden boy. I adored him, but I was jealous. He was bigger, stronger, smarter, and generally perfect. Everyone loved him. Our teachers favored him. They tried not to show it, but, well...." I shrugged, reminding myself to stay detached. Always hard when remembering Aaron. "He was the archetypal good boy, with whom I could never compete, so I devoted myself to being the opposite. I was good at being bad. I fucking excelled at that."

"Seriously? Is that the way you thought about it back then?"

"What teenager thinks? I was just a seething mass of feelings. Did I consciously set out to walk on the dark side because my brother had already claimed the light? Maybe not, but in retrospect it's obvious.

"I caused trouble, talked back, acted out, disgraced the family, brought shame upon my house—the whole thing. Petty crime, drugs, girls, and the MCs. I wallowed."

"I think I have a soft spot for the bad boy in you."

I chuckled. "I know you do, you badass. But I carried things to extremes. It's amazing I didn't end up dead or in prison. I harmed myself and I hurt a lot of other people. My family, especially." I paused again as my buried pain rose up to sabotage my nonchalance. "I loved Aaron, though. He had the sweetest, most generous nature of anyone I've ever known. Even when I was at my worst, being a complete asshole to him and everyone else, he never gave up on me." Fuck it. I was getting choked up. "It just about ruined me when he died."

She squeezed my hand hard. "That must have been a nightmare."

"Yeah." I stayed silent for a few moments to compose myself. "You mentioned your mother being lost after your dad died. I get that. I was lost, too."

"But you got your true self back."

I snorted. "My true self? Who would that be? I play a good game, that's all. The stains I put on my soul during those years remain. You can't do shit like that for as long as I did and come out clean."

As I said this, I knew I still wasn't clean. I'd been through a long period of hell after my brother had died. I'd missed him. I'd felt guilty. No one knew what my brother had been doing in that motorcycle club bar that night. The general belief was that he'd gone there to try to get me to stop fucking around, drinking, and hanging with the kind of folks who frequented the place.

As if she read my mind, she said, "What happened to your brother? I've heard a couple of different versions of the story."

"Have you heard the version that I set him up to be murdered so I could step into his place in the pack?"

"No!" She sounded shocked. "Who the hell says that?" She sat up straighter, looking the way I must have looked a few minutes ago when I'd been all primed to take off for Scotland and avenge her mistreatment. "That's bullshit! You would never do such a thing."

"You're right, I wouldn't. The possibility has always existed that someone else did, though."

"That's what Grandpa told me, too," she admitted. "That maybe someone had killed him on purpose, except that it seemed unlikely because he had no enemies."

"Yeah. Believe me, I suspected everybody for a while. Including other members of the pack."

"Like who?"

I shrugged. "This is probably just another example of me being jealous, but I had my eye on Brandon. While I was dicking around as a teenager, he'd come along and endeared himself to everybody. Including my father. He's a strong alpha and ambitious. I don't like him or trust him."

"I don't, either."

"You hardly know him," I pointed out. "Anyway, he was Aaron's friend, not mine, and Aaron liked him well enough. Brandon seemed just as devastated by Aaron's death as the rest of us were, and there was no evidence against him. He did challenge me for leadership, though. I thought we were going to have to fight it out with an old-style dominance duel."

"But you didn't?"

"Nope. Before Dad died, I'd proved myself with the pack a bit. Resurrected myself would be more like it. Dad ordained me as the leader at the end. There was an election that I won. Brandon accepted the results."

"What about Suzanne?"

"You don't like her, do you?"

"Actually, it's she who doesn't like me."

"Probably not. You're a threat to her. I think Suzanne wanted Brandon to fight me. But he declared in front of everyone that he respected the democratic process. To my astonishment, he bent the knee to me. I thought Suzanne was going to fucking kill him."

"She wanted to be the alpha female."

"You got it. She still wants it."

"Your mother is the alpha female."

I looked at her, not speaking. She probably knew what I was thinking: You're my mate, Jess. It should be you.

CHAPTER TWENTY-FIVE

Cade

I figured it would be pushing my luck to ask Jess to tell me any-thing more about her past, but now that we were finally talk-ing, I didn't want to stop. Usually I didn't give a shit about hear-ing my hookup's bio, but things were different with this woman. It was partly because I was starting to feel some affection toward her and partly because her damn elusiveness fascinated me.

And let's face it—I also really dug her enthusiasm for sex. I was grateful as hell that whatever had happened to her in the past hadn't frozen her sexuality. That was always a risk when a woman had been stalked and assaulted.

I thought of her strange collar, which she hadn't brought with her. Not that I didn't like it. I found it kinky as hell and I loved that she seemed to glow with submissive desire when she was wearing it. What kind of magic did that thing possess?

If it was just an erotic prop, then I was a fool to ignore the signal—she was obviously turned on by roleplaying my pas-sionate slave.

Well, that was fine with me.

I tweaked her breasts. Her nipples were rosy and hard and I couldn't resist pinching them. She gasped and twisted her limbs against mine, not pulling away but pressing herself harder against me.

"Horny, my love?"

"Hmm. We did get a bit distracted when we were doing that bondage thing."

"Happy to pull out my ropes again. Or, wait, got another idea." I flipped her over onto her belly. Handling her body made me feel as if I was burning inside. Lust, but not just physical. Something deeper. I slapped her ass. "Up. On your hands and knees."

She scrambled to obey, rising to kneel on the mattress.

I smacked her inner thigh. "Spread 'em, babe." She did it and my hand dove in between her legs and played with her pussy lips. "I want full access to you. You're mine now—every part of you." I pressed my thumb into her butthole. She screeched. I chuckled. "Unexplored territory there? You've got a treat coming, hon." I went on gently fondling her clit and soon she was moaning and jerking back against my hand.

I loved how responsive she was.

As I continued to caress her, she arched and cried out. She was all woman, delicious and wild. I loved the way she squirmed. I crouched down behind her and ducked my head to lick her pussy. I held her down firmly with one sparkling hand on her ass as I probed and sucked her, stabbing my tongue into her.

Inching toward her clit, I teased and circled for a few before skating my tongue across the engorged bud. She gasped and my cock throbbed.

I couldn't wait any longer. I had to take her, and roughly. I went up on my knees and held her hips steady for me as I slammed into her weeping slit. I bent forward over her body, one hand grabbing a breast to squeeze and the other slapping her heaving thigh.

I wanted to hear her scream my name. She was mine now and it was time she knew it.

I could see the static sparks or sevmelle or whatever the hell it was everywhere my fingers touched her skin. It radiated in a hazy glow from all the places where our flesh met. My mate. The sparks and the glowing proved it. I was fucking claiming her. Every part of her.

As I pumped fiercely into her amazingly soft, tight sheath, I felt myself slipping away. Wildness reigned. Her scent was intoxicating. I wanted to nip her and bite her and roll in the dirt with her, my lover, my mate.

Whoa. I was starting to shift. Fur ran up my arms and my fingers turned to claws.

Holy shit. Not cool. I never lost control like that, not even in any excess of rage or passion. But Jess was bringing out the beast in me.

And it was tempting…oh so tempting, to just let it happen.

"Don't stop," she cried and I wasn't sure what she was asking for. Did she realize? Another moment or two and my cock would knot itself inside her and stopping wouldn't even be an option.

"Shift with me," I gasped.

She stiffened. Dammit! She didn't like shifting. If I let this happen, she'd probably freak.

Gritting my teeth, I pulled back out of her before I totally lost it. I took a moment to force the transformation to cease. No bones had changed yet. I dragged my claws and the sprouting fur back inside, becoming smoothly human all over again.

Fuck…that had been close.

She rolled over to her back and raised her hand to my face. "What? Are you okay?"

"I'm fine." I slid between her thighs. "Let's try it the old-fashioned way."

She tilted her hips for me as we joined again. We kissed as we moved together, establishing a rhythm, experimenting with different angles of entry, different depths, different tempos. Everything we tried felt wonderful. "I want to fuck you so hard that you scream."

"Do."

I began to do just that, piston-ramming while she arched off the bed and met me thrust for thrust. I was half afraid to hurt her and half loving the ferocity of it. She was just as rough with me—her nails were carving welts into my back and shoulders.

She gasped out a scream every time her clit impacted my groin, which happened so fast and so often that her sounds were constant. I slammed so hard into her I could feel my balls slapping against her ass. We writhed together in a frenzy.

"Come for me, baby."

Howling with pleasure, she obeyed. She screamed as she came, throbbing rhythmically on my cock. I followed with just a few more pounding strokes, groaning as the climax squeezed a shower of pleasure into me.

It was only then, as we were both coming down, that I thought again about how she hadn't been wearing the Highland Choker. I'd almost shifted, but despite her fears, she had maintained her human form throughout.

I slid my fingers around her throat and squeezed gently. "No choker. Why do you like that thing so much?"

"Don't ask me."

"How can I not? I'm the alpha and a curious man. I have a need to know all manner of things for the good of the pack."

She laughed. "Nice try."

I nipped her ear. "I should cuff you. Slap you down as the dominant wolf would instantly do to an insubordinate underling."

"If you're going to cuff me, I'd prefer the other type of cuff. The leather ones."

My turn to laugh. "I'll bring my bondage stuff home with us—how about that?"

I stroked where she usually wore the neck thing and then let my fingers drift down over her breast. I took one of her nipples between my finger and thumb and squeezed. "You have a collar already. Why not other types of restraints?"

Her green eyes were sparkling. "I wouldn't say no."

"You would obey your leader?" I rained delicate kisses down her throat. "Your master?"

"If I were in the mood, I might."

I was beginning to like this woman a lot.

Chapter Twenty-Six

Cade

"Can I ask you something else?" she said a little later.

"Only if you answer my question about why you refuse to shift."

She rolled her eyes. "I'll take a dare rather than do that."

"I'm teasing. You needn't take a dare."

Her chin tilted stubbornly. "Give me a dare. When I agreed to your stupid game, I meant to follow the rules." She winked at me. "I suppose it'll be some sexual thing. Good luck trying to think of something I wouldn't eagerly do."

"I refuse to be so predictable." I thought for a moment. "I dare you to come with me the next time I go hunting."

Her face changed. She went pale for a moment before looking pissed off. "If you think you're going to force me to shift in some underhanded fashion—"

"Not running as a wolf hunting. Pheasant hunting. With Barney. And a shotgun. No shifting. You and me'll hunt ourselves some dinner."

"That sucks. You know how much I hate hunting. I won't shoot a gun. I won't kill a bird."

"You don't have to. You just have to be my hunting partner. There'll be no blood on your hands, I promise."

She hesitated.

"You can still change your mind and answer the question."

She shook her head violently, her dark strands of hair scattered across her shoulder. "I'll go hunting."

"Fine. I'm gonna hold you to it. Now what was your question?"

"OK. This is my question—I heard some talk today about a murder. Who got killed?"

Damn. Had the other members of the pack been gossiping? Well, there was no harm in her knowing. I hadn't told her because I hadn't wanted to worry her.

"You mean the guy who got his throat torn out last month?"

"I guess. I overheard some pack members discussing it. Somebody was killed by a shifter? That's something you've never mentioned to me."

"It's not a secret. I didn't think you were interested in pack business."

"A murderer on the loose sounds like something more than pack business to me."

Okay, she had a point. There had been some discussion at the Council meeting today about the killer. I hadn't realized the talk had continued during the socializing afterwards, but since I hadn't told anyone to exclude Jess from pack business, I couldn't really fault anyone.

It emphasized how messed up our situation was, though. When the alpha wolf takes a mate, it's expected that she'll become an intimate part of the pack. Hell, if we were ordinary wolves in the wild, the alpha and his mate would be the primary mating pair and would produce the young wolves that the rest of the pack would help raise.

Maybe our marriage had been intended as temporary, but Tom's conditions in his will had trapped us more neatly than we'd realized. Everyone had expectations of us. Hell, I was beginning to have expectations.

"What do you want to know about it?"

"Who got murdered and why do you suspect a shifter?"

"A man was killed. A human. He was a drug dealer and thug who belonged to one of the local motorcycle gangs."

She raised her eyebrows. "The MCs again? Could that be a coincidence?"

She was quick. "Seems to be. The guy didn't have anything to do with our pack, as far as I know. The dead guy, Jock Nichols, was a dealer, so we thought there might be a drug link. But there's no evidence at present that any of the young idiots in our pack were buying from him."

"So no one in the pack does drugs?"

"I wish that were true. But there are other dealers. As far as we know, none of us had any kind of relationship with the creep.

We're thinking that the killer might be a lone wolf. Somebody passing through the area."

"Could it have been any other kind of shifter? Like a bear?"

"I don't think so. I saw the body. It actually happened that night when I was first at your place. Remember I got that phone call and had to leave? That was Jake, and I went to join him at the hospital morgue."

When I said this, Jess turned white. She dropped back against the pillows looking as if she felt faint. Maybe I shouldn't have mentioned the morgue? "What, babe? Are you okay?"

"That was the first time we hooked up?"

"Yeah, awesome night. So?"

She pressed her palms together. Her hands looked shaky. What the fuck?

"You're sure this man was killed by a wolf shifter? Absolutely sure?"

"Yeah. If the killer had been someone else, there'd be no reason for our wolf pack to investigate."

"It couldn't have been a grizzly? Or, or anything else?"

"Anything else like what?"

She looked away. Her skin was flushed and I could see from the way the pulse fluttered at her throat that she was agitated. What the fuck was going on with her?

I tried to get her to tell me, but of course she wouldn't. Silence and secrets had fallen between us again.

Jess

I didn't dare fall asleep. For the first time since I'd started sharing my nights with Cade, I wasn't wearing the Highland Choker. After the way he'd hassled me about my refusal to shift, the last thing I wanted was for it to happen involuntarily.

Which could happen. It had happened to him. Did he think I hadn't felt it? He'd nearly shifted to his wolf and I hadn't even minded. He was damn sexy in any form. The only thing I'd minded was that he'd wanted me to shift, too.

My cousin must have been wrong about fucking being a stress reliever. I was having lots of sex, but my darkling self felt closer to the surface than ever. The rough way we tended to have sex didn't help—it brought out the wilder parts of me.

If it should happen by accident when we were together, he might be in danger. His wolf was powerful and strong, but my darkling might be stronger still. I could hurt him. I could maybe even kill him. He didn't realize he was harboring a monster at his breast.

And now I'd learned that someone had been murdered by a shifter. What if that killer was me?

I lay awake while Cade slept by my side, trying to convince myself that I'd had nothing to do with this stranger's death. I didn't know anybody from a motorcycle club. I couldn't imagine where I might have met such a person, let alone stalked, attacked and killed him.

I don't think I'd have worried about it at all, except that the murder had occurred on the same evening I'd returned to the ranch with blood on my hands. The conditions had been right that day for my demon to emerge. I'd been crazy stressed out over Grandpa, and I'd had no sex for weeks. I hadn't even pleasured myself.

If my darkling self had run into a cheap thug, as Cade had termed him…if he'd mocked or insulted me…or if I'd liked the smell of his blood, maybe I'd assaulted him? If he'd fought back and pulled a knife or gun, I'd probably have ended him. Darklings liked violence and had no problems killing, especially in self defense.

But all I could really remember about that experience was waking up under the oak tree behind my grandfather's ranch. With the taste of blood in my mouth.

My one consolation was that if I had done such a horrible thing, it wouldn't have looked like a wolf attack. No, the investigators would have been worried about things even more mythic than werewolves. The dead guy would look as if he'd been bitten and drained by a vampire.

CHAPTER TWENTY-SEVEN

Jess

"I'm going hunting today," Cade said early one morning a few weeks later. I was still in bed, not fully awake, my mind hazy with fantasy. I was reliving the previous night's lovemaking. Our naked limbs entwined, flesh hot, eager and tireless. His husky voice whispering sensual commands; my excitement as I complied.

"Want to come?" he asked.

"Mmm, yes, I want to come," I laughed.

He was standing there beside the bed, grinning down at me. There was a familiar glint in his blue eyes that spoke of pleasure and promises. "Hunting," he said again, more loudly. "Don't try to tempt me into anything else, you witchy woman."

"Hunting in your wolf form?"

"No. I'm taking my gun and my dog and going pheasant hunting." He jerked the curtains away from the windows, making me groan because the sky was still dark, with only the faintest glimmering of dawn showing. "Come on, gorgeous. Rise and shine. You're coming with me."

I woke up at that. Was he really calling in the Truth or Dare debt? I snuck a look at his face. Yup. He was serious.

Okay, fine. He hadn't violated his side of the agreement. No more questions about why I wouldn't shift, although I knew he was still curious. It seemed that when he made a deal, he kept it.

He'd been treating me a lot better than I'd expected when I agreed to this fake marriage. I'd thought nothing would happen between us but some incendiary sex, and that at the end of our six months, we'd probably both have had our fill of that. But somehow or other, I'd started to care about him.

I wanted to do something nice for him that didn't involve my tongue or my pussy muscles. I guess it wouldn't kill me to show some interest in his damn hobby.

"Surely even the pheasants aren't awake yet," I struggled to stand, reaching for the warm flannel robe that was hanging from the bedpost.

"Lazy-bones," he teased me.

"I'm only coming because we have nothing for dinner. This is strictly only kill what we intend to eat, right?"

"Absolutely. I'll get breakfast ready while you dress. Wear plenty of layers. It's a cold sport."

Climbing into the Jeep with him a little while later, I hoped this wasn't going to be a big mistake. The hunting season was in full swing; every day I could hear shotguns booming in the distance.

Cade had already hunted a couple of times with his friends, coming home with game he'd cleaned and cooked. He was a good cook, and I'd had to admit that I'd enjoyed the fresh, juicy flesh. I knew he was a responsible hunter and that he'd been raised to love the chase. My objections to hunting rose from a different place than Cade even knew. It wasn't as if I was a vegetarian or an animal rights activist.

So I wasn't of a mind to quarrel with him about hunting. Or about anything.

Something was happening between us. I guess we were compatible. With the collapse of the physical barriers, some sort of subtle emotional bonding had been taking place.

Was it due to the sevmelle? Were we truly mated souls? I would have liked to believe it, but I couldn't quite. Cade still hadn't seen all of me.

I was still a bit worried about the death-by-shifter of some unknown motorcycle club member, even though it seemed unlikely that the crime had had anything to do with me. I would have felt much better if only I could remember what I'd done that night.

But all that had come back to me were the dark shadows of the woods and the bright gleaming of the stars overhead. The smells of dying leaves and growing mushrooms and the goldenrod in the meadows…autumn setting in.

My vivid imagination kept envisioning the murder—the blood, the tearing of claws and the snapping of powerful jaws. When I forbade myself to think about it, the images moved into my dreams. Cade had held me and comforted me on several occasions when I'd awakened, sobbing and trembling, my pulse a-thunder, my skin slick with sweat.

At night, I made sure to wear the Choker when we were in bed together. I didn't like sleeping in it because it was tight and heavy, but my fear of waking up outside, dark wings unfurled and my husband staring at me in horror were enough for me to insist that he leave it on until morning.

Although I'd told him its purpose, he still thought it was a sex thing—a fetish of mine. He liked that idea and he capitalized on it. He made wearing the collar exciting and fun.

"We're not hunting in the forest?" I asked when Cade parked the Jeep on the shoulder of a dirt road that led toward a large, open meadow. Two other vehicles were already parked there.

"Not for pheasants," he reminded me as we clambered out to unload the truck. Barney leaped about inside, eager and excited, whining to get out.

"If I were hunting ruffed grouse, which I love to do, I'd seek them in a hardwood forest with hilly terrain. I'd take my 20-gauge Parker for that. But for pheasant hunting I've brought this 12-gauge, double-barreled Winchester." He removed his shotgun from its case as he spoke, handling it gently, with reverence.

I rolled my eyes. Men and their guns.

CHAPTER TWENTY-EIGHT

Jess

"Good morning, Cade." I whirled, not having sensed the two people who came up behind me, dressed as Cade was in hunting duds and orange jackets. Cade, however, showed no surprise.

It was Brandon and Suzanne, both holding shotguns and accompanied by their own hunting dog.

Some nameless sensation rippled through me. I did not like these two.

"Jessica," said Suzanne, raising her perfectly penciled eyebrows. "You look as if you're all tricked out for the hunt. I thought you weren't fond of the sport?"

"Good morning," I said as courteously as I could manage. "I'm partnering my husband today."

"It's a good location," said Brandon. "Shall we all hunt together?"

"Nope. I have a special spot I want to show my mate." Cade flashed a grin. "I'm sure you can understand."

Brandon laughed. Other people seemed to find his laugh pleasant, but it grated on me. "Of course. Still enjoying your honeymoon? You both look—" he paused while his gaze flicked over me with what seemed an awful lot like lusty male appreciation "—well-satisfied."

Cade tensed and Suzanne scowled. What the hell?

"We are," I cooed, sliding in closer to Cade and slipping my arm around his waist. He gathered me close and matched Brandon, smile for smile.

The wolf inside me sensed the silent battle of wills, and I saw for the first time how much of a rival Brandon must have been during the leadership election. He was clearly an alpha, albeit a highly controlled and careful one.

What was his story, I wondered. He'd come to Montana from Texas when he was a teenager, but he had never mentioned his family or how he'd ended up attached to Cade's father's pack.

"Which way are you two headed?" Cade asked. "We're going east, towards Great Meadows."

"Then I guess we're going west," Brandon said affably. Suzanne bit her lip as if to argue, but she held it in.

"Sounds like a plan," said Cade. "Good hunting."

"Good hunting to you, too," Brandon said, and Suzanne muttered an echo. Then they hiked off with their gear and their dog.

"That was awkward," I said.

"Happens too often. We all know the best hunting sites. That's why we start early. First come, first served."

Unless you're the alpha, I thought. Then you get first choice.

Cade glanced at me sideways. "Was it my imagination, or did he send some vibes your way?"

"I thought it might be *my* imagination, but if you noticed it, too...."

"I'd kill him if he ever touched you." He said this casually, but there was a steely hardness behind his words.

I went up on tiptoes and kissed his mouth. "I'd kill him if he ever touched me, too. And I'd kill her if she ever tried to touch you again."

"Don't worry about that. Suzanne hates me now. Her loss." Some of his old bad boy cockiness came out in the way he dismissed her, and I elbowed him in the side.

"You're such a jerk, Derringer."

"I'm taking that as a compliment. Let's go. We've got roast pheasant on the menu for dinner tonight."

He let Barney loose. The dog bounded joyously out of the Jeep and erupted into the field. Cade whistled for him and Barney stopped, looked back, and reluctantly returned to Cade.

The purpose of the hunting dog was not only to sniff out birds, but also to corner them and, at the right moment, make them fly. Because Barney was a young animal in his first season of hunting, Cade explained that things weren't going to go as smoothly as they would with a more experienced dog.

"He's eager to please, and he knows instinctively what he's supposed to do, but he doesn't understand how to work as a team. He's liable to make some mistakes."

"What sort of mistakes?"

"This gun has a range of about forty yards. If Barney flushes a pheasant at a distance beyond that, I won't be able to hit him."

He hefted the shotgun, then stuffed the pockets of his hunting jacket with more shells. "Put that orange vest on, and we'll get going."

As I did so, he added, "Please remember everything I told you about gun safety."

"Yup." I knew plenty about gun safety, but I'd listened dutifully to the lecture on the subject he'd given me during the drive.

"Stay behind me. If you hear the sound of a bird being flushed, stand still, don't move. Don't run toward it or do anything that might put you into my line of fire."

"Not likely. Last thing I want is for you to shoot me by mistake." I nodded to his shotgun. "Aren't you going to load it?"

"I was just about to. It's a double-barrel so it can take two shells at a time. These are the shells." He took two from his pocket and held them in the palm of his hand. "Number Four shot—that refers to the size of the pellets inside."

"The smaller the prey, the higher the number code of the shot, but the smaller the individual pellets."

He gave me a quick, reassessing glance. "I wouldn't have expected you to know that."

"Yeah, well, you'd be surprised what I know." I took the shotgun from him, broke it open, took one of the shells from his hand, loaded it in the right barrel, grabbed the second, loaded it in the left barrel, closed the gun, then checked to be certain the safety was engaged. I handed it back to him, grinning at the expression on his face.

"So," he said after a moment. "You've handled firearms before."

"I did grow up in Montana. Grandpa taught me."

Cade opened his mouth, but no words came out. Then he grinned at me. "Fuck me. I feel like a fool now. Did Tom take you hunting?"

"If he did, it was so long ago, I've forgotten." But as I said it, something stirred inside me again, nudging sharply, alarming me. Shit. Maybe this had been a bad idea.

It was a quiet morning, cool and misty with a stiff breeze. In the east, the sun was rising with the promise of lovely weather to come. As we moved slowly through the tall, dry grasses of the autumn meadow, Cade said, "This is one of the things I love about hunting." He stopped and I nearly walked right into him. "Look at the sky. D'you see the way the mist is shimmering as the sun climbs higher? And listen to the birdsong."

"It does seem louder than usual."

"Exactly. Everything seems louder, clearer, sharper, more distinct. That's because we're more alert. More tuned in to our surroundings. Like when we're shifted."

"But without the superior sense of smell."

"If I were a pheasant now, would I feel safer feeding in that clump of tall grass over there, or would I rather feed down in that hollow? When I hear the dog, which way will I run? At what moment will I panic and fly? The hunter must become one with the prey."

I tried not to roll my eyes too hard.

There," he said pointing, his voice low and excited. "Barney's picked up the scent."

I felt my own adrenaline start to pump. As much as Cade or Barney, I wanted to find that bird. There was something deeply primitive about being hot on its trail. I missed that feeling. I missed the hunt, the chase, the kill.

CHAPTER TWENTY-NINE

Cade

Barney was running around, back and forth in front of a long, narrow patch of briars, wagging his tail and whining. "He's making game," I told Jess as I moved through the tall grass, my shotgun at the port arms position. "Hurry. We're almost out of range."

She followed.

"The birds have been feeding in the grass, but now they're retreating into the thicker stuff." I slowed to a quiet, careful walk now that we'd come up a few yards behind the excited dog, who was looking for a way through the briars to get at the birds. "They'd rather run than fly, but they'll fly if they think there's no alternative."

"Where are they?" She mouthed as I stopped and remained motionless, watching Barney.

"There. Wait. Any second now."

Barney looked back, wagged his tail harder, then turned and plunged into the briars. I raised the shotgun to my shoulder even before the clap of wings. Three things happened in quick succession: I identified the bird as male and fair game, I took aim, and my finger froze on the trigger as I envisioned the expression that would cloud Jess' face when my prey tumbled from the sky.

The pheasant flew on, and my gun barrel followed, but in a split second, the shot changed from easy to difficult. A moment later, the damn thing was out of range.

I lowered the shotgun. Barney, looked back toward me, as if to say, "Hey, what happened? There was supposed to be a boom and that bird was supposed to fall down and I was supposed to run and fetch it. I did my job. Why didn't you do yours?"

But Jess smiled at me. And then she moved toward me and enveloped me in a hug. "Thank you. You could have killed him, I know. But he was beautiful. Thanks for letting him live."

Shit. What the hell had just happened? I should have taken the shot. Why hadn't I pulled the fucking trigger?

"It was the wrong thing to do. I confused the dog."

I'd invited her along because things had gotten to a certain point with us—the point where, to my mind, we either moved closer or we moved apart. I'd wanted her to see the primitive, elemental side of my nature. She wouldn't shift and run with me. She wouldn't acknowledge the predator. This was the next best way. I wanted her to accept me for the man I was.

Fuck. What kind of sentimental fool was I turning into?

Look at her, grinning, almost gleeful. She thinks she knows me, she probably thinks she's tamed me. But guess what? She's wrong.

If I'd been alone, that bird would have been supper.

I stalked off to find Barney, to praise and reassure him. I shouldn't have brought her hunting. Damned if I'd do it again.

Fifteen minutes later, Barney was into another bird, and this time I didn't hesitate. I moved quickly in the wake of the dog, leaving Jess behind, making no attempt to wait or explain or palliate the experience for her. This is me, I felt like shouting at her. I love hunting. Fuck, I'm a wolf, an alpha. This is what I am.

When the cock pheasant flew this time, I had the shotgun to my shoulder. It was smooth and sure, like a thousand times before, perfect: The arc of the creature's flight, the swing of the gun, the gentle squeezing of the trigger and the cartwheeling plunge of the bird from the sky, carefully observed both by me and by my dog.

Even before the body hit the ground, Barney was running, and for several moments both bird and dog disappeared in the thigh-high meadow grasses. Then he came bounding back, the bird held gently between his widely spread jaws, his retriever instincts arrowing him to his master. With great solemnity and pride, he presented me his trophy.

"Good dog," I praised him, patting him and taking the bird, which was cleanly dead. Even seasoned hunters tended to feel a twinge of guilt over the game we didn't instantly kill. "You did everything right that time, Barney. Last time, too, for that matter. You're awesome, boy."

Only then, after making an appropriate fuss over the dog, did I turn to Jess, who'd lingered several yards behind. Walking back to her, I could see that she was pale and stiff-limbed. There was an unnatural shimmer in her eyes.

Staring at the dead pheasant, she shook her head. "I'd like to go home now, if you don't mind."

"Fine. We've got supper. Let's go home."

Her gaze dropped to my bird. She started and one hand went to her throat. She gasped, and pointed at the bird, whose feathers were ruffling in the stiff wind. "It's not dead. Oh my god, you're torturing it."

"Of course it's dead." I was certain of that.

She swayed. She put her hands up to her face, covering her eyes, swiping away her hair; then she bent over, as if she were about to be sick. Whoa. I got worried. What the fuck?

"They died so slowly. He tortured them."

"Shit." I didn't know what was going on, but I dropped both the shotgun and the bird and rushed to her side just in time to grab her as her legs collapsed. Clinging to me, she sank to her knees in the tall grass.

"Jess?" I knelt beside her and put my arms around her. Her skin was like ice and she was trembling. "Hon, what's the matter? It's okay." I was stroking her shoulders, her hair. "I've got you. I'm here, Jess, it's okay."

She shoved me away. It was a strong, powerful shove that sent me sprawling.

I sat up, shocked. She wasn't usually so rough.

I heard the crack of bone and the groan of muscle. Sounds that were familiar to me, except that I'd hardly ever heard them from her. She was shifting, and from the sound of it, the change was violent and extremely fast.

I stared, feeling as if someone had put a fist around my throat. The air crackled with magic and it was hard to breathe. Clouds must have covered the sun because the whole meadow turned dark and chill.

I thought for a moment I was going mad.

Jess, my wife, my lover, my mate, was gone. In her place was no sable wolf, but a shadow, a phantom, a creature—something that I'd never seen before. Unless…I remembered that I had seen something, vaguely, through the fog on the night that Tom's SUV had almost collided with my motorcycle.

Something I hadn't understood, or believed. Afterwards, I'd figured I must have imagined it because of all the adrenaline that had spiked through me as I'd fought to control my bike and not spin off the road.

Fuck.

It…she…Jess was in the air about six feet off the ground, held aloft by huge, black wings. She soared higher, rising over the treetops. She caught the air currents and flew back and forth over the darkened meadow. She moved at incredible speed while I gaped up at her from the ground, trying to process what I was seeing.

She looked like some gigantic bird of prey, except that, but for the wings, she had a human form. She was Jess—her face, her arms, legs, and body. But it was as if all the color had drained from her, transforming her into shadow and bone. Her body seemed thinner and longer than usual. Her face was lily white, except for red lips and with eyes that burned with emerald fire.

She looked like an apparition. A dark angel. Or even a demon.

And yet, she was strangely beautiful.

She glided back down, deadly yet graceful. Her green gaze seared into me as she fluttered in the air for several moments while I fumbled to understand. What was she? Was this real or was I hallucinating?

There were stories, of course. There were always stories—beings who could take more than one shifted form. Beings who weren't really shifters, but Something Else. The Fae? Demons? Faerie folk slipping through from a parallel world?

You don't really know me, Cade. You don't know all of me. There are dark things inside me.

Was this what she had meant?

Of course. This was her secret. The reason she would never shift for me. Whatever she was, she hadn't wanted me to discover it.

The cracking came again, like a sigh this time. Agony. Defeat. The powerful black-feathered wings crumpled and collapsed. Her entire body blurred. She fell to earth and lay crumpled among the wildflowers, an ordinary human body, curled up at my feet.

My heart slamming, I dropped to my knees beside her, terrified that she was dead. I could swear I'd seen death in her pale, strange face. I could almost see the skull beneath her skin.

Chapter Thirty

Cade

Thank God she was breathing. I gathered her into my arms and sat in the dirt, holding her in my lap and feeling her heart beating frantically against my chest. I thought she was unconscious until I heard her voice.

"You saw. Cade? Oh my god, I'm so sorry."

"Ssh. It's okay. You're okay." I was just grateful she was alive and speaking. That she knew me. That she was still here. As I thought this, I felt the heat in my fingertips, the sparkly glow where they stroked her skin. The sevmelle. Whatever she was, she was still my mate.

"You saw me. What I have inside. What I am."

"I did. You scared the shit out of me. I thought you were dying."

"I'm so sorry. Usually I can control it. Keep it inside. But sometimes something triggers it and then it happens so fast that I can't stop it."

"What are you, Jess?" I didn't want to ask, but I had to know. "I didn't know it was possible to have a human form with wings and…" my voice trailed off. And power, I thought. I'd felt it. Immense power. "Are you some sort of angel?"

She laughed softly and the sound flowed through me like clean water. I was glad she could still laugh like an ordinary human. Er, shifter. Neither of us was an ordinary human.

"No. I'm a multiform shifter."

What the fuck was a multiform shifter?

"You mean you can change into more than one creature?"

She nodded. "My mum and I, we're related to a powerful clan. The Mallochs. From Mallochbirn. Have you heard of it? It's a place in the Highlands."

"Yeah, you've mentioned your family there."

"My mother is a Malloch, and the Mallochs all have different forms or aspects. Wolves, lions, hawks, bears, and even sea dragons."

Okay. But she hadn't been any of those things. A hawk? A big gigantic hawk with a woman's body? She hadn't really been an animal, had she? She'd looked like a human in most respects, but she'd had wings. And clothes that were different from the clothes she had on. What was that about? No one shifted with clothes.

Her original clothes were back now, too. Looking as if they'd never been shed. Could she shift her clothes?

I tried to back up a step. "Something spooked you, didn't it? Something about my shooting that bird? What caused you to shift like that, Jess?" There were too many mysteries here. "You looked a little like the angel of death. Or maybe a vampire."

She went cold and still. Fuck. I shouldn't have blurted that out.

"My other aspect is a darkling. That's what you saw."

I felt that chill again. I'd heard of darklings, though I'd never met one. They were a rare creature who supposedly lived in some shadow world that ordinary beings found difficult to enter. They were reputedly long-lived and strange. They had a taste for blood. Humans tended to confuse them with ghosts, ghouls, and vampires…none of which I'd ever believed in.

But fuck. Now I wasn't sure of anything.

"I've sensed your wolf. How can you be a wolf as well as a darkling?"

"I am told it is very unusual. Believe me, if I had any choice in the matter, I wouldn't be."

I wanted to understand and deal with this. In part because I was curious now and in part because Jess thought I couldn't handle it. Was that why she hadn't told me? I could tell by the tremor in her voice that she was terrified by this revelation.

In truth, I *was* kinda appalled, but I couldn't let her see that. I schooled my features as best I could and said, "Jess. I don't care what you have inside you. She looked kickass to me. Like a superhero. Maybe a dominatrix superhero." I tried to joke about it, but I wasn't sure it came off as funny. "What I want to know is what spooked you? Because I don't think I'm getting the whole story here."

"Can we go home?" She folded her arms around herself and shivered. "I'm cold."

"Sure, babe. Let's go home."

CHAPTER THIRTY-ONE

Jess

I couldn't stop shivering, not even when we were home in front of the warm fire that Cade built. What a fool I'd been. I never should have gone hunting.

My loss of control had been almost as terrifying as the surge of memory that had caused it. But worst of all had been the look of horror on my husband's face when he'd seen me hovering in the air above his head. He had tried hard to hide his feelings, but darkling vision and perception were far better than those of a human. Or a wolf. I could read his naked emotions and they'd been everything I'd always feared.

Ever since we'd gotten home, Cade had tried to get me to talk about it, share what I was thinking and feeling. Give him an explanation. Free him from what I could see in his ravaged countenance was a burden of dread.

What kind of thing had he married? What the fuck had his old friend Tom stuck him with?

I tried to find the words, but I felt really numb. Not until he threatened to call Jake, the physician, for help, did I manage to shake off my lethargy. "No, please. I don't need a doctor. I'll be fine."

"Prove it. Talk to me. What set you off like that? Why did you think the bird I shot wasn't dead? This has something to do with your attacker, doesn't it? That Jonathan guy?"

I nodded.

"What the fuck did he do to you?" His voice was heavy.

"It's more what I did to him. I killed him, Cade."

I expected him to shudder, but he didn't. He held my gaze steadily and his hand tightened on mine. His blue eyes opened wider for a moment. Then he smiled. "*You* took him out? So... not just beautiful but badass too? Good. I love it. I need a strong mate at my side."

He was giving me his acceptance and it helped. My story came pouring out.

"From the time my darkling first emerged, my mother warned me to suppress her. It's dangerous to have such a form. There are actual darklings in Scotland. Shifters and darklings are ancient enemies there."

"So the legends about darklings are true? They're real?"

I nodded. "I've never met a purebred darkling. My mother and I are believed to be members of some diluted genetic line where, generations ago, a darkling and a shifter mated."

"So your mother is one, too."

"No. She's a multiform shifter like me, but her other form is a bird. A hawk. All the Mallochs are multiform shifters, but the forms they can take vary. Mine—the darkling shift—is the rarest. Well, mine and the sea dragon—that is rare, too."

"But there are non-shifter darklings? Do they really live a thousand years?"

"Some do. That's why they aren't too interested in humans or ordinary shifters. We're like mayflies to them—we hatch and mate and die. We're insignificant. Anyway, it's hard to keep my darkling self contained. The pack in Scotland used to control me with the Choker."

"Wait—the Highland Choker? Your collar?"

"Not the one I have now. My cousin Cam gave that to me. In Martin's pack, they used to make me wear one, sometimes as a punishment and sometimes just because they could."

He growled in anger.

"I hated it. I tried to shift anyway, but you can't shift and the more you try, the more it hurts. I didn't realize it, but I was training myself not to shift. The more I tortured myself in the attempt to shift, the more my brain connected shifting with pain and suffering."

"Fuck! How did your mother allow this?"

"Martin had total control of my mother. They kept most of us in those collars. The women, especially. He made a slave out of my mother."

"Jesus."

"Jonathan hated it when I was in my wolf form because I was much more powerful than he was. His wolf was a runt. He got his power from weapons—he was obsessed with guns. And with hunting."

I drew a deep breath to steady myself. The rest of the story was hard to tell. "He liked to trap small animals—mice, baby rabbits, birds, chipmunks—and torment them. When he went hunting, he shot to injure, not kill. He was an excellent marksman, and he knew how to hit areas that weren't vital. The poor thing would fall and the dog would retrieve it, but it would still be alive. Jonathan would stand there, smiling, and watch it exhaust itself trying to escape. Then he would...God, I can't even describe the things he'd do."

Cade groaned. "No wonder you feel the way you do about hunting."

I closed my eyes, wishing I could roll up like a hedgehog. But I had to go on. If I stopped, I'd never finish. "As we got older, Jonathan added sex to his list of ways to bully me. He was such a strange and hostile kid that no girls would go out with him. We weren't related, he pointed out to me, so why not?"

"Shit."

"I refused, but that meant nothing to him. He didn't care about my feelings. He pursued me, grabbing me when I least expected it, kissing and fondling me while I fought him off. When I resisted or threatened to tell his father, he captured some small animal, killed it slowly, and brought me the body."

Cade made an inarticulate sound. His hands were clenched and he was breathing much faster than usual.

"I had a puppy. A Labrador retriever named Dusty. She looked a little like Barney. Jonathan knew how much I loved him."

"Oh God."

My heart was pounding so hard now, I could scarcely speak. "If I didn't fuck him, he was going to torture Dusty. He described how he'd do it. Every gory detail. I knew he meant it. I also knew that even if I gave him what he wanted, he'd kill my dog anyway. He was getting crazier all the time."

Cade reached over and took my tense hands in his. His fingers tightened on mine. Where our hands met, sparks flickered. "It's a damn good thing Jonathan is already dead. Or I'd be out the door right now on my way to the Highlands to track the fucker down."

"He's dead. Very dead."

"How did you escape this hell?"

"I told my mother. I don't know why I had never told her before. I'd been raised to be self-reliant and she had basically checked out on motherhood ever since my father's death."

I paused. My head was aching.

"She didn't believe you?" he guessed.

"No, she did believe me. In fact, it was as if she suddenly woke up. Once she got her head together, she was great. She planned everything. When my mother gets angry, she can work wonders. We drugged them all with some narcotic she'd procured. We snuck out of camp. We fled to London."

"London is not that far from Scotland."

"But it is city and Mum said Martin would never come to a city. He'd never go anywhere where he couldn't rule the roost, and the only place he could do that was in the outposts."

"What happened to your dog? To Dusty? Did she escape with you, too?"

My mind went dark. Even now, after all these years, I couldn't bear to think about Dusty.

I nodded and hurried on to the next part: "My mum and I'd both had enough of shifters and wolf packs, so we lived as humans in a suburb of the city. I went to school, where I had a lot of catching up to do. We stayed out of the shifter networks. And I continued not shifting."

"And at some point, Jonathan came after you?"

"Yes. It was several years afterwards. He'd graduated from torturing and killing animals to raping and assaulting girls. The women he preyed upon always looked like me—same build, same eyes, same dark hair. But I didn't find that out until later.

"His own father had exiled him from the pack—that's how much of a threat he'd become. Without the pack, his only social connection, he turned to criminal enterprises. He was arrested several times, but he broke jail and escaped."

"It's hard to keep a shifter in prison."

"He became a player in the trafficking nets that operate on some of the islands off the Scottish coast. It's really horrible. Wealthy people put in orders for unique slaves. They love to capture shifters. What a novelty…can you imagine? They use the chokers on them, too, doing things like putting a wolf shifter in a pen with a pack of wild dogs, but in human form and wearing the choker. So when attacked, they can't shift to defend themselves."

"Fucking hell. I've heard rumors about stuff like that—I think it happens here, too. But I hoped the stories were false."

"Nope. Sadly true. Anyway, I left Scotland. I went to college here in the States, majoring in fine arts. I thought I'd put the whole nightmare behind me. I didn't know he was still stalking me, or that I had become his obsession. He wasn't obvious about it.

"After I graduated college, I went back to Scotland for a while when I was figuring out what to do with my life." I shivered, wanting to hurry through this part as quickly as possible. "That was where he grabbed me. I was driving on a country road to Inverness to visit my mum. He overtook me and stopped me, pretending to be a traffic cop, and next thing I knew I was bound and gagged in the boot of his car.

"He took me to an isolated hideout. He was going to sell me to the slavers. What was left of me after he was finished. He had quite a program planned. He described it to me in exquisite detail."

Cade had risen and was stalking about the room, his face an angry red and all his muscles clenched with rage. He growled a couple of times and I thought he was going to shift, but he stayed human.

"He started in on me. With a knife. But he'd forgotten something."

"Your darkling?"

I nodded. "It had been years since he'd seen me shift at all. And he'd never seen my darkling. He didn't know about her. If he had a Highland Choker, he didn't use it. Big mistake.

"When threatened, my darkling isn't exactly docile. She came out and attacked."

A heavy silence hung over us. I could tell that Cade was reluctant to press me too hard. I was thankful for that.

"She—I—went for his throat. His wolf emerged, too. I guess that attack and defense instinct is strong. We fought. But he was no match for me. No wolf is." Not even you, I was thinking. "You've seen her. You're right—she's like a superhero. Or maybe a super villain."

I didn't want to continue, but I needed to spit this out. "I killed him. I tore open the blood vessels in his throat and watched while he bled to death. Slowly. Then I ripped his body to pieces. Sometimes I can still taste his blood and feel the sticky grit of his fur in the back of my throat."

Cade didn't look away from me for even so much as a moment. His voice was firm and strong as he said, "Good. Fuck him. He got what he deserved."

Relief flooded me. But I kept speaking. I had to. "It wasn't over. I'd committed a crime against our kind. And I'd done it as a darkling at a time when shifter/darkling relations were uneasy, at best. I wanted to run away and hide, but I knew I'd be hunted down if I did. So I went to Mallochbirn to be judged."

"What do you mean? Here we decide such matters in the pack. As the leader, I'm also the judge."

"As a multiform shifter, I am subject to the judgment of the laird of Mallochbirn, who is the head of all the Scottish multiform shifters and many of the other shifters as well. That's Ross Malloch, my second cousin. His twin, Cameron, is the head of something called the Council of Protectors. I'm not sure what they do, but they seem to be in charge of all sorts of things, including fighting criminals like the shifter trafficking outfits."

"Wait. Isn't that the man your mother wanted you to marry?"

I nodded. "That was later. I didn't know my cousins when I first went to Mallochbirn, so I didn't know what to expect. I just wanted it all to be over. If they condemned me, I was prepared for that. I couldn't forget my darkling's rage. It haunted me. It still does."

"Anyway, there was a trial and I told my story. It was judged to be an act of self defense, so no punishment was forthcoming. But I was ordered to learn to control my darkling. Cam warned me that even in Scotland, darkling shifters—and he is one also—are regarded with great suspicion and fear. Should she kill again, I'd be screwed."

"So you're afraid of that? Of her? That's why you don't let her out?"

"Yes. She's wild. Completely without conscience. She enjoyed what she did to Jonathan. That's why I lock her away. Her ferocity and savagery scare me. I don't know what she might do next."

"I get that," he said slowly.

I wondered if he did. I don't think he felt as much of a division between his human side and his wolf side as I did. Cade had never been forced to lock his wolf away, or been punished for releasing it.

"I want to meet this badass darkling who saved your life."

"You have met her."

"I've seen her. I want to spend some time with her."

Surely he didn't mean that? No, he couldn't. He was trying to make me feel better about myself. Which I really appreciated.

Funny. At the beginning, I'd thought him an arrogant ass. Now what I thought was that I didn't deserve him.

CHAPTER THIRTY-TWO

Cade

During Jess' confession, I'd restrained myself as long as I could. I wanted to grab her, hold her, reassure her with my body. She'd gone through a terrible ordeal, but she seemed to think she was somehow responsible for everything she'd suffered. And that killing the bastard had been wrong.

I needed to make her stop thinking that.

I slid over on the sofa where we were sitting and pulled her to me, stroking her hair, offering her my strength and compassion. At first, she was tense. I could feel her quivering, hanging on desperately to her control. Then, she softened, relaxed and started kissing me. She heated up fast and became the aggressor.

She rolled onto her back and pulled me down upon her, cradling me between her thighs. Tilting back her head, she searched for my mouth. Her kiss was passionate, frantic. Her hands moved into my hair, clutching me so hard, it hurt. "I need you," she whispered. "Fuck me."

Fine by me. I started stripping off clothing, hers first and then my own.

"Wait. Put the choker on me."

As far as I knew, that damn collar was upstairs in the bedroom. "Nah, we don't need it."

She started to get up. "I'll get it."

I caught her hand to stop her getting away from me. "Why, Jess? I'm not going to freak if you shift. Besides, why do you willingly wear the object that was used to subjugate you?"

She hesitated. "I know it must seem strange. But I got used to it. And Cam thought it might help me gain some control if I wore it of my own choice."

"Cam, your cousin?"

"He tried to help me. He's the only other darkling shifter I know. Maybe I should call him and try to figure out why this is happening to me."

I had an irrational desire to punch this Cam guy in the teeth. She didn't need him to help her. She had me. "We'll figure it out together."

I'd thought the Highland Choker was one of her kinks, which was okay with me. I'd been getting off on the master/slave vibe. But now I understood that she wanted it to prevent herself from turning into whatever the hell she had shifted to out in the meadow. That darkling kickass. Could she even have sex in that form?

Why not—she'd had a female form with breasts and, I presumed, genitals. She'd looked pretty much like herself except with wings and a boost of several inches in height. Her arms and legs had been longer, her waist tinier, her skin paler. Her hair had been the same. Her eyes had glowed. Her fingernails had looked like claws and although I hadn't gotten a good look at her teeth, I suspected she'd had fangs.

Was my wife a vampire?

Stop being a fucking idiot, Derringer.

"We don't need that choker, Jess. If you were trying to hide your other forms from me, it's too late now. And I don't believe you're gonna shift spontaneously while we're fucking, anyhow."

"I don't want to take that chance."

"Yeah, well, I need you to stop being afraid of what you are. I don't know any other multiform shifters, and I don't know why you were raised to be afraid of it because I think it's cool. In my pack, we're not ashamed of who we are. Or what we are. You're my wife, Jess, and I'm fine with it."

At least, I hoped I was fine with it.

"It's just that I'm dangerous when I'm sleeping. Sometimes I shift in my sleep. I get up, go outside and hunt. Afterwards I have only the vaguest memory of what I've done. I come back with blood on me, but I don't remember what—or who—I've hunted."

Who? Did she mean she was hunting humans?

No, I didn't believe that. The body might change form, but the inner self remained the same. A nasty human was a nasty wolf. A friendly human was a friendly wolf. And a woman with a pure heart like Jess' could never be a cruel wolf…or, surely, not a cruel darkling.

Right? Only problem was, I didn't know shit about darklings.

I knew my mate, though. At least, I was coming to know her. And to trust her. Hell, I was even beginning to think I might be falling in love with her.

Whatever she was, she couldn't be evil or cruel.

CHAPTER THIRTY-THREE

Cade

The next morning, I stopped over at the Derringer compound to talk to my mom. She was surprised to see me. She looked as if she'd just gotten up. Her hair was still wet from the shower. I thought she seemed a bit uneasy, but maybe she wasn't completely awake yet.

She sat me down at the kitchen table and offered me coffee. The rich scent of it was stronger than usual and mixed with other scents I didn't recognize. Was my mother wearing perfume at this hour of the morning? That was odd.

"Haven't seen you for a while, Cade. Is something wrong?"

I wasn't sure how to respond to this query, so I ignored it. I took a large sip of my coffee and then said, "Remember when you asked me about Jess' mother's family? What do you know about them?"

She looked wary. "Why are you asking?"

I was in no mood. "Look, Ma. I'm the alpha of the pack. You got information, I want it. Now."

"That's something of a harsh tone, Cade," a voice said from behind me.

I'd scented the man a split second before I'd heard him, and I was on my feet almost as swiftly. But I recognized the voice. And the scent. What shocked me was the way Heck's scent was mingling with my mother's.

"Heck?" I said as my father's old lieutenant entered the room and helped himself to a mug from the cabinet. Mom had given me a mug from the kitchen table. One of two sitting there, waiting for morning coffee.

Holy shit.

My mother was shacking up with Hector. How long had that been going on?

"Morning," Heck said. He pulled out a chair and sat down. Mom looked from him to me and sighed.

"We were going to tell you," she said. "Soon."

My mind was spinning wildly as I tried to come to terms with this new knowledge. Dad had only been dead for two years and she'd loved him. Hadn't she?

Of course she had! Two years was a long time. Had I ever gone two years without sex?

Maybe it was just a thing? The idea of Mom having a thing with anybody messed with my head. "How long?" I asked, because I couldn't think of anything else to fucking say.

"Not long," Heck answered in his calm, loose-limbed manner. He'd always been the solid, reliable one. My dad's right hand man. His beta. "Few weeks." He glanced at Mom and I could feel the love rolling off him. "But I've loved your mother for years. She never even looked at me, though. Not that way."

Mom reached over and took Heck's hand, squeezing hard. I was embarrassed. Damn. She loved him, too. "Sometimes friendship ripens into love," she said.

I wondered if I ought to leave. It had never occurred to me that I might be interrupting something. "So, um, congratulations. Does this mean another wedding is in the offing?"

"We'll see." My mother was noncommittal. "What was it you wanted to know about your wife's family?"

Yeah, right. I glanced at Heck, who looked as if he were staying put. I could order him out and he'd have to obey. Unless he was planning to challenge me. Take the official alpha female, my mother, because I still hadn't claimed that position for my own mate. I hadn't cleared the way for Jess. Why hadn't I?

Was that even possible now? Would the pack ever accept her if they knew what she was?

I saw in my mind again the creature she'd become in the meadow. The memory gave me a little chill. She'd carried some sort of darkness with her, like an aura.

Dammit! What the fuck was wrong with me? I'd demanded that she accept herself. What if I was the one who couldn't accept who or what she was?

Could I really be that much of a dick?

"I wondered how much you knew about the Scots relatives. Jess was, uh, telling me some things about her mother's side of the family that seemed a little far-fetched."

"I know Jess' mother is a multiform shifter, if that's what you mean," his mother said calmly. "She is related to the Mallochs of Mallochbirn."

"Yeah, she told me." I looked from my mother to Heck. I noted that the latter didn't seem surprised by the subject. He was nodding as if he already knew this. Did everybody know who the fuck the Mallochs of Mallochbirn were except me?

I was never that good at shifter lore and history. Aaron had been interested in that kind of thing, but I'd rebelled against learning it. Why study dusty old tomes about the history of shifters when I could be out getting wasted with my friends?

Damn. I'd been such a fuckup. Why the hell had Aaron died? He'd have been so much better at this pack leadership gig than I was.

"You guys better fill me in. I obviously didn't learn all the things I needed to know for this job."

They didn't rail on me about it, at least. Heck, who'd always been knowledgeable about all sorts of esoteric shit, said, "There are a lot of myths and legends about the Scottish shifters. It was supposedly somewhere in the northern Highlands that shifters first entered this world. Through some kind of rift from another dimension. Some even claim that Mallochbirn is sitting on a tiny island right near the place where the worlds crack open.

Beings from one of the other Nine Worlds can sometimes slip through into ours."

Right. The Nine Worlds legend. I'd heard that one. I'd always thought it was utter bullshit. "So shifters aren't native to this planet? According to this myth? There's, like, a shifter world somewhere long long ago and far far away?"

"Something like that," Heck agreed. "It's a classic origin myth, for people who believe in those. The important thing is that the family at Mallochbirn has maintained a certain status in the British Isles for generations. Centuries, in fact. They appear to have special powers that are uncommon among other shifters."

"They can shift to more than one animal form," my mother said. "At least, the direct descendants of the ancient Malloch clan can. No one knows how many Malloch descendants have this ability, but clearly some do."

"Some reputedly have two animal forms, like a wolf and a hawk, for example," Heck continued, "Or a bear and a lion. Others may be capable of more than two. The most famous Malloch creature is the sea dragon."

Even I'd heard that story. "The dragons who fell from the sky, losing their fires and condemned to the deep?"

"Even so," Heck agreed. "No one's ever seen a fire dragon in the sky, but there are definitely a few sea monsters in the oceans."

I mulled this over for a couple minutes. How many forms did Jess have? Given how scared she was to shift, maybe she didn't even know?

"Is Jess a multiform shifter?" Mom asked. She didn't sound shocked by the prospect. She had probably been expecting it.

"She has another form, yes. But she was always discouraged from shifting, so it doesn't feel natural to her. She keeps it locked up inside. I'm trying to encourage her to be more open and accepting of her shifter nature."

My mother nodded. "That's wise of you. It's not good to keep the other parts of one's self locked away."

I hesitated. But I needed advice, so I said, "What if you can't control the actions of the other parts of yourself? What if you have something inside you that's ferocious and—" I cast around for the right word "—alien?"

Both the older folks looked mystified. My mother set her coffee cup down. "Cade, do you object to your wife's other animals?"

"No, of course not." I was beginning to wish I'd never initiated this conversation. "She hardly ever shifts, except when she's stressed out. She was raised to believe it was wrong to shift at all. Not by her mother, but by her mother's asshole second partner. Her pseudo-stepfather. They weren't actually married. But the guy had a son who was some kind of psycho. He assaulted her and tried to rape and murder her, so she shifted to defend herself."

And ripped him to shreds, if her account had been accurate.

"How terrible for her," my mother said, with the empathy and concern that she was known for. "Did this happen when she was in Scotland?"

I nodded.

"Where's her attacker now? Is he still stalking her? Do we need to be on the lookout for him?"

"No. Her attacker is dead."

Mom and Heck exchanged a quick glance, and they both nodded. "Good."

I was pretty sure they understood who'd killed him. Not that there would be any trouble over that. It was accepted within the shifter community that when you were attacked, you had the right to defend, even unto the attacker's death.

My mom reached out and covered my hand with her own. "It sounds as if she has a lot to work through. But Jess strikes me as a strong woman. She'll be okay. I hope she'll begin to feel more comfortable within our community. No one is going to judge her, son."

"I hope not." I honestly wasn't sure what people would think if they saw her darkling.

"As for her other forms, if she has trouble accepting those sides of herself, the best thing you can do is be open to them yourself. Encourage her to shift for you when she feels the need. Keep your own animal restrained if you fear some conflict. If she has a big cat, for example, your wolf might not take to it at first."

A big cat. Hell, that would be easy.

I overheard my own thought and felt ashamed. This was Jess. How was she going to learn to accept herself if her own mate was a little freaked out by her?

Fuck my life. I'd better get over my wariness or whatever the hell it was, because Jess needed me.

Enough. I couldn't tell them anything more, and I had to get out of there.

CHAPTER THIRTY-FOUR

Jess

It happened again. I rose from our bed and shifted. Cade was asleep. I felt it coming on and I fled into the bathroom. Once it started, it couldn't be stopped, but I did try to control it. I managed to shape myself into my wolf, furry and panting with the effort. I tried to settle into that more familiar form. But I could feel her, my demon, struggling to get out.

The shift helped relieve some kind of tension in me that no longer seemed to be released by sex. Damn my cousin and his worthless advice. I was having lots of orgasms these days, but they weren't preventing my darkling's insistence that she be freed to wreak her violence on the world.

I couldn't understand why this was happening. Ever since the day we'd gone hunting it was as if a fire had been kindled inside me that kept roaring hotter and hotter. Was I going mad? What did she want from me?

But I knew. It wasn't what she wanted from me. It was what she wanted from him.

She wanted Cade. I wasn't sure exactly what she wanted to do with him, but she definitely wanted to get her fangs and claws into him.

What I hadn't confessed to him about that morning in the meadow was that when she'd burst out of me and shown herself, she'd caught the scent of his blood. It had inspired in her a wild lust that was even stronger than anything my human self was capable of feeling. Which made it pretty damn strong.

A dominatrix superhero. Yeah, no joke. But I didn't think dark-lings knew limits or respected safewords. I was afraid she would hurt him badly, maybe without even realizing that she was being rough.

I succeeded in keeping her inside me that time, and, at least, as morning was graying the sky, I was able to shift back to human. I slunk back to bed and as I slipped in beside him, Cade rolled over and wrapped his arm around my waist. "Cade. Are you awake? Put the choker on me."

"No way," he said in a sleepy, slurred voice. "No choker." He'd been refusing to lock that thing around my throat ever since he'd learned my secret. He'd actually come home yesterday with a hand-made leather bondage collar and a pair of matching cuffs that he'd ordered online. "You want to do the kinky, we can use these."

"Those are cool, but it's not the same."

"I know. But you're not hiding any part of yourself from me anymore, babe. You wanna sleep shift? Bring it on. If you're into shifting during sex, bring that on, too. I'm up for it. Sounds like fun."

I loved him for the way he was so willing to welcome any aspect of me, but I was afraid for him nevertheless.

He pulled me closer now, and next thing I knew he had dragged me under him. I don't think he was even fully awake, but his cock was hard and jutting. As soon as I felt it, I turned wet. "Sleep fuck," he muttered and proceeded to do just that. I don't think it took more than a couple of minutes for us both to come, and afterwards, I was able to sleep peacefully.

Maybe Cam was right. Maybe I just needed lots and lots of fucking.

But the next night, it happened again. And this time I couldn't stop my darkling from emerging. She burst out of me before I could escape to the bathroom, but she was unusually quiet about it. The distinctive shifting sounds that should have awakened Cade did not. He slept on, oblivious, while she—I—stood over the bed, just a few inches away from his exposed throat, my huge wings spread and poised as if to fly..

But she didn't fly. She—I—stared down at the man I had married with a vastness of hunger that my human self could scarcely comprehend.

But she didn't attack. She didn't do anything violent. She just stood and watched and yearned.

My own terror of what might happen warred with her desire for nameless things. As Cam had told me, we weren't ordinary creatures. Our desires were dark. Evil? I didn't even know. When I was her and she was me, I lost all sense of the difference between darkness and light.

I don't remember what happened after that. But when I woke up, I was lying on the cold floor beside the bed. I was naked and freezing. It was Cade who found me there. He hustled me into bed and warmed me with the quilts and his body. "You should have put the choker on me," I said, torn between dread and anger.

"You shifted? I didn't hear it."

"Did I hurt you? I don't remember. I was looking down on you, but then it all faded to black."

"You didn't hurt me Jess. I'm fine. Nothing happened. You probably dreamed it."

"I didn't dream it. I was standing over you hearing your heartbeat thunder in my ears and wanting to feel it under my tongue. I want to drink your blood, like a fucking vampire."

"I'd like to see you try."

Oh God, such an alpha. He still didn't take this seriously. He probably thought that if I ever attacked him, he could defend himself. He probably thought he could win.

CHAPTER THIRTY-FIVE

Jess

I was at my easel and Cade was working over at his compound when someone knocked at my front door. I growled, hoping they'd go away. I was into my work.

But the knocking persisted, and I finally put down my brush and went to the door, wiping my hands on a turpentine-soaked rag.

I was surprised to find Brandon on the front porch. I looked for Suzanne, since they seemed to travel as a matched set, but there was no sign of her. Brandon was dressed casually, like everyone around here, in thigh-hugging jeans and a flannel shirt and jacket. It was cool today; one could feel that winter was on the way.

A stiff breeze ruffled his golden hair. If I hadn't been so wrapped up in my own man, I might have found him attractive. He was tall and fit with a bladed nose, a firm jaw, and fathomless gray eyes.

"If you're looking for Cade, he's at the compound."

"Actually, I dropped by to see you."

There was some kind of edge to his voice, and all my instincts warned me to be careful. Instead of inviting him in, I grabbed my jacket from the hook near the door and slipped it on, thrusting my paint rag into my pocket. Stepping out onto the porch, I said, "I was just about to take a little walk. You're welcome to come along if you want."

He gave a twisted smile that told me he knew this was a lie, but he didn't object. I didn't care for the idea of being alone with him in the house. Nor did I think Cade would be too pleased about it if he came home early. "Where's Suzanne?"

He shrugged. "At home, I guess. I wanted to speak to you alone."

"What about?" I remembered the way he'd looked at me when we'd run into each other hunting a few days ago. If he was going to make a move on me, Cade would probably kill him. Or else Suzanne would.

I led him over to where the chickens were rooting around in their pen. I decided to feed them since it would give me something to do. I headed for the barn where the chickenfeed was keep. Brandon paced alongside me.

I grabbed a bag and started tossing handfuls to the chickens. They waddled over and started pecking the ground.

"What can I do for you?" I asked.

"You can answer a few questions."

I blinked at him, bemused by his harsh tone. I barely even knew the man, but he sounded accusatory. "Are you serious? Questions about what?"

He took a step closer to me and I felt aggression rolling off him. Whoa. What was going on? "You're not a wolf shifter, are you?"

Shit. Where the hell was this coming from? "Of course I'm a wolf shifter."

"No one in the pack has ever seen your wolf. Why is that? How do we even know you're really Tom MacLeish's granddaughter?"

What the fuck? "You may not have grown up in this town, but I did. People know me…I'm not some stranger. Why are you asking me this?"

"You've been gone a long time and you're obviously fooling a lot of people. Darklings can do that. I know what you are."

I felt the blood rush into my cheeks. How did he know? "Are you out of your freaking mind? Why would you think something like that?"

"Don't bother to deny it. I saw you fly over the treetops on the edge of Great Meadows the other day when we were out hunting."

My throat closed or I might have squawked like a chicken, too.

"If you'd intended to hide it, you should have told Cade to pick a more private place. There were several other hunters in the area. The pheasants are thick there."

Shit. Could he be bluffing? I hadn't flown for more than a few seconds that day. But he had been in the area, and a bird hunter would probably be watching the sky.

Even though my heart was skittering, I decided to play it cool. I glanced from the chickens to Brandon, feigning disinterest. "So I can fly, huh? Was I riding a broomstick? Playing quidditch, maybe?"

He moved closer, asserting his own alpha dominance. I stood my ground. He wasn't my alpha. "You're a darkling. That's why no one in the pack has seen your wolf. You're not one of us. I don't know what the fuck Cade was thinking when he married you, but the sooner this marriage ends, the better for all of us. Shifters don't mate with darklings."

"That sounds like a bigoted opinion. Are you equally prejudiced against all races?"

"So you're admitting it."

"I admit nothing. Sounds to me as if you were seeing things. Or doing drugs."

"You know, I am crediting myself with a good deal of rational thought on this matter," he said pleasantly. "I haven't told anyone what I saw. I didn't even share it with Suzanne, whose attention was elsewhere at the time. I've let a few days go by because I didn't want to act precipitously." His mouth hardened. "But I'm here now, and this is what I've decided."

What he'd decided? Who the hell did he think he was?

"You're going to leave. Go back to Scotland or wherever you came from. I'll give you two days. If you're not gone by then, I'll tell everyone in the pack who and what you are."

I'm not sure what I'd expected, but this took my breath away. Inside me, something stirred. The air around me turned sharper and my fingers flexed. The aggressive forces were sick of being restrained. It wouldn't take much for them to burst their bonds. I could hear it in my own voice as I said, "How dare you threaten me? You have no idea what you're talking about."

"You're wrong. I've dealt with darklings before. I might be the only one in this pack who has. A vicious darkling clan in Texas murdered my entire family. That's how I ended up here, in Montana, when I was a young teenager on the run. If you think I'll let another one of those foul creatures destroy this pack, you're motherfucking mistaken."

"I'm not a darkling. I'm a wolf shifter." I was mad at myself as soon as the words were out of my mouth. It sounded defensive, and it was a bad idea to get defensive with an alpha because he would seize the advantage and walk all over anyone who did.

"Right," he sneered. "So I was hallucinating? I saw you. You've already killed one person, haven't you? That biker who died a few weeks ago was torn apart by a paranormal creature. We were afraid it was someone from the pack, but it was you, wasn't it? Did you sate yourself on biker blood? How long until you turn on one of us?"

That was a kick in the gut, since I'd feared the same thing myself. I couldn't let him see it. But I could feel the perspiration breaking out on my palms and the tingling running up and down my spine.

"I don't know why Cade married you or what hold you have over him, but you're alone here. One darkling, powerful though you may be, is not enough to do battle against the whole pack. And if Cade takes your side in this, we'll destroy him, too."

"That sounds like what you've wanted all along. To take his brother's place in his family? To lead the pack? But you didn't defeat him in the election and you're sure as hell not going to do it now." I took a step toward him. "Maybe one darkling can't take out the whole pack, but she can easily deal with a single shifter."

I caught the flicker in his eyes, even though it only lasted for a split second. If he feared darklings from whatever had happened to him as a child, he controlled his emotions well. Had his family really been murdered by darklings? Full-blooded darklings? So they did exist on this continent?

He gave no ground. I understood now why he had been considered a worthy rival to Cade. Brandon had a core of steel.

"Kill me, darkling, and you destroy yourself. The entire pack will be down upon you before the day ends. Even your precious lover will not be able to let that crime stand."

I could see only one way out of this, and transforming to my darkling self and ripping out his throat wasn't it. But could I do it? The fear that I couldn't control my own shifting had been tormenting me now for months.

Focus. Control the shift. You decide which aspect to present to the world. You are the alpha of your own being.

"If you're deluded enough to challenge me over some mad fantasy of yours, let's play it out in the ancient manner."

I went inside. I reached for my wolf and focused on her form, her senses, her bones, her blood.

Pain wracked my body as I began to shift.

It hurt more than usual because I was so tightly wound, so desperate to do it correctly. I needed to keep the wilder and more ferocious darkling in. I summoned my wolf. I'd have pleaded with her to come and the other to stay contained, except I needed discipline now. Not weakness.

My fingers elongated as my claws sprang forth. My skin prickled everywhere as it flowed differently over breaking, changing bones. Silky fur sprouted as my spine cracked and my muscles remolded. My skull screamed with pain as bones reshaped and pressed my brain into a different conformation. I had the familiar sense of my brain being compressed, rewired, certain connections vanishing and others taking their place.

It was always traumatic, and the lore proclaimed that some shifters suffered more than others in the process. But when it fully formed, my shifted body felt strong and lithe, and my senses of smell, sight, and hearing magnified a thousand fold.

I sprang into the air and thought for a moment all was lost. But no, it was the leap of a wolf, not the flight of a darkling.

New scents swirled around me as the air pumped into my lungs, I pranced among the chickens, who scattered, shrieking.

I was not the only wolf in the yard. No sooner had I begun to shift than Brandon did the same. He completed his shift before I did, too, probably because he was much more practiced at it. He was a gray wolf, large and majestic. Bigger than I was and probably stronger. Male and dominant. He stood stiff and straight, his tail high, ready to attack.

We circled one another, both of us snarling. I stared at him through my wolfish eyes. I caught his smell as he caught mine. And I sensed his surprise.

He knew about darklings. But apparently he did not know about multiform shifters. He was trying to unravel the fact that he believed he had seen a darkling. But what he now saw before him was clearly a werewolf.

He growled. I lowered my tail a smidgen to let him know that I did not really want to fight him. I had made my point. I'd said I was a wolf shifter and I'd proved it.

Your move, alpha.

I remained still and let him approach me. I was damned if I would exhibit any submission to a male who was not my mate, but I did let him sniff me. Suck it, Brandon. When I was a wolf, I was all wolf. He would not find a trace of darkling in me now.

We were still assessing each other, narrow-eyed, when my ears pricked up at the sound of an engine approaching. Motorcycle.

The same engine my wolf had first heard on the night of the accident.

Cade was home.

CHAPTER THIRTY-SIX

Cade

"What the fuck is going on here?"

I don't even know if they heard me because I was already shifting and streaking across the final hundred yards to the barn before the whole sentence was out of my mouth. My body turned from flesh into white-furred lightning. My brain was a seething red explosion of rage. That was Brandon—I saw him, smelled him and yet could hardly believe he would dare to approach my mate in my absence, especially in his wolfen form.

But what really ripped my mind into shreds was the sight of my own wife, who never shifted—who refused to shift for me—standing still in the yard in her own wolf form and letting another male fill his lungs with her scent.

I wanted to fucking kill them both.

I chose him to attack first because it was the natural thing to do. He had been my rival long enough. It was time to end the bastard.

I was airborne before I even hit the barnyard. Brandon rose up defensively on his hind legs and we crashed together in a vicious embrace. My claws and my teeth ripped at him, fully ready to destroy him. We'd never done battle for the alpha wolf position. Fine. We could have that brawl now.

He whined as I clawed him. I went for his throat, but he twisted away and dropped to the ground, cowering before me as bones cracked and Jess' aura shimmered. She shifted and a naked woman crouched where a gorgeous sable-colored wolf had stood a moment before.

"No Cade," she screamed. "He made a mistake, but not the kind of mistake you think. He's submitting. Back off."

He was submitting. His proud tail was now down between his legs. Despite the fury in my blood that urged me to kill him anyway—easy now when he wasn't even fighting me—I tried to get a grip on my temper.

I whirled instead on my mate, my lush, naked, big-breasted wife who roused me to full virility no matter whether I was wolf or man. Damn her for shifting back. I wanted her wolf crouched in the dirt before me. She had shifted for another man? I'd mount her and fuck her into oblivion.

I snarled at her and herded her human body back against the side of the barn, pressing my fur against her silky skin. I was tempted to claw her, just to see my mark of ownership on that smooth white skin.

There was another groaning of flesh and bone as Brandon shifted. Now there were two naked humans, either of whom I could lunge at and kill. Fools. Didn't they know how angry I was?

I thought of the body of the biker who'd been murdered by a shifter. The mess of blood, the wounds, the horror on his frozen face. My rage leached out of me. That was what was left when a wolf went postal on a human body—ruin and devastation.

"She's right, Alpha," Brandon said as he slowly got to his feet. He backed away from me. "I came over because of something I thought I saw. I realize now that I was mistaken."

I had no clue what they were talking about, but I knew my brain would make more sense of this if I resumed my human form. So I, too, shifted. As soon as I did, I found myself beset by new feelings of anger at the sight of my wife's bare body. How dare she show herself to another man? Such a thing had never upset me before. The whole pack ran around naked as we shifted in and out of human form. But the first words I barked at her were, "Cover yourself."

She found her clothing on the ground, tattered and torn, which meant she had shifted precipitously. She pulled on a shirt and jacket that provided at least some modesty. Brandon made no such attempt to get dressed.

"What mistake?" My voice felt hoarse; I still sounded more like a wolf than a man.

"He saw something on Sunday when hunting. Probably a vulture or some other large bird of prey." Jess' eyes were intent on mine and I got that she was signaling something to me. She added, speaking slowly and clearly, "He thought he saw a mythical creature. A darkling. He thought it must have been me."

Fuck! I recalled that Brandon and Suzanne had been in the area on Sunday when I'd taken Jess hunting, but I'd sent them off in the other direction. Not far enough away from us, it seemed.

"There is nothing mythical about darklings," Brandon said. He was still breathing hard. "They decimated the town I lived in as a boy. But this was the first time I'd seen one in Montana."

"Since he had never seen my wolf, Brandon came up with the theory that this creature he thinks he saw was me. Now he knows that I have a wolf inside me. How he believed anything else when he knew my grandfather, I can't imagine."

"I apologize."

He looked as if he meant it, and I concluded he didn't know there were shifters who could take the form of a darkling. Since I hadn't known it either, I felt a brief glimmer of sympathy.

He shook his head, his eyes puzzled. "I still think that's what I saw. It was my error in believing it arose from the same spot where you and your wife were hunting. There were others out hunting pheasant that morning. I shouldn't have jumped to conclusions without more evidence."

I cleared my throat as I sorted rapidly through the implications. This would cause confusion among the pack members, if it hadn't already. Jess' secret would not remain a secret for long. I didn't think it should. I wasn't going to lie about my wife's super powers or whatever they were.

She might want to deny her identity, but I wasn't the secretive type. I'd always lived my life defying custom and convention, acting on my feelings even when that meant I was being an ass. This is who I am—take me or leave me. And who I was now was a wolf shifter who loved a rare creature with a darkling side.

She would fucking well shift on my command now. I couldn't believe that she'd brought out her wolf to show Brandon after refusing to do so for me. I wanted to tie her to the bed and thrash her ass until it was fiery red and then fuck her until she screamed for mercy.

"Put your clothes back on and get the fuck off my property. And don't ever come to visit my wife again or I'll rip out your fucking throat."

CHAPTER THIRTY-SEVEN

Jess

Cade was spitting mad at me. "I can't believe you shifted for him when you've refused all these weeks to shift for me!"

"I had to. It was the only way I could think of to prove I wasn't a darkling. He told me darklings murdered his family in Texas."

"I've asked you to shift to your wolf a million times. Dammit, Jess. You let him sniff your butt!"

"Sniffing my butt was proof that I'm a wolf and a shifter."

"Yeah, well, you're not, are you? You're a multiform shifter and you do have a darkling inside you. How long do you seriously think you can hide that from the whole pack? It's gonna come out sooner or later and I would like to control how it does."

"Why, because you're the alpha? It's my body. I've never agreed to be a formal member of your pack and you don't control me."

"You're my wife!" he roared.

"Soon to be ex-wife! Maybe even sooner than you think!"

We were having our first real fight. Facing off in Grandpa's living room, with the dead heads of various hunting trophies staring down on us, we were both bristling like a couple of skirmishing wolves.

"Next time you have a problem with someone in my pack, tell them to fuck off and bring their complaints directly to me."

"You're acting like a jealous idiot."

"No one sniffs my mate's butt but me."

"Fine! You wanna sniff my butt?" I ripped down the jeans that I'd grabbed from the closet as we'd stormed into the house. We always had fresh trousers and shirts nearby, but didn't bother with spare underwear. I turned my back on him and stuck my ass in his direction. "Well here. Go ahead."

Mistake.

He grabbed me, sank down on the leather sofa, and manhandled me across his lap. "I can think of better things to do with your bare ass."

The flat of his hand landed hard across my butt cheek and I let out a shriek—more anger than pain. I squirmed as I tried to get away, but he hooked one leg over my ankles and his free arm over my shoulders and whacked away. I could feel my ass getting red, and it fucking hurt, but since every swat drove my pelvis into his thigh, my clit was soon reverberating with that crazy hot sensation.

Angry sex. Damn. With the right person, it could be hot as hell.

And Cade was the right person, or so my body had believed ever since we'd met.

His hand on my ass was fiery hot. He was soon punctuating his spanks with downward slides of his fingers along the flaring lips of my pussy. His other hand pushed my top up and freed my breasts. They hung down over the edge of his thighs where he could stroke them and play wicked games with my nipples while the spanking continued.

He leaned down so his face was brushing my tangled hair. "You're mine. My mate. My wife. I've claimed you, and we have the static or sevmelle or love lights or whatever you want to call this thing. He raised his fingers away from my ass and held them just a few millimeters above the surface of my skin. I could feel the current zapping between us—a faint shock of sensation that felt a whole lot better than any static electricity had ever felt. "I can see it and feel it and so can you. I don't know what the fuck it is, but it's real."

He jerked me up and rolled me over. I was panting with arousal and a lot less eager to get away. In fact, since I was missing half my clothes, it was time for him to join me. I reached up and pushed my hand under his T-shirt. I went straight for one of his nipples and squeezed it between my thumb and forefinger until he made a low sound in his throat. He liked it rough? Fine. I could retaliate.

"You're full of shit," I told him. "I'm your temporary bride and that's all I am, so stop trying to make this more than it is."

He ripped off his shirt, exposing all that fine hard-muscled flesh for my appreciation. "You need to stop trying to make it less than it is. I obviously haven't used you hard enough, Princess, if you're still defying me."

I laughed in his face, but he kissed me into silence. I struggled with his clothes and mine, not entirely clear whether I wanted them on or off. They all came off—shirts, pants, shoes and socks—and were tossed wildly around the room. At one point, I wrenched free of him and made a brief escape attempt. He leapt over the back of the sofa and caught me up against the wall, under the goddamn stag antlers.

Next thing I knew we were wallbanging, my arms spread-eagled against the wall and my legs wrapped around his waist. I was dripping wet for him and aching with lust. Every time he thrust into me, I moaned, reveling in the slide of his thick hard cock inside me. The trophy over our heads shook and I hoped it wouldn't crash down and knock the two of us unconscious. But I soon forgot about that worry as he drilled into me and my pussy convulsed violently around his cock.

He held me there, pinned to the wall, even after we had both climaxed. I was clinging to his arms now, my head on his shoulder, my hair crushed between our bodies and the pleasure spasms still flooding my insides. He plastered my face with kisses.

"You drive me crazy, Jess. I swear, there's never been a woman like you."

I started laughing and he joined in. That happened a lot with us. Wild crazy sex made me laugh afterwards, partly because it felt so amazing and partly because I was so overwhelmed with other feelings that I didn't want to confront.

I didn't want this to be temporary anymore.

I did want the light-flickering phenomenon to be the sevmelle.

Could the alpha wolf's fated mate ever be a multiform shifter who was part vampire or whatever the hell I was?

Was that even possible?

He backed us off the wall and carefully set me on my feet on the carpet. He captured my wrist and pulled me toward the staircase. "I'm not done with you yet. I'm taking you up to bed. I'm gonna spend the rest of the night proving you're mine. Not for six months, but for as long as I want you. I'm gonna own your body. And then maybe I'll take your soul."

"That's hot."

He pressed another savage kiss on my mouth. "No sassy commentary, babe. There'll be more spankings coming your way."

"Bring it on, Alpha," I laughed.

Cade

When I got her up to the bedroom, I made her kneel before me on the carpet and suck me for a while. I was only half-erect at first, but it was amazing how that clever tongue could get me going again, even after the explosive climaxes we had both had downstairs.

"You're a good little cocksucker," I told her, deliberately going for the rough talk she sometimes chided me for. I knew she liked it, when she was in the mood. If she wasn't in the mood again yet, she'd better get there soon, because I wasn't anywhere near done with her.

She leaned back and grinned up at me. "You're pretty good under the sheets yourself."

I fisted her hair and forced her back onto my dick. I pumped in and out of her mouth, getting harder every second. After another minute of this, I pushed her down on her hands and knees and dropped to the carpet behind her.

"I hope you like it wild, because my wolf is feeling damn near the surface."

She moaned slightly and moved her hips invitingly.

Kneeling behind her, I reached around to find her breasts. She groaned and arched her spine, her back against my belly, her ass cheeks cradling my dick.

She'd been seared upon me, body and soul. She was my mate and I was going to claim her in the way of the wolves. Maybe she wasn't truly at peace with her own wolf nature, but I could no longer suppress mine. That static electricity or whatever the fuck it was ought to have proved to her that she was mine to hold, mine to own, mine to keep.

Enough of this temporary marriage bullshit. I was going to put an end to that crap once and for all. Jess had sworn an oath to accept me as her husband and dammit, she was stuck with me. For better or for worse.

My wolf was no longer going to be denied. I couldn't chain him much longer anyway.

I stretched my neck and nipped her on the shoulder. I was still human, but she must have felt a hint of my fangs.

Her silky skin felt so soft and tender compared to my own bristly muscles and tendons. Every time I touched her, I felt reverberations in my cock. If any more blood pumped into my genitals, I'd burst before I'd given her what she needed.

Much as I loved touching and stroking her in my human form, especially when my dick was swollen, I couldn't help wondering what it would be like to meet face to face as our elemental selves. To run with her hard into the night. To nuzzle, groom, and mount her. To feel her accepting me in every possible way.

The more I envisioned it, the closer to the surface my beast rose.

I had to fuck her again. Deep. Hard. I felt as if I hadn't come for days.

"Open nice and wide for me, babe."

She stretched her legs apart. I took my dick in my fist and massaged it, just to torture myself, I think. Then I bowed my hips and plunged inside her. As her pussy clutched and held me, I let out a snarl. I continued to nail her, my genitals burning with intense lust. Wolves mated roughly sometimes. Once the male was inside the female, they would stay locked together, with him knotting and expanding inside her until he came. No way would he withdraw or let her go until he'd was fully satisfied.

That was the way I felt. Hungry like a wolf and determined to milk this thing for every ounce of primal pleasure.

"If I gave you a dare now," I breathed near her ear, "Would you do it?"

"If you're going to dare me to shift to my wolf," she gasped, sounding rather growly herself, "Yes. I would. For you, I would."

Ha. Not just to prove something to Brandon, then? Okay.

I squeezed her breast as hard as I could. I figured she deserved a little more punishment for that ass sniffing thing. "Stay human. I will, too. But after we finish here, we're going for a run in the woods. You and me. The alpha wolf and his mate. That's how I want you tonight and that's how I'll have you."

She nodded, her breath heaving. It felt so right. Together, we found a common rhythm. She scrunched her ass backward to meet my every thrust. Her pussy muscles clenched around me as if to stay clamped to me forever.

I kissed her neck and rubbed her clit. And then I slammed my dick into her until we both dissolved in bliss.

When we'd recovered, I took her hand and led her downstairs and out into the back yard.

"Now," I ordered. "Shift for me, Jess."

With a groan of bone and muscle, she kept her promise. Her majestic sable-furred wolf took shape before me, and in her intelligent canine face, I could see the pride and dauntless spirit of Jess, my wife.

I, too, shifted. I walked haughtily around her and, very deliberately, sniffed her delicious ass.

If a wolf could laugh, she did it then. A moment later, she bounded off toward the woods, and I quickly followed. With a thousand stars lighting our way, we ran together as wolves.

Chapter Thirty-Eight

Jess

The next few weeks alternated between being joyous and rocky.

Cade and I continued to have amazing, hot, wonderful sex.

When we weren't jumping each other's bones, we lived together in relative contentment. I finished a painting and did piles of good work for my graphic art clients, designing websites and book covers and doing a couple of nature photoshoots. I wasn't a super good photographer, yet, but I'd been getting into it since it fit so well with my other visual work. In the past, I'd mostly used my camera to take shots that I might want to paint, or use as inspiration for painting, but now I'd begun to use my camera as a tool for more art.

I also started designing the mural Cade wanted for the large empty wall in his house. We spent some time over at the compound, hanging out with his mother, whom I really liked, and with Heck, who had turned out to be her lover. But I was still avoiding most of the other members of the pack. I wasn't ready to be upfront with them about my dual shifter nature.

The bad was that I still felt like a person plagued by multiple personalities, and I think Cade was growing impatient with that. "You're just you," he kept insisting. "Like I'm me whether I'm a man or a wolf. Don't try to convince me it's any different just because you have this rare darkling aspect. She's still you, Jess."

Yeah, a nasty violent me with a penchant for drinking blood.

Because he absolutely refused to put the Highland Choker on me, I did sleep shift on several occasions. When I shifted to my wolf, he could always sense it somehow. He would wake up and follow me out. I would nudge open the back door and run down the back porch steps into the barnyard. Wolfen Cade would run with me, and together we would race across the fields and into the woods, where we would prance and dance, flirt and play.

We stayed away from other wolves, so it was just the two of us—mates who enjoyed our time together, even though this sometimes meant that we got little sleep and woke up to the human world bleary and in need of large quantities of caffeine.

But on the nights I shifted to my darkling form, he usually didn't wake.

She didn't wake him, either. She just stood over him, gazing down and struggling with her own dark desires. Listening to his heart and lusting for his blood.

I was now able to remember what happened when she came. When I was in the form, I was surging with deep-seated emotion, yet at the surface, where flesh touched the world, I was cool. My heart hardly beat, my fingers were cold, and I needed very little air. Cade didn't wake because I was cloaked in an aura that made me stealthy. When I touched an object in the room, like the bedposts, my fingers left a faint impression of frost.

Cam had told me many months ago that darklings could wield something he called chilling magic. "We can slow objects around us. Briefly, at least. You should practice. You'll get better at your magic if you use it."

Sometimes I wanted to practice, but I was still too scared of my darkling self. Every time she emerged, my soul seemed to be divided. Part of me was in her, trying to learn her, control her, *be* her. But the rest of me looked on in horror, afraid of what she might do.

One night, not shifting, but dreaming, I woke perspiring and disoriented.

We'd been playing with Barney that night before bed—he was a sweet puppy whom I had grown to love with a passion that reminded me of how I had once felt about my dog, Dusty. In the nightmare, I saw Dusty again and wept over her.

When I jerked awake, I felt as if I was tied down, helpless, I couldn't move. It felt so real. There was a man's body, strong, merciless, holding me down. He was going to hurt me. He had a knife.

I fought to get free, thrashing, trying to throw him off, feeling him restrain me, screaming until a hand covered my mouth and smothered my cries.

I knew his scent at once. It flooded in, calming me. But just as suddenly, I felt angry at him because I thought he must have tied me down again—put me in bondage without warning me. BDSM was okay; I loved, it in fact, but I didn't like to be surprised with it.

"Ssh, Jess, it's okay. It's me, hon. Take it easy, you're safe."

The hand moved away from my mouth and I tried to relax. As full consciousness returned, I realized I wasn't bound at all. That must have been part of the nightmare. Cade wasn't restraining me, but holding me. In sleep, our limbs had become entangled.

As my coiled muscles loosened, tears welled up in my eyes. I squeezed them down. "I'm sorry. I was dreaming."

"I figured. You're okay, babe. I've got you."

Somewhere in the room, a dog whined. Panic washed through me again. The dreams—and the memories—were still so close. I knew it was Barney and that he was probably dreaming, too. But the dog I saw in my mind's eye wasn't Barney.

"I misled you about Dusty," I blurted. "I couldn't bear to remember it. We didn't all escape safely together. Jonathan killed my dog. Just as he'd threatened to do. I wouldn't have sex with him, and he slaughtered Dusty."

I burst into sobs.

"Holy fuck," Cade growled as he comforted me. "It's a good thing that creep is already dead, or I'd rip him to pieces myself."

When the sleep shifting and the nightmares didn't stop, I slipped out of bed one night, took my phone downstairs and called Cam. We hadn't talked since before my wedding.

"I told you to fuck some cowboy, not to marry him," he said as soon as he recognized my voice.

"I guess you heard."

"Oh aye. Your mum had a hissy that could be heard all the way to Edinburgh."

"Yeah well, she was hoping I'd marry you."

"No. No offense, but no. Although, it would be an interesting experiment to see if we could breed a full-blooded darkling."

"Shut up. Whatever darkling DNA I have in me is more than enough. Is there any way to get rid of her all together?"

"If that's why you're calling, forget it. Yours is part of you just like mine is part of me and the Zrakon is part of my twin. She giving you trouble again?"

"I've been sleep shifting again. My darkling comes out at night and I think she wants to drink my husband's blood."

"So? He's a shifter, right? It won't kill him. He'll probably love it; they usually do. Frenzied orgasms for both partners, in my experience."

"But what if she takes too much?"

"Fuck, you're such a worrywart. You're strong, but you're not all-powerful. If the guy's such a weakling, leave him and come back to Scotland. I could use your talents here."

"Doing what?"

"We're having some darkling problems, actually. There's a truce in place now between the races, but skirmishes are always breaking out. People like us, who can temporarily take the form of a darkling, are useful go-betweens and mediators."

He'd offered before to train me to do just that. Become a mediator. Which I suspected was just another word for a spy. Or worse.

"Then there are the slave nets, which you had your own unfortunate brush with. Human trafficking has always been a thing, but shifter trafficking has been increasing. We want to stop it. Put an end to those fuckers once and for all. Darklings or even darkling shifters could be really useful there because of our chilling magic. The creeps mostly use guns and we can stop bullets. You can be both a hammer and a shield in the battle against evil."

"What are you, a superhero recruiter? I don't want to battle evil. I just want to stop myself from committing any!"

"You're rare and valuable, Jessica. The way I see it, you're wasting your talents in Montana. You could be here doing something useful. Do you even know how to use your magic?"

"Not really. I've poked around with it a bit, but I haven't practiced. How exactly does it work? Could you teach me to be a shield instead of a hammer?"

"I suppose. But anyone can be a protector. You could be something special. You could be an avenger."

"I've told you before—screw that. I'd rather protect than avenge."

"Fine. I can teach you that, but you'll have to come to me. Your magic will be stronger here, anyway, closer to its origin and source."

"I wish I could just be an ordinary wolf shifter instead of a freak."

My cousin muttered something about not having time to listen to me whine and hung up on me.

Sigh. I didn't want to go back to Scotland.

What I wanted was right here in Whittier, Montana.

CHAPTER THIRTY-NINE

Cade

"I've been thinking about a short trip to Scotland." Jess spoke casually, as if jetting off to the Highlands was a minor thing. "I just got email from my mother. She's invited me to come and spend a couple weeks with her soon. Around Christmas."

It was an early December morning. We were eating breakfast together in the kitchen. Outside the sky was gray and it looked like snow.

I looked up from my coffee cup. I'd been staring into it, my mind elsewhere. And she'd just dropped a fucking bomb.

"What the fuck? You can't do that. By the terms of Tom's will, we have to live together for six months. There are still three left."

"Surely that's a technicality. Everyone in Whittier knows we got married." She was nervously fingering the silverware, rubbing her thumb over the tines of a fork. "I'd like to visit my family."

"Your family or your fucking cousin Cam?" I knew she'd talked to that guy. Did she seriously think she could get out of bed and go downstairs to make a call without me hearing?

She rolled her eyes. "There's nothing between him and me. I don't even like him. But he does know something about darkling shifters and he might be able to teach me. There's a lot I still don't know."

"No way," I said, pissed.

"I'll come back in a couple of weeks. And then before we know it it will be March and we'll be free to divide up the property and file for a divorce."

"Who the fuck said anything about a divorce?"

"This was never meant to be a permanent arrangement."

"Don't be an idiot, Jess. And don't make excuses. I know you're having a hard time right now, but it'll pass. We got married. We're staying married."

"Stop dictating to me."

It was as if a serpent had entered our garden. Or a monster with dark wings and claws.

Ever since I'd seen her darkling aspect, Jess had been moody and upset. Well, not all the time. She could still laugh and have fun and sass me and sex me into cock-spewing paradise, but I could tell she was not at peace with herself.

I didn't get why, though.

And it was frustrating because she made me feel very content and happy. It was harder and harder to imagine my life without her. I wasn't going to let her go running off to Scotland.

The last week or two, she'd been ducking out on me, either by going to bed early or by insisting on doing her artwork downstairs until she thought I was asleep. When I pushed it, she always complied, but she'd reverted once again to not talking to me much and not telling me what she was feeling.

It burned me the fuck up. For the first time in my life, I *wanted* a woman to tell me her thoughts and feelings, and my own wife refused to do so!

Plus we were still arguing over that damn Highland Choker. She wanted me to put it on her every night, and I was fucking sick of hearing about how she was going to shift in the night, attack me viciously, and suck out all my blood.

I gulped what was left of my coffee. I had an image of her stretched out on her back, her hair tangled, her lovely bare skin damp with the exertions of lovemaking. What was happening to us? Was I failing her somehow? Was this my fault?

I'd probably over-reacted during that dust-up with Brandon. Was she afraid I was some kind of jealous, possessive bastard who might go all psycho on her someday like that shithead rapist, dog-killer Jonathan?

In the past, I'd always been the one who'd refused to commit to a serious relationship. My methods of avoiding intimacy had been extensive and varied, most of them unrecognized by me until enough time had passed for me to gain perspective. More than one lover had accused me of distancing myself from a short affair without even being aware of what I was doing.

I'd been aware, though. I hadn't loved any of them.

But now? I had no experience with love. Not romantic love. I'd loved my brother. And my dad, even though I'd picked an asshole way of showing it for a few years. I loved my mom. I might not ever say so, but they'd known it, right?

Ever since our wedding night when she'd come apart in my arms, I'd felt bonded to Jess. Sometimes it felt as though we were speaking mind to mind, without words, the way legend said fated mates sometimes could.

But she was still hiding part of herself from me.

I guess I'd pushed a few women away. Maybe I was pushing Jess away, too?

But I didn't want her to leave.

"Are you giving up on us? Is that what you're telling me?"

"On you and me, no. But why do we have to be married? Such a formal relationship makes it look as if I'm your fated mate, and that's always going to be problematic for your pack. Given who and what I am."

"That doesn't matter. We're great together. We even have the sevmelle."

She rolled her eyes. Rightly so. I couldn't believe I'd just said that.

"I know there are some issues. But you needn't be so worried about people getting to know your darkling self. She's kickass."

"Cade, you're a wolf shifter and I'm a multiform shifter. That means we're just not compatible."

I jumped to my feet, flinging my chair backward so hard it nearly fell over. I started pacing across the kitchen the way my wolf stalked back and forth. "That's bullshit! We've lived together all this time with scarcely a ripple of discontent, except for this darkling business. You're the first woman I've ever spent so much time with who hasn't driven me nuts."

I stopped beside her chair. When she tried to turn her face away, I cupped her chin and forced her to look at me. "Jess, I love you. We have to work things out."

She didn't answer. I was shocked. I guess I'd never expected that I'd say I love you to a woman and not hear her say it back.

"Shit!" The flat of my hand slammed down on the top of the table, setting the dishes clattering. "I'm not willing to accept silence from you." Moving closer, I leaned over her and gripped her shoulders between my palms. "I love you, Jess. Look at me when I say that. I love you."

She pulled away. "You must know that I don't want to leave you. But you're so stubborn and you won't let me wear the Choker and I'm afraid I could lose myself and attack you, Cade! Hurt you. Maybe even kill you. Don't you see? I'm terrified of that."

There she went again with the I'm-so-deadly-and-dangerous-to-you thing. I was a fucking alpha wolf, dammit. Did she seriously think she could hurt me?

"I can't take this. I need to think." Blindly, I strode into the study, jerked a shotgun from the glass case and jammed a few shells into my trousers' pocket. I grabbed my jacket and my shooting vest from the hook near the front door and yelled for Barney.

"Cade—" Her voice was wavering, wretched.

"Do what you have to do. I'm going out to murder a few birds."

With Barney trailing happily at my heels, I went out and slammed the door.

CHAPTER FORTY

Jess

I sat motionless at the kitchen table for what must have been close to an hour.

What was I afraid of?

I'd assumed from the start that this thing with Cade wouldn't amount to a real relationship. I guess that's what I'd wanted. I'd initiated our first sex. In fact, I'd initiated sex every time he tried to get me to open up in any other way. I'd known he was a player so I figured it would be easy and uncomplicated—he'd want nothing more than a quick fuck. I could enjoy him and escape with my heart still free.

When had that plan gotten fouled up? Even the temporary marriage hadn't alarmed me over-much. Six months and then "see ya."

I wasn't supposed to fall in love with the jerk.

I wanted to go back to being ordinary. Not deadly and not scary. I'd been hoping that I'd grow accustomed to never shifting and passing for human for the rest of my life. I didn't want to fantasize about tying my husband down with his own bondage gear, climbing on top of him and riding him like a stallion while I sated myself on the blood from one of his veins.

"We could try that," he told me the other night when I'd confessed I'd had such a fantasy. "Sounds kinda hot."

"I might kill you!"

"I'm a magical fucking creature, Jess. You can't kill me. You make a wound, I'll shift it closed. Jeez, I'm a quick-healing shifter and strong as fuck. Why aren't I the perfect partner for your damn darkling dominatrix?"

He had a point.

Rousing myself, I climbed the stairs to the bedroom I'd been sharing with Cade, intending to pack a few things and get out of here before he returned from hunting. I wouldn't go to Scotland. I'd go somewhere I could practice summoning and controlling my demon.

My wolf loved to play with his. Mate with his. Our marriage might have been arranged by my grandfather, but some force beyond our ken had decreed that we were true mates. The sevmelle that glistened around us when we coupled proved it. Why was I still denying it?

For some unknown reason I remembered my father. He had died when I was not quite thirteen and it still hurt. I'd missed him so much. I'd been absolutely furious with my mother when she'd started hooking up with Martin. The bastard and his son had nearly ruined us both.

"You defended yourself," Cade had said. "You had every right."

No one had condemned me for what I'd done. Why couldn't I stop condemning myself?

As I rose from the bed, I noticed the white flakes dancing past the window. Snow. Probably just a squall. Did it mean he would be home soon? Could he hunt in a snowstorm?

Come home, Cade. Come home and make love to me. The truth is, I don't want our marriage to end.

Chapter Forty-One

Cade

It wasn't a great day for hunting. It was fucking cold, for one thing, and the sky had that gray glowering look that threatens snow. Pretty soon it actually was snowing and the wind had picked up. Was that in the forecast? I'd been so messed up in my head when I'd left the ranch that I hadn't checked.

Barney and I'd flushed a couple of birds in the first hour of hunting, but I'd failed to bring any down. Lately, though, we'd had no luck in finding game. After a couple more hours of tramping, feeling the temperature dive, the wind accelerate, the moisture from the precipitation soak my clothes, I decided that all the ruffed grouse must have taken shelter from the storm. My enthusiasm for hunting dwindled.

The words to an ancient folk song began repeating themselves over and over in my brain.

Western wind, when wilt thou blow,
The small rain down can rain?

289

Christ, that my love were in my arms,
And I in my bed again!

When the wind turned bitter and several inches of snow clogged my footsteps, I whistled for Barney, who came bounding back toward me.

"Good boy, Barn." His golden coat was matted with dampness, but he was still happily wagging his tail. "Not much luck today, huh? Come on. Weather's nasty. We'd better head back."

As I reversed our direction, Barney looked faintly disgusted, but was soon running ahead again, avidly sniffing for any scents he might have missed. He had gone around a bend, out of sight and off the path, when I heard an ominous metallic snap, followed by a loud whine of canine agony.

Fuck! I started running toward my dog. Barney must have stepped into a trap left carelessly and illegally in the woods by some unscrupulous hunter.

This was exactly what I found—Barney, confused and frantic, startled yelps of pain issuing from his throat as he jerked at his imprisoned leg. It was raw and bleeding, locked within the rusty jaws of an ugly leg-hold trap.

Fuck fuck fuck. Ranchers occasionally set traps for coyotes and other predators, and I'd heard rumors of wolves—the non shifter variety—in the vicinity, who'd been raiding livestock. But it was illegal to hunt wolves with traps. There were bears, too. Shifter bears, even. We left them alone and they left us alone. We all hated traps.

I knelt at Barney's side, talking softly to calm and reassure him, while I examined the spring and how best to release it. "I know, I know, fella, but you're going to have to relax. I know.... Fuck it! Just let me get a grip on the blasted thing. Whoa, Barney. Stay down."

His brown eyes wide, Barney remained still long enough for me to manhandle the trap open. Reflexively, the dog pulled out his paw, but screamed again when he tried to scramble to his feet and put his weight upon it. I disarmed the trap and threw it aside in disgust, then took my dog in my arms.

"Down, boy. You gotta lie down and let me get a look at that."

It was bad. There was profuse bleeding from the deep, jagged wounds where the teeth of the thing had penetrated. It also looked like the foreleg had been fractured. I applied pressure to the wounds to slow the bleeding.

Barney was already drenched from the snow, which would exacerbate shock. There was no way he was going to be able to walk back to the road.

Which left me with a dilemma. I considered shifting, but I could help him better in my human form. I was going to have to carry him. Which wouldn't be trivial since Barney had filled out in the past few months and must weigh sixty or seventy pounds by now.

I felt the first pricking of concern about the mess we were in. I wasn't sure how far away the Jeep was. I hadn't really been hunting today; I'd been sulking.

Which meant I'd been out of touch with the forest, the birds and the weather. The snow was swirling around us, tossed on a powerful wind. Visibility had been cut and would be diminished more if the storm's intensity increased. I hadn't even listened to a weather report before venturing out. Shit. I couldn't think of a time when I'd been so careless.

I dug my cell phone out of my pocket and switched it on. Battery was fine but there were no network bars. Fuck.

What I did find were a couple texts from Jake. I must have had cell service when they'd come in, but the sound on my phone had been turned off. He'd tried to call me, too.

The first text said, "Something's come up. Call me."

The second was longer: "Another shifter attack, clearly connected. Victim talked. Where the fuck are you?"

Fuck. "I screwed up, Barney. Big time. Stuff is happening, you're hurt, and we're stuck out here. Goddammit."

CHAPTER FORTY-TWO

Jess

I spent several hours trying to work on a painting I had started the previous week. I guess it was about mid-afternoon when I heard sounds at the front door. I ran to open it, thankful that Cade was home at last.

But when I pulled it open, it wasn't Cade who was shaking the snow off himself on the threshold. It was the doctor, Jake Cartwright.

My heart seemed to stop. Why was he here? I looked past him at the snow swirling. I'd been so involved in my work I hadn't noticed that the snow had turned heavy. Shouldn't Cade be home by now?

Jake had given me the bad news once about my grandfather. And there was something odd about the expression on his face now. "Jake? What is it?" My voice was so dry I could hardly croak out the words. "What's wrong?"

He stamped snow on the mat and stepped inside. "Cade here? I need to speak with him."

"No, he's not here. He's out hunting. I didn't realize the weather had turned so bad. Do you know where he is?"

His gaze swept me and he must have taken in how alarmed I was. "Hey, it's okay," he said quickly. "No, I've no idea where he is, but I'm sure he's fine. I drove over because he wasn't picking up his cell, but that's no surprise. Cell service sucks out here in the woods." He took my arm and walked with me into the living room.

"I know. Sorry. I saw you and panicked."

He grinned. "Happens to me all the time. But no worries. Cade's a woodsman and a wolf. A little storm isn't going to bother him."

I was relieved by his confident tone. "I'm just feeling guilty because we had a bit of an argument before he left."

"Ha. Well, in that case, maybe he's stopped off at a bar on the way home to get himself some sympathetic male companionship. Totally normal."

I remembered my manners. "Do you want some hot coffee? Or something stronger?"

"No thanks, I'm good. When Cade does get home, I want to talk to him. Will you give him a message for me?"

"Of course." I noticed that his face had grown worried again. "What's going on?"

"Yeah, I got some news. There's a Council meeting tonight, but I'd like to tell him before the meeting, assuming cell service comes back."

"It's been spotty lately. Is this something you can tell me? I'll make sure he gets your news before he heads out to the meeting."

For a moment, he looked uncertain. "Does Cade talk to you much about pack business?"

"He didn't in the beginning, but now he does. You can count on me to be discreet."

"Okay, good." He pulled of his down jacket and sat down. "It's disturbing news, truth to tell. That's why I wanted him to hear it before the meeting."

Damn, something was definitely up. Despite his physician's sangfroid, I could tell by Jake's demeanor that he was upset. Had someone died?

"Do you know about the murder we had a few weeks back? Motorcycle gang member attacked by what looked like a shifted wolf?"

"Yes. Cade told me. What about it?"

"Late last night, there was another attack. Same method. I was on night duty at the ER when the patient was brought in."

Alarm washed through me again. Seriously, it seemed I was living in a bath of adrenaline these days. I was so over-sensitized that full-blown panic erupted at the slightest thing.

"The victim came in a little before dawn. She was still alive, but she'd been severely clawed and bitten and there wasn't much I could do for her. She'd already lost a huge amount of blood and she wasn't in good health to start with. Druggie. Connected with one of the MCs."

"We stabilized her and she came to and started talking. But she was on a combo of drugs, so it's hard to tell if she was making sense."

"What did she say?"

"I'll tell you, but pass this news on carefully, okay? Make sure Cade understands that the woman was raving. There's no evidence that she was telling the truth. Anyway, she claimed to be poor Jock's old lady, and a hanger-on in the Rockets MC."

"Jock is the man who died?"

"Yep. Seems like this woman had been treated real bad by the other members of the club since his death."

No doubt. From the little I knew, women associated with motorcycle gangs didn't fare too well under any circumstances.

"Anyway, she claims Jock was killed because he was stupid enough to try to blackmail a shifter. But this is the real kicker: she said that the person Jock had been trying to extort was the same person who hired him to take the hit on Cade's brother four years back."

The hit? "Cade told me that Aaron was caught in the cross-fire of a shootout. Now you're saying he was assassinated?"

"It could be complete bullshit. This is a drug addict and a prostitute talking, and she was out of her head. Not the most reliable witness."

My heart was pounding now for another reason. If Cade's brother turned out to have been murdered, all the horror his family had lived through would be brought back. Plus, he'd want to know who'd done it. He'd want revenge.

"Did she say who this shifter was?"

He shook his head. "She claimed Jock hadn't told her that."

Something else occurred to me. If these two shifter attacks were related, then it was unlikely that I'd had anything to do with the first attack. I hadn't really been worrying about that lately, but it was still good to know.

"Is this witness safe? If someone attacked her last night and failed to kill her, they might try again."

He looked down at the floor. "That's the thing. They didn't fail. She seemed to rally for a few minutes, but then she crashed. Massive circulatory system failure. She'd lost too much blood. We couldn't get her back."

"So she's dead."

"Yeah. And we have no way of verifying her confession. If it even was a confession rather than some crazy fantasy. But Cade'll want to know about it. And to look into it, no doubt ."

I nodded. Yet another problem to deal with. "Is there anything to suggest that she was telling the truth?"

"Well, we do know Jock was at the bar the night Aaron died. His story was that he didn't see anything, didn't do anything. Didn't even have a gun on him." Jake rolled his eyes at this. "He didn't get caught with one, at least."

"The police must have investigated."

"They did. Aaron's and Cade's dad did, too, you can count on that. He didn't believe a damn thing anybody in the MC had to say. But if there really was a hit on Aaron, it's never been proven. He was a popular guy. Everybody loved him. Who would want to kill Aaron?"

We looked at each other. "Someone who wanted to replace him as future leader of the pack?"

"You're not referring to Cade, I trust."

"Of course not! I'm referring to Brandon. Wasn't he Cade's competition for the post?"

"Yeah, he was. But he submitted, didn't he? And Brandon and Aaron were best friends."

"I don't trust him."

Jake shrugged. "Neither do I, but he's been loyal since Cade took over. I'd be the first to jump on him if I had any excuse, but he's buckled down under Cade's leadership, considering he's a strong alpha himself."

"I wouldn't be surprised if Suzanne put him up to it."

He shrugged. "I don't think even Brandon would go against the pack and against the man who was his closest friend on account of a woman."

I couldn't really find the right words to argue with that.

"Anyway, if Cade could share the news with his mother, I'd appreciate it. Obviously, Lorna has to be told. I hope for her sake it's not true. Would be cruel to drag it all up again."

"If there's any possibility that Aaron was murdered, Cade will want to bring that person to justice."

"Me, too. Aaron was a friend of mine."

We shared a long look and I felt like a real member of the pack. Cade's mate. Jake had told me something important and I would have a part to play. I just wished Cade were here now, so he could help figure out how to handle it.

For the first time, I felt the responsibility of my position as mate to the leader of the wolf pack. It pressed down on my shoulders like a boulder. Fuck. I wasn't going anywhere, after all, was I? My own bullshit seemed trivial in comparison with this.

CHAPTER FORTY-THREE

Cade

Sweating with exertion and weariness, I stumbled, falling to one knee in the deepening snow. I managed to keep hold of Barney, whom I was cradling in my arms. The dog whimpered loudly, a sound that wrenched my heart. But it reassured me that he was still conscious.

Gently, I set him down, speaking softly to him. Barney kept trying to lick his injured leg, which had swollen to twice its normal diameter and must have hurt like hell.

I tried to get my bearings, but it was difficult to recognize any landmarks. The poor visibility combined with the snow-shrouding of trees to make everything look the same. I could only estimate, from the time I'd been hiking, that I'd made it back about half the distance to the road where I'd left the Jeep.

I was fucking tired. My back and shoulders were aching from Barney's weight. My legs were leaden. Worse, although I felt hot while tramping, it took only a couple of minutes of standing still in the wind for me to start feeling cold. At least the wind had been behind us. If we'd had to walk straight into it, we probably wouldn't have gotten this far.

I thought about shifting, but it would expend energy that I needed to save. Although I'd be warmer as a wolf, I'd be unable to carry Barney.

Barney stopped worrying his leg and curled up into a tight ball. He was shivering. I figured we had less than an hour of daylight left—if you could call this snow-gloom daylight. Not enough time to find my way out of here before conditions *really* got bad.

"Guess it's time for Plan Number Two, boy." The dog lifted his head to the sound of his master's voice, a good sign. "We gotta get ourselves into some shelter. See any caves around here, fella? Or maybe a nice big boulder slanted so it has an overhang? We find something like that and we can make ourselves a little hut. You stay here, boy. I'm going to scout around."

As soon as Barney perceived I was leaving him, he let out a piercing series of yelps that didn't stop even as I pitched my voice to its most reassuring tones. "I'm not leaving you, Barney. No way I'm leaving you. No, boy, stay. Good dog. Stay. You usually do the sniffing around for me, but now I'm doing it for you. Watch me. I'm moving in a circle, I'm keeping an eye on you. I'm hunting for a downed tree, or a large rock, or anything that we can use as a buffer against the wind. Take it easy, boy. I'm trying to save your life."

The yelps devolved into whines of pain that tore at my heart. This is all my fault, as usual, I thought. Me, the big hunter, the alpha wolf, the skilled woodsman, storming out into a goddamn blizzard. Smart. Real, goddamn sensible.

"Maybe I deserve to freeze. But you don't, dammit, so keep your chin up. I'm going to get us out of this mess, don't worry."

I'd do the worrying for both of us.

Jess

As I watched the snow fall thicker and heavier, I began to worry. Cade didn't usually hunt all day. Why wasn't he home yet? What was the point of hunting birds in heavy snow? Didn't they all take shelter like any sensible creature?

I called his cell, but as Jake had indicated, there was no answer.

I tried to remember how he had been dressed when he'd left. Was he warm enough? Dry enough? Did he have anything to eat or drink? The wretched storm was turning into a blizzard. What if he was lost?

Don't be silly, I yelled at myself. He's a shifter. A wolf with a warm layer of fur. Storm or no storm, he wasn't going to freeze.

Yeah, he was probably sitting in a nice, cozy bar somewhere, drowning his sorrows in a bottle of whiskey.

By the time it started to get dark, I'd begun to imagine all sorts of dreadful things. I ruined my fingernails, chewing on them.

Something about this whole thing felt wrong. Someone had been murdered last night, possibly by the shifter who had killed

Cade's brother. Now Cade had not come home. What if the same person who had shot Aaron had now gone after Cade?

Find him, a voice deep inside me said. *He needs you.*

The voice was insistent, and I usually trusted my intuition. *Go out and look for him.*

Fine. Where?

I could search for his Jeep. If I found it, I'd know what part of the wilderness he had entered.

So where might it be? There were several roads to search, and I didn't know where to begin. With the snow falling and the hours of daylight limited, I'd have to narrow it down somehow. Was he hunting in the fields or in the forest?

I went into the room that was now serving as Cade's office and opened his glass-fronted gun cabinet. Four of the five weapons that were kept there remained. Thoughts of Jonathan flashed. I felt a little dizzy. Get a grip, for God's sake.

I knew guns. I didn't like to think about that now, but I'd grown up with them.

The 12-gauge, with the bigger barrel and the bigger shells, was for shooting pheasant, a relatively large bird. There were two 12-gauge, double-barrel shotguns in the case.

One of the other weapons was not a shotgun at all—it was some sort of automatic rifle. Not a hunter's gun.

The last gun in the case looked old and beautiful. It had only a single barrel, which was the same diameter as the other two. Another 12-gauge. Which meant the missing weapon was Cade's

20-gauge shotgun. It had a narrower barrel and would be used for shooting smaller birds like grouse.

I remembered what he'd told me—grouse hunting was usually conducted on hilly terrain. Forests, woodlands. If he'd stayed in this area, there were only a couple of places where he could be.

I called the compound before going out looking. I wasn't sure what time the Council meeting was scheduled for, but it would be stupid not to check to see if he'd simply gone there directly instead of coming home. I hoped someone else from the pack besides Lorna was there. I didn't want to worry Cade's mother.

It was Suzanne who answered. Shit. She was the last person I wanted to speak to. I forced myself to remember what Cade had told me—that there was bound to be some rivalry and that I'd just have to suck it up.

But I knew it was more than simple rivalry. Susanne had wanted to be alpha female. She still wanted it. And it pained me to have to admit to Suzanne that I didn't know where my husband was.

Plus Suzanne was Brandon's mate, and if there was anyone I could envision as a killer, it was Brandon.

"I was wondering if Cade was there? He went hunting this morning and he's usually back by now."

"Haven't seen him all day. Where did he go to hunt, do you know?

"He didn't say. I suppose he might have hit a bar on the way home," I said, trying not to sound as if I was really worried about him. "Only thing is, he had his dog with him. He couldn't take Barney into a bar. Nor leave him for long in a cold car."

"That is odd," Suzanne's offhand tone told me that I'd sparked her interest. "Do you know what he was hunting?"

"Grouse, I think."

"There are only a couple of prime grouse spots around here. I guess I could ask Brandon to check them out for you."

"Is Brandon there with you?" I asked, trying to make the question sound casual.

"Yeah, he's here? You want to talk to him?" There was an edge to her voice now.

"No need to bother him. Is Jake there yet, by any chance?"

"Nope, not yet. There's a Council meeting tonight. Cade'll be late if he doesn't get home from his hunting gig soon."

"Is Lorna there? May I speak to her?"

"I wouldn't want to worry Lorna." She sounded falsely solicitous. Man, didn't anyone else see how fake this bitch was? "After all, she's already lost one son."

"And she's not going to lose another," I snapped. "If Cade is late to the meeting, please alert the pack and send out a search party."

"Absolutely. I'll do that now. We should be able to track him down and make sure he's safe."

Chapter Forty-Four

Cade

The shelter I located was in a small clearing in the woods, in the lee of an old uprooted tree. Its ample root ball, fallen in such a direction as to cut off the bitterest blasts of wind, was roughly circular and a good six feet in diameter. It was tilted in such a way to allow me to scrunch down under it and have a roof over my head and body.

I added to this effect by carving off several sturdy evergreen branches from the surrounding trees with my hunting knife and filling in the empty spots on the root ball. I then laid a thick bunch of sticks and branches on the surface of the snow under the make-shift roof and dug around in the dirt until I found some large stones that I could heat in a fire.

"It ain't much, Barney, but it's home." I made a soft nest of dry leaves and pine on top of the evergreen floor before getting him underneath the shelter. "You rest now. I gotta see about building us a fire."

I hollowed out a circular well in the snow in front of the shelter. On a flat rock nearby, I laid out what gear I had stowed in my hunting vest and pack:

One half-empty bottle of water.

One cell phone that couldn't find a network to connect to.

Four 20-gauge shotgun shells—I'd only grabbed a few on my way out of the house.

One Swiss army knife complete with various small tools, none of which were especially useful at this moment.

One snakebite kit, never used.

One tin of gun oil.

One topographic map of the Big Horn River area of Montana, a couple hours' drive east of here.

One duck-call whistle that had never worked.

One battered compass.

One can of waterproof matches.

One ancient, white-tinged chocolate bar.

One scrunched-up twenty dollar bill.

I re-stowed everything except the matches, the map, the water and the twenty. I hesitated over the candy bar, the sight of which sent hunger pangs shooting through me, but I figured I might require its energy later on. Besides, I was loath to eat something that Barney couldn't, and a lot of dogs were hypersensitive to chocolate.

I could kill some supper for us, once I had the shelter snug and the fire burning.

I gathered wood, deliberately choosing the types that were most resistant to damp and snow. I stripped a dead birch of its bark for kindling, using that, together with the twenty dollar bill and the topographic map to get my fire started.

As the fire caught, smoking from the damp kindling, hissing as the snowflakes fell into its flame, I visualized Jess standing naked as a goddess in front of our blazing fireplace. Her thick black hair. Her generous breasts, curvy hips, and long legs. Her lovely, entranced face, eyes dreamy, mouth soft. Her sexy, husky voice. Such a strong woman in so many ways. Honest, courageous and full of love and laughter. Yet holding within her such darkness.

She'd had knowledge of, and intimacy with, the most vicious forms of evil. Of course she was hurt, of course she was scarred. Yet there must be a way to bring her out of that darkness and into the light.

You could let her go to Scotland, if that's what she needs to do. To that fucking cousin she kept talking about. Cam Malloch. The guy who might have something useful to teach her about controlling her darkling self.

No fucking way. The cousin probably wants to nail her. What red-blooded man wouldn't?

Fuck that. Jess and I are mates. No other man is ever touching her. You want blood-rage? I'll give you blood-rage. No jaunts to the Highlands. We are solving this problem right here.

I shook myself. Despite the warmth of the fire, I was getting dozy. A bad sign. I laid the stones I'd found into the campfire. When they got hot, I'd put them under the branches in our shelter so they could radiate some heat.

In the meantime, though, the cold was getting to me.

I only had my jacket to keep me warm, and Barney just had his golden fur. At night, in this kind of weather, it might not be enough. If we were going to survive, I'd better use the snow itself as insulation by piling it over the root ball and the branches. Once we had a good cozy den, we could settle down inside and wait for the blizzard to subside.

CHAPTER FORTY-FIVE

Jess

T he snow was coming down heavily when I drove my car out of the driveway. I wished he'd left me the Jeep, which would have been more reliable in this weather.

I silently gave thanks that the car had front-wheel drive.

Fortunately, I knew the road accesses to the trails that led to the most likely grouse-hunting areas. I found the Jeep at the second spot I'd tried. It was parked in a hollow on the side of the road near an area that Cade had once pointed out to me as the best damn ruffed grouse hunting territory around.

There was no sign of Cade or Barney at the Jeep. Any tracks they might have left had long since been obliterated by the falling snow.

I climbed into the Jeep, which was covered by a foot of snow, and stuck my key into the ignition. It started sluggishly. I hammered on its horn. My elation at having successfully located the Jeep was beginning to fade as other thoughts crowded in. Why hadn't Cade returned to his vehicle? Was he lost in the woods?

Injured? Had there been some sort of hunting accident? Had the murderer come for him?

My mind shied away from the last possibility.

I switched on the satellite phone I found in the glove compartment and tried again to reach Cade on his cell phone. Nothing. I used it to call Jake and tell him where I was. That I'd found the Jeep and that Cade must be nearby. He promised to come immediately and bring the pack.

I wasn't going to wait.

Jumping out of the Jeep, I shaded my eyes against the driving snow and gazed into the woods. The wind was roaring out of the forest, striking me head-on. The trees were ghostly, and all evidence of any woodland trails was buried under several inches of snow.

Miles of upland forest swept away from this spot. He was out there, yes. I was damn well going to find him.

A particularly strong gust of wind assaulted me, bringing with it the faint cry of an animal in pain. Barney? Was he injured? Was that why they hadn't made it back to the Jeep?

The rational part of my mind protested that it was unlikely I'd be able to recognize a dog's cry at a distance, in a blizzard. But I was in a heightened state, and all my paranormal senses seemed to be operating. It didn't sound like a wolf's howl, but a dog's whine.

I delayed only long enough to search the Jeep for supplies. If Barney was injured, we would need—what?—a blanket. I found one tossed in the back along with an old windbreaker and a filthy pair of leather gloves. I collected them all. From the glove compartment, I took a flashlight, a first-aid kit and an ancient box of raisins.

There was another blanket in the front of the Jeep, so I grabbed it, too.

Unfolding one of the blankets, I dumped my hastily collected gear in the middle and wrapped it into a bundle, which I flung across my back. It was heavy. I adjusted it as comfortably as I could, hoping the trek wouldn't be too long. Maybe I should shift to my wolf and run? But then I wouldn't be able to carry anything.

Wind could carry sound a long distance. It could confuse the direction of the sound, too, especially in a storm.

I wasn't even sure that the sound I'd heard was real. Yet something was pulling me out into the blizzard, away from the Jeep, my own car, and the small degree of safety they offered. I was going to have to trust my instincts, and hope I wasn't making a mistake. If I miscalculated, there might be three of us lost in the forest this evening.

Jerking the hood of my jacket as far down over my face as possible, I plunged into the woods.

I hadn't gone more than 20 yards when I realized this wasn't going to work. The snow was up to my knees, making my progress painfully slow.

I had to find them. And I could only think of one way to do it. I had to shift.

No point in shifting to my wolf form, either. She could bound over deep snow to some extent. Maybe she could even find an animal trail that my eyes could not see. But she would be slowed up by the snowfall too.

My darkling, though, could fly. And because her body was in most respects human, she could carry supplies, too.

My heart thundered as I tried to decide what to do. If I allowed her to emerge in this world where she was such a dangerous blood-hungry predator, could I control her actions? She was fascinated with Cade, but so far she hadn't hurt him. She wanted something from him, and I wasn't even sure what it was.

While I debated, she decided.

She caught his scent and went into a frenzy. All that I was clutching in my arms fell into the snow as my bones began to crack and roar. Then Jess was gone and she took over.

The predator lurked in the shadows, downwind from the clearing. She scented blood, which excited her. The heavy, wet snow had dampened any instinct for hunting, but the smell aroused her. Its sharp scent penetrated the cold, white blanket that cloaked the forest and had driven her prey to ground.

Cautiously, she advanced toward the clearing. The wind brought her the acrid smell of smoke.

The smell of blood was stronger now, too. Was her adversary weakened? Injured?

That would make things a whole lot easier.

A wounded animal lay in the clearing, hiding underneath a fallen tree. The dog, not the man.

Another smell drifted toward her over the blood and the smoke. Yes. He was there.

The wounded dog sensed danger—he whined, sniffed the air, tried to move.

Along with blood, the shifter could scent fear.

Soon. Soon it would be time to move, to lunge, to savor the hunt.

She stood poised, watching, waiting for the right moment. A good hunter knew how to bide her time.

CHAPTER FORTY-SIX

Cade

Barney shifted and whined loudly, jerking me upright and alert. Shit, I almost lost it. I must have been exhausted because I think I'd just dozed off for a few minutes. That was a good way to freeze to death. What the fuck was wrong with me?

I checked my dog, aware that his cry had sounded less like a whine of pain than a whine of alarm. Barney's head was up, his ears cocked. Did he hear something? Or was he smart enough to register alarm at the sight of his master taking a fucking nap in a blizzard?

Actually, the snowfall seemed to have let up a bit. Maybe even stopped. It was difficult to be certain in the semidarkness, with the way the wind was blowing the stuff around. I hoped it was stopping. That would make things marginally easier.

I rose, stretching my freezing limbs. Gotta move, gotta do jumping jacks, gotta do something to get warm. Gotta shore up this shelter somehow—with more branches, saplings, leaves and dirt and snow. Snow's an excellent insulator. A good woodsman uses what he's got, and what he's got here is lots and lots of snow.

When I climbed out of the shelter, I loaded my shotgun and took it with me. The long hike with Barney on my shoulders had depleted my energy reserves. We had a fire; I could cook. Once we'd eaten, we could both huddle in the shelter after I'd insulated it with more snow. I'd shift to my wolf to keep myself warmer and huddle up under my down jacket with Barney to share our body heat.

The fire wasn't looking too healthy at the moment, though. Needed more wood. Some logs, if possible. I dusted off the flat rock near the fire and put the gun down. "Be right back, Barn. Gotta find us some firewood."

Barney whined and made as if to get up. "Stay," I ordered him. "Good boy. You guard the campsite. I'll be back soon."

Barney sniffed the air and whined again.

When I got back with an arm full of firewood, Barney was freaking out. Whining. Trying to bark. I was about to soothe him when I realized I'd been stupid again. Far stupider than I had any right to be.

My dog wasn't barking at me. He was barking at *her*.

CHAPTER FORTY-SEVEN

Cade

The figure approached our little fire like something out of a dream. I was startled because I hadn't expected anyone to track me down in this weather.

Especially not Suzanne.

She was dressed in hunting clothes and carrying a rifle. She was on snowshoes, which made sense. Too bad I had not grabbed a pair myself.

"What the fuck, Suzanne?" I said, not graciously. I looked beyond her for Brandon, since I rarely saw one without the other, but there was no sign of him. I could probably use some help, but I hated to admit it to them. "Are you the rescue party?"

She glided into the firelight. Barney knew her, but he kept on growling. He'd never liked Suzanne much.

"You need rescuing, Cade?"

There was something strange about her tone. She was brittle. Sharp in a way I'd never seen in her. Well, maybe I'd seen it, but I'd averted my eyes. I'd grown weary of her attitude a long time ago.

"I don't, but my dog does. How'd you find me?"

"Your silly little wife told me you were hunting grouse. In a blizzard, Cade? Not too smart."

My silly little wife? What was eating her…the bitch ought to know better than to speak to her alpha that way.

"What's wrong with the dog?"

"Trap got his leg. It's bleeding, broken. Do you happen to have a sat phone? Cellular network is unreachable."

She lifted her rifle and pointed it at Barney. "No problem. I'll end his pain. Couldn't do it yourself?"

What the fuck? Not funny.

"Say the word, Cade. It'll be a lot quicker than a trip to the vet."

A wave of sickness wrenched me as I realized she was serious. For a second all I could think of was Jess, sobbing with the memory of the creep who had murdered her dog, Dusty. Rage swept through me. I couldn't quite make sense of it yet, but Suzanne was *not* the rescue party.

"Suzanne," I barked at her. "Lower the fucking rifle." It was a rifle, not the sort of shotgun she might use for hunting grouse. "Shoot my dog and you're dead."

She adjusted her aim so she was pointing at me. There was a steeliness to her jaw and a glitter in her eyes. My brain was racing through my options, but they weren't good. And I was listening hard for Brandon, whom I expected to emerge at any moment. Two against one was bad odds.

"What the fuck is wrong with you?" Jake's enigmatic texts surfaced in my brain. He'd needed to speak to me. Another attack. The victim had talked. Named the perp?

Did this have something to do with Brandon and Suzanne?

I thought fast. Since my hands were still in my pockets trying to keep warm, I silently pressed a couple of buttons on my cell phone. The battery wasn't dead. I couldn't make a call, but I could record everything that was said here. In case I didn't make it out, which was beginning to look like a distinct possibility.

"What's wrong with me? You. You're the one who's wrong, Cade. You always were. Wrong for me and wrong for the pack."

"I guess I'm not surprised," I drawled, while my brain sorted through the possibilities. I took a chance. "Jake got through to me before my phone died. He had some news for me."

Yeah, too bad I didn't know exactly what the fuck it was.

She swallowed the bait. Suzanne was wily, but she had never been all that smart. "So you know. My mistake. I should have made absolutely certain Jock's bitch was dead so she couldn't spill any deathbed confessions."

Holy fuck. "It was you who killed that MC drug dealer. Are you using? Need a little high now and then? What'd he do, sell you and your boyfriend some bad shit?"

She laughed. "You don't even realize, do you? Haven't figured it out yet, alpha? Jock's old lady didn't admit she was also trying to blackmail me? She deserved what she got for that, the stupid cunt. What made either of those lowlifes think they could black-mail a shifter and live?"

"If you're planning to shoot that thing, hurry up about it. It is fucking cold out here."

Weird as this was, I didn't think she would shoot. I mean, hell, I'd fucked her. She'd even been a little in love with me. She sure had not been pleased when I'd ended things. But that crap about hell hath no fury was total bullshit, right? Brandon, though…smile and smile and be a villain. He'd blast me if he had the chance.

Or…light dawned. If I were dead, Brandon would be elected alpha leader. Which was what she'd always wanted, once both my brother and I had fucked her and dumped her and she'd taken up with Brandon instead.

And then I knew.

It was as if a slot opened and revealed the inner workings. The pieces came together and I fucking knew.

"You shouldn't be where you are. No one ever expected it. Aaron, yes. He had charisma. But not you."

"Hey! I got charisma." I was stalling because I couldn't reach my shotgun. I could shift to my wolf and leap for her throat, but she had the advantage there. I'd hunted with Suzanne and Brandon many times. They were both expert shots and Brandon was probably in the trees somewhere with a bead on my skull at the moment, anyway. The wind direction meant I couldn't catch his scent, just as I hadn't caught hers.

"You didn't have the skills to be pack leader. If you had, I'd have held onto you, honey. But it didn't take long before I knew you were flawed clay."

Flawed clay? If I hadn't been so fucking cold, I'd have laughed at the metaphor. If she meant I'd have cracked in the pottery oven, I wished to hell we could test it out. I could use a nice baking right about now.

Besides, I'd been the one to dump her.

She adjusted her rifle. I blinked, snowflakes in my eyes, still not quite believing what my brain knew to be true. Maybe because I was so fucking cold, all the pieces didn't quite fit. Where the fuck was Brandon? He wasn't the type to lurk in the background while allowing his mate to take all the risks.

"It was you, wasn't it? That shoot-out four years ago was some kind of set up. You had my brother killed because you thought Brandon would take his place as pack leader. Like so many others, you didn't take my candidacy seriously. You figured once Aaron was gone, you'd rule the fucking roost with your mate."

"Took you long enough to figure it out."

Fuck. This bitch had killed my brother? The fury that was rising in me was starting to be beyond my ability to control.

"What about Brandon? Did he set this up? The two of you worked it together? Shame he lost the election, then. That must have come as quite a shock." I was trying to keep my head. Make a plan. I'd been weakened by my own stupidity in this fucking storm, but I needed a way to defeat or outwit her.

My adrenaline was high and all my senses were evaluating the surroundings at quantum speeds. I was part wolf already in that respect. My body ached to go full wolf, but wolf against rifle was never good odds.

I remembered the night the two of them had tried to run me off the road. Had that been an actual attempt to kill my ass? Instead, they'd startled poor Tom so much that he'd careened into a curve and lost control.

The same night I'd fallen for Jess.

What they'd done was almost unthinkable. Brandon could have fought me for pack leadership. That was the old way, no longer practiced very often, but still considered legitimate. Turned to their wolf forms, rivals could battle it out for dominance.

For the loser, the fight marked the end. If he survived, he'd be driven out of the pack. As it happened in nature, so it was in a traditional shifter wolf pack.

But murder? Humans did that shit, not shifters. At least, not the shifters in the Whittier, Montana pack.

"Where's your partner?" I sneered. "I get why you, a weak female, feels the need of a weapon, but I'd have expected Brandon to be brave enough to fight me man to man."

"Brandon knows nothing of this. He's a better man than you are, but not even he had the guts to challenge the Derringer dominance of the pack. If I hadn't taken the initiative, your damn brother would still be alive, and Brandon would be kowtowing to Aaron even more than he kowtows to you."

The thought of Brandon kowtowing to anyone was laughable. Was she telling the truth? I sensed she was. She had nothing to lose. She was planning to kill, and I wouldn't be giving away her secrets. Unless someone found the recording on my phone.

With me gone, Brandon was the logical heir. Suzanne would become the alpha female to Brandon's alpha male. She might even murder my mother and Heck. Why not? Suzanne's hands were covered with blood already.

Fuck my life, I'd underestimated her.

Enough. My clothing fell away as I started to shift. And no one shifted as fast as I did.

This bitch should have pulled the trigger while she had the chance.

Chapter Forty-Eight

Jess

I was soaring over the trees, my black wings beating more rapidly than ever before. I had powers and senses as a darkling that were unavailable to me in any other form. And yet I'd spent so little time exploring them that I didn't even know what I was capable of.

"I'll train you," my cousin Cam had said. "You'll be able to do things you never even dreamed possible. You can use that bloodlust, baby. That natural ferocity. There aren't many of us, but we're the fucking Special Forces of the shifter world. Join my cadre of elite dark rangers and we'll put a stop to the kind of brutality you were subjected to by the psycho who kidnapped you."

"You want to train me to be a killer?"

"An avenger. Together we'll put the slave traffickers who prey on our kind out of business. Your people need your abilities. I'll make sure you're taught everything you need to know."

I'd given up the chance to learn from him because I hadn't wanted to be a killer.

I was thinking clearly about this, even though I was in my darkling form. I wasn't a mass of rage and fury. I was me...except I was immensely powerful and I was flying through a snowstorm. Speeding towards my lover.

The scent of smoke was strong, and in the gathering darkness ahead, I thought I caught sight of a flicker of red.

It was a fire—not much of one, it looked like sputtering coals instead of cheerful flames—but what could one expect in this weather? The air around me was sharp like crystal and the sky above me was clearing.

I heard again the whimper of a frightened dog. Barney. Not just frightened. He was in pain.

My brain reeled as I remembered another dog's agony.

Who the fuck would harm a dog? Someone who didn't deserve to live.

I dived lower, skimming trees and brush and thickets, up a slope and over a rise....Yes, there was a fire and beyond it, a makeshift shelter. I smelled blood, and it enraged me. No sign yet of Cade, but I could smell his intoxicating scent. I could tell he was aroused, but not with sexual chemicals. Like me, he was burning with fury.

There was someone else present. A figure dressed in a parka and hood, turning like a whirlwind, rifle poised to shoot at a moving target...Barney? No, my blood surged and my heart flew toward him.

Cade.

I'd found the camp. But another hunter had beaten me to it.

CHAPTER FORTY-NINE

Jess

With superhuman speed, I assessed the situation. I could smell the same kind of sly aggression that I'd encountered once before—a being who would blot out others for the sake of aggrandizing himself. Or herself, in this case. Suzanne was sighting down the barrel of her rifle at a white wolf in mid-leap who was springing at her throat. Which was faster—a bullet or a maddened werewolf?

A bullet, of course. Without even knowing I could do it, I threw up a shield of icy air between my beloved white wolf and the bullet. Magic flowed out of me, but it was protective magic, not the vicious deathly magic I'd used on the lowlife who'd thrust a knife against my throat while he tried to rape me.

It did not stop the bullet. But it must have slowed it. Maybe altered its course. The bullet still struck Cade, but it penetrated his shoulder, not his heart. And without the impact it otherwise would have had.

The wolf had knocked the weapon from the killer's hands before she could get off another shot. I was on her by that time, too, fangs and claws ready to tear her open.

She had tried to kill my lover. For that, she deserved to die.

The white wolf faltered in the snow, blood blossoming from his injured shoulder. Barney barked and Suzanne, our enemy, stumbled backwards, shrieking, "It can't be! You're a wolf. He saw you. He said you were a wolf!"

The claws of my right hand grabbed her around the throat and squeezed. As I lifted her off the ground, a variety of deaths flooded my mind—drop her from a great height? Rip her apart and drink her blood? Dash her brains against a rock? Impale her on the leafless branches of a tree? Or I could peel off her skin, strip by strip. That had been one of Jonathan's favorite ways of killing the animals he tortured.

Something rebelled inside me at that idea.

I realized that, unlike the first time this had happened to me, I was thinking clearly.

I had control. I wasn't out of my mind with bloodlust. I could make a reasoned decision about what to do to the bitch.

A kind of exultation took me.

I shook Suzanne until her body flopped. I dropped her into the snow. She landed hard, but she was nowhere near dead.

I didn't have to kill her. The pack would have a means of judging and condemning her. All I had to do here was protect my husband and our dog.

The crack of bones echoed all around me as Cade shifted back to his human form. At almost the same moment, Suzanne summoned the energy to shift to her wolf. Both were bleeding. The scent of blood made me half crazy. But only half.

It had been a long time since I had enjoyed a few mouthfuls of blood.

Cade

I didn't know how Jess had found me, but her arrival had been timely. I'd twisted as I'd shifted, popping out in a different location than Suzanne had expected. She'd had to rotate to aim, and I'd already been airborne in my lunge for her throat when she'd gotten off the shot.

She would have hit me anyway, probably with a kill shot, but Jess had done something. I had no clue what, but I'd felt magical energy roar into me. It had seemed as if the air around me had coalesced for a second, turning into thick, icy soup.

I'd felt the bullet penetrate my flesh by degrees. I'd been shot once before and I'd felt nothing until well afterward. This time every millimeter had burned, but the good thing about it was that I knew it had not gone in too deep.

The slug was still there in my human body, and my shoulder hurt like hell, but I'd survive, thanks to Jess. Suzanne would not.

I dove for the shelter where I'd left my gun. Barney was crouched inside, half growling, half whining, thoroughly spooked by what he had just seen. I grabbed the shotgun, then changed my mind. I can't claim my brain was operating too clearly. I leapt for and took up the rifle Suzanne had dropped when Jess had swung her up off her feet.

Jess had flung the bitch away and Suzanne had shifted. She had started to run now, somewhat impeded by the deep snow. Jess, the ultimate predator, took off after her. My darkling was chasing after the fleeing wolf like a black-winged falcon zeroing in on her prey.

Suzanne had to die for her crimes. But I didn't want Jess to do it. If she did, she would probably torment herself over Suzanne the same way she'd agonized over killing that pond-scum, Jonathan.

I took aim swiftly and fired. The shot wasn't perfect. It hit her, but not in a vital area. She faltered but kept running. Shifters were strong and fast. As I lined up another shot, I shouted for Jess.

"Let her run," I yelled. "She can't go far."

I didn't know if Darkling Jess would respond to my shout, but I yelled it again, imbuing the words with every ounce of alpha command I still held within me.

Normally I'd never have allowed a wounded animal to flee without delivering the coup de grace, but I wasn't feeling chari-table to my brother's murderer.

The great black wings dipped and the darkling twisted in the air. Faster than I could even grasp, she came streaking toward me. She landed deftly in the snow in front of me. I was tall, even when stooped over with pain and cold. But dark winged, dark shadowed dark haired glorious Jess was taller still.

The darkling shift made her body long and thin in a way that was so different from her ordinary self, yet still alluring. She gave me a smile that looked a little odd on such a demonic creature. Were darklings really the origin of the vampire myth? Well, vampires had an offbeat sexuality, didn't they?

The more I stared, the less she resembled a vampire. In fact, she looked a lot like Jess. Her eyes were more luminous—the green had turned brighter and those eyes shone in the dark like a cat's.

But she gave me an old-fashioned curtsey and said in a low, husky voice, "You ordered me to stop and I did. But she was going to kill you. She must be found and brought to justice."

"She will be. You saved my life, Jess. That was totally badass, and I love you, no matter what form you take. But I need my clothes. I'm fucking freezing."

"Just a second. Let me take care of that bullet for you."

She bent her face to my shoulder, where the blood was seeping out. I think at any other moment, I might have felt a pang of concern, because, weirdly beautiful though she was, she sure seemed deadly. But I relaxed when she set her mouth against my bleeding shoulder and started to suck.

Magic roiled around us once again. Everywhere we touched felt warm and bright. Her wings folded around me, sheltering me from the cold and the snow. All pain vanished. The sensation I felt as the bullet withdrew was blissful.

She spat it out on the snow and swallowed the blood that had been leaking. As she did so, her eyes flashed a deeper green and my cock pulsed with unexpected pleasure.

She licked my wound languorously with her tongue and drew back. "It should heal fine now."

CHAPTER FIFTY

Jess

The rest of the pack arrived within the hour, some on snow-shoes and skis, the rest in their wolf forms. I explained to Cade that I'd called in our location on the sat phone that I'd found in the glove compartment of his Jeep.

I made sure that Cade was once again warmly clad and ban-daged up his shoulder with the stuff in the first-aid kit. I ban-daged Barney's leg, too and dispensed some pain-killers to them both.

I wondered how badly injured Suzanne was and whether she was still alive. Cade played the recording he'd made on his cell phone. Until I'd heard it, I hadn't really made sense of everything.

"Do you believe her that Brandon wasn't involved?" I asked him.

"Not sure. Maybe. I've had my eye on him for a long time, but I've never seen him do anything more than mildly rebellious. Even on the night when they tried to run me off the road, I think it was her, not him, who veered her bike into mine."

I did not shapeshift from my darkling form. For the first time ever, I felt calm and confident with this aspect showing. I did adjust my appearance somewhat, though. I could fold my wings back and collapse them into my shoulder blades. As Cam had tried to explain when he'd been mentoring me, darklings are also shifters, and can change their humanoid bodies to a certain extent—retract the claws, the fangs and the wings and minimize the elongation effect that makes us appear so tall and slender. I didn't really like being a bony, insubstantial creature—I had grown accustomed to my voluptuous, curvy self.

I smiled at the thought of having body issues over being too skinny.

But I no longer felt the need to hide my darkling aspect from the other members of the pack. Yes, I liked the taste of blood, but I could use that trait to heal, not kill. And yes, I could prevent myself from tearing another being apart, even when I was enraged and ravenous.

I knew what Cade had been trying to do when he'd shot Suzanne, though. He hadn't wanted me to take her death on my conscience. I was grateful for that. He was the pack leader and the one most sinned against. It was up to him to dispense justice.

Jake was the first to find us. He came running up, in his wolf form, panting. Several other wolves, including Lorna and Heck, weren't far behind. Brandon came alone and changed to human almost instantly.

"Where's Suzanne?" he asked. His voice was harsher than I'd ever known it to be, and for once the expression on his face was readable. He looked stunned. Crushed. And angry. "She took off without telling me where she was going."

"What about last night?" Cade said harshly. "Did she take off then, too?"

Several other members of the pack had gathered around now, most of them still in their wolf forms. A few were staring at me in mystification, but I noted that they seemed in awe rather than frightened or repulsed.

"She was out most of the night, yeah." He swallowed hard, looking around the makeshift camp. "What happened here?"

Cade switched on his cell phone and played the recording.

Some members of the pack exclaimed in shock or disbelief. Brandon sagged and squeezed his eyes shut. "I should have realized. Fuck it, I ought to have known."

Cade turned on him, cold and hard. I could hear his alpha voice resonating. "She claimed you were not involved and that you knew nothing of this. Is that the truth? I want to hear it from your own lips."

Brandon dropped to one knee, naked in the snow. His head bowed, his spine arched. If he'd had a human tail, it would have been tucked between his legs. "On my oath, Alpha, I didn't know."

"She is a murderer. She killed my brother and two other people."

Brandon did not reply. His shoulders heaved, and he shook his head in denial or disbelief.

"You heard her. She confessed it. When she's caught, she will pay the full penalty for her crimes."

Brandon's voice was low but clear as he said, "I understand." He looked up, his face a blank. "She's still alive, then?"

"I shot her, but I didn't get a clean shot. She's still out there, injured, bleeding."

"Oh God."

"If you are indeed loyal, prove it. Stand up."

Brandon did so. His head remained bowed.

"Choose some wolves. Lead them. Hunt her down." He paused. "Look at me, Brandon."

The naked man raised his eyes.

"You know what has to be done. Do it."

Brandon nodded once, his expression a mask again. But I could see the agony in his eyes.

I realized that Cade had just given an execution order.

Brandon nodded to several other members of the pack. They gathered around him. With a crack of bone, Brandon shifted, and the wolves began to run, following in the direction where Suzanne had fled.

CHAPTER FIFTY-ONE

Cade

I was lying on the carpet in front of the fire in the living room with my lovely bare-assed wife sitting on my hips. Every time she moved rhythmically up or down, I moaned with pleasure. My cock was deep inside her, being expertly massaged by the astonishingly powerful muscles of her pussy.

Her darkling body was skinnier than I liked (although I would never let on that I preferred her curvy, big-breasted self), but she had other advantages that totally made up for it. Her domme side was exciting and fun for a change—I liked just about every kind of sex I could imagine, and I could imagine all sorts of kinky stuff.

She smiled wickedly as I hit the plateau just before orgasm. I caught a glimpse of the sharp pointed fangs hidden behind her lips as she seized one of my wrists and put it to her mouth. The tiny pain as her teeth sank in sent me over the edge. I shouted as pleasure pooled in my belly and then flashed into every cell of my body.

She sucked a small amount of my blood. Her expression changed from predatory to blissful as her pussy gripped me even harder and began to convulse. Her tongue sealed the tiny wound she'd made and her back arched as she leaned back, her hair thrashing the air, and rode my bucking, throbbing cock.

We both collapsed together, entwined and panting. I felt the magic swirl around us as her body reformed to human. It was a smaller change than the wolf transformation. Now that she'd grown comfortable with letting her darkling self emerge, she and I had both realized that bony, winged Jess wasn't all that different from curvy Jess.

The bloodsucking thing was off-the-charts hot. She'd been working on the timing—if she did it right before we came, we both were flipped into some kind of erotic wonderland. It made my orgasm harder, longer, and gut-wrenchingly awesome. I might have wanted it that way all the time except that it shut us both down sexually for quite a while afterwards. Sometimes it was sweeter to have the pleasure doled out in smaller portions so we could do it over and over again.

Several weeks had gone by since the events of the early December snowfall. Christmas had come and gone and the real Montana winter had settled in. Both wolves and humans were hunkering down now, staying warm and waiting for spring.

I got up, stretched, and threw a couple of logs on the fire. I tugged Jess off the floor and onto the leather sofa. Barney came over, wagging his tail, and poking his snout at me for a pat. I obliged. His leg had mended nicely, although he now walked with a bit of a limp.

We'd all recovered well from that night. My bullet wound hadn't been deep and Jake was surprised when he started work on it to find that it was already partially healed.

"Come a little closer, Darkling Wife."

She scooted nearer, but not quite near enough. I caught her wrist and pulled her to me. She pushed her hair aside, and on her face I saw a smile so radiant that I was dazzled.

"You look happy, Jess."

"I am. I feel bad sometimes, being so happy, given everything that's happened. I mean, you were nearly killed, and other people did die, and you learned about your brother—"

I sank a hand into her thick hair and pulled her face to mine. I kissed her mouth, cutting off any further reminders. The truth was, I was happy too.

Aaron had died four years ago and I'd suffered the worst of my grief for him then. This time the memories hadn't been quite as cruel. I think having it all dragged up again had been harder on my mother than on me. She'd had Heck to comfort her, though. And Aaron's killer had finally been brought to justice.

The subject of Suzanne's villainy was still painful. It had been difficult for everyone in the pack to realize we'd been betrayed by a person we'd trusted. It had been hardest on Brandon, of course. But he and the others had followed my orders. They'd tracked and trapped the wounded Suzanne. Marta, who had been among the trackers, had reported back that while Brandon had given the command, he hadn't participated in ending Suzanne's life. When it was over, he'd held her in his arms and wept over her body.

I guess he'd really loved her.

Afterwards, shoulders drooping as if he were carrying a mountain on his back, he'd informed me that he was leaving the pack. He couldn't stay among us, not after what had happened. He would become a vagabond, a lone wolf.

I'd granted him his release from the pack. I didn't blame him. If it had been me, I wouldn't have stuck around either.

"I've been thinking about something," Jess said.

"Yeah? What?"

"I'd like to do something for everybody in the pack. To brighten up the winter a bit. And to thank them for the way they all came out in a blizzard to find us that night."

We'd both already thanked them a bunch of times, but I sensed there was something more to her musings.

"Sounds good. What were you thinking of doing?"

"We could hold a big celebration, with feasting and dancing and running together as wolves. And booze. Lots of booze."

"Okay. Are we celebrating anything in particular?"

Her green eyes twinkled at me and her lips curved in a mischievous smile. "I thought a ceremonial wolf pack wedding might be in order. You know—the kind that is held for fated mates when they marry."

I swallowed hard. "Are you trying to tell me something, Jess?"

She nodded, looking away from me into the fire, her black hair partially covering her face.

"So say it."

"I love you, Cade."

I leaned back. "You want to run that by me once again?"

She raised her eyebrows and crept a little closer on the sofa. "I love you."

"You love me?"

She punched me lightly in the arm. "Yes."

"Crude alpha male that I am?"

She giggled. "Yes, you jerk. I'm in love with you and I want everyone to know it."

"You're not still thinking about running off to Scotland?"

"I didn't really want to do that anyway. But no, no running away."

"And you don't still want a divorce?"

"Nope. You're stuck with me."

"So we're really married now, huh? Forsaking all others, till death do us part?"

"It's what we vowed."

"And your other aspects? Your darkling? Your wolf?"

"It's all good. My darkling turns out to be a shield, not a hammer."

Whatever that meant.

"And as for my wolf, wolves mate for life, don't they?"

"Yeah. They sure do. Come here."

She scooted over.

I hugged her close for a moment, threading my fingers through her fine, dark hair. "I love you, too, Jess. It's your face I want to see on the pillows at night, at the breakfast table in the morning and over the heads of our children someday."

She smiled and pressed her mouth against mine. "I want that, too."

Later, much later, I noticed she was smiling. "What are you grinning about now?"

"I was thinking about my grandfather. Wondering what he would say if he could see us now."

"Well, I reckon he'd be tickled pink."

"He was right about you. And right about our marriage."

"Hmm, yeah. Well, all I can say is, I sure never expected, during all those great fishing expeditions we took together, that my good buddy Tom would stick me with a bride."

She laughed.

"Suppose we go upstairs to bed, Mrs. Derringer."

She jumped up and ran toward the stairs. "You'll have to catch me first," she cried over her shoulder.

"I'm right behind you, lady."

She led me straight to bed. Great place to be.

"I love you, Jess," I said as we settled under the covers.

"I love you, too."

"We are mates, you know. I think those fizzy lights really are the sevmelle."

"Never thought I'd hear you admit it, Alpha."

I snorted and slapped her bottom, grinning when she murmured, "Ow."

We kissed with great tenderness at first, then hotly, ardently. Whoa. It didn't usually happen so soon after one of those vampiric orgasms, but my cock was stiffening again.

The woman was gonna kill me, but not in the way she'd feared.

I hoped someday I'd expire in her arms, fucking at the age of ninety-nine or so. What a glorious way to go.

Jess

Cade had saved me.

I was thinking about it a few days later after we'd celebrated our union with the entire pack.

He'd done what my cousin Cam could never have done for me. When he'd taken up his gun and shot Suzanne that terrible night during the storm, he'd removed my temptation to rip her apart the way I'd killed Jonathan. When I'd sucked on his shoulder to remove the bullet, I'd realized that my darkling's desire for blood could be used to heal instead of to harm.

Using my magic to act on behalf of someone I loved had given me the power to control my darkling's natural aggression.

My natural aggression. My pronouns were changing now, too, as I grew more at peace with the entirety of my nature. I was a multiform shifter with a wolf and a darkling aspect. And I could live with that.

Cade had allowed me to be the shield instead of the hammer. He was my forever lover. The true mate of my soul.

The pack had accepted me too, especially when they had learned my role in saving their leader from Suzanne's attack. Instead of being appalled or frightened by my dark bony self with my ability to fly and slow a speeding bullet, they treated me like some kind of superheroine.

"You're so badass," one of the teenage girls in the pack had said to me at our mating ceremony. "I wish I could fly."

"You're a beautiful young wolf," I'd told her. "Maybe you and your friend could pose for me one day? I'd love to paint you."

She'd giggled and agreed, and I'd been making plans for the wolf pack mural that I was now sketching on Cade's massive living room wall at the compound.

"There's no doubt about it now," Cade told me. "You're the alpha female of the pack, whether you like it or not."

"I do like it. I like it a whole lot better than I thought I would."

"Yeah? Convince me. Not that you haven't already, but I like the way you convince me, babe."

I laughed and shifted to my wolf form. I could do it confidently now. It was as if something had clicked into place inside me and I knew now how to do what I'd struggled with for years.

I trotted over to my sexy husband. I nudged him with my snout. Then I wagged my tail and crouched down with my forelegs lowered and my butt in the air in standard "Come play with me" mode.

Barney barked delightedly and Cade grinned. His handsome form melted and reshaped itself into a gorgeous white wolf. His blue eyes were burning. My heart was full of him. He nipped me gently on my shoulder and led me out into the wilderness where we could frolic together under the bright Montana moon.

THE END

Author's Note

For more alpha male shifters, check out
The Zrakon's Bride and *The Zrakon's Curse*.

More Books by Linda

If you like Bad Boys:
Stephen: I want it all: whips and chains.
Hearts and kisses. *The Dangerous Hero*
Nick: She thinks I'm dominating. Cruel. But
I've got a dirty job to do. *Uncover Me*.
Daniel: She's a psychic? With a reincarnated
cat? Don't make me laugh. *Blazing Nights*.
Connor: She accepted a ride with me? Her troubles
are just beginning. *Color Me Blue* (novella).
Shane, the ultimate bad boy Navy SEAL: *Badass*
(co-written with Alana Albertson).

LINDA'S BIO

Linda Barlow is the author of 25 novels, with more on the way. She lives in New England with her spouse (who sleeps during the day, which has often made her wonder if he's a vampire) and their equally enigmatic and nocturnal cat.

Linda has written in various genres, including historical and contemporary romance, romantic suspense, paranormal romance, New Adult romance, family sagas, and general mainstream fiction. Publishers have included Doubleday, Dell, Penguin, Warner Books, Hachette, New American Library/Signet, Berkley/Putnam, Silhouette and Harlequin.

Linda is a *New York Times* and a *USA Today* bestselling author. She's proud to have earned a few awards over the years, including the Rita from Romance Writers of America for *Leaves of Fortune*; New Historical Novelist of the year from *Romantic Times* for *Fires of Destiny*; and a Career Achievement award from *RT*.